ALL GOOD DUKES COME TO AN END

Dukes in Danger
Book 12

Emily E K Murdoch

ARE YOU SIGNED UP FOR DRAGONBLADE'S BLOG?

You'll get the latest news and information on exclusive giveaways, exclusive excerpts, coming releases, sales, free books, cover reveals and more.

Check out our complete list of authors, too!

No spam, no junk. That's a promise!

Sign Up Here

www.dragonbladepublishing.com

Dearest Reader;

Thank you for your support of a small press. At Dragonblade Publishing, we strive to bring you the highest quality Historical Romance from some of the best authors in the business. Without your support, there is no 'us', so we sincerely hope you adore these stories and find some new favorite authors along the way.

Happy Reading!

CEO, Dragonblade Publishing

Additional Dragonblade books by Author Emily E K Murdoch

Dukes in Danger Series
Don't Judge a Duke by His Cover (Book 1)
Strike While the Duke is Hot (Book 2)
The Duke is Mightier than the Sword (Book 3)
A Duke in Time Saves Nine (Book 4)
Every Duke Has His Price (Book 5)
Put Your Best Duke Forward (Book 6)
Where There's a Duke, There's a Way (Book 7)
Curiosity Killed the Duke (Book 8)
Play With Dukes, Get Burned (Book 9)
The Best Things in Life are Dukes (Book 10)
A Duke a Day Keeps the Doctor Away (Book 11)
All Good Dukes Come to an End (Book 12)

Twelve Days of Christmas
Twelve Drummers Drumming
Eleven Pipers Piping
Ten Lords a Leaping
Nine Ladies Dancing
Eight Maids a Milking
Seven Swans a Swimming
Six Geese a Laying
Five Gold Rings
Four Calling Birds
Three French Hens
Two Turtle Doves
A Partridge in a Pear Tree

The De Petras Saga
The Misplaced Husband (Book 1)
The Impoverished Dowry (Book 2)

The Contrary Debutante (Book 3)
The Determined Mistress (Book 4)
The Convenient Engagement (Book 5)

The Governess Bureau Series
A Governess of Great Talents (Book 1)
A Governess of Discretion (Book 2)
A Governess of Many Languages (Book 3)
A Governess of Prodigious Skill (Book 4)
A Governess of Unusual Experience (Book 5)
A Governess of Wise Years (Book 6)
A Governess of No Fear (Novella)

Never The Bride Series
Always the Bridesmaid (Book 1)
Always the Chaperone (Book 2)
Always the Courtesan (Book 3)
Always the Best Friend (Book 4)
Always the Wallflower (Book 5)
Always the Bluestocking (Book 6)
Always the Rival (Book 7)
Always the Matchmaker (Book 8)
Always the Widow (Book 9)
Always the Rebel (Book 10)
Always the Mistress (Book 11)
Always the Second Choice (Book 12)
Always the Mistletoe (Novella)
Always the Reverend (Novella)

The Lyon's Den Series
Always the Lyon Tamer

Pirates of Britannia Series
Always the High Seas

De Wolfe Pack: The Series
Whirlwind with a Wolfe

CHAPTER ONE

1 November 1811

A DAM SEYMOUR, DUKE of Gilroyd, hated weddings.
Had always hated them. Even before—

He wasn't going to think of that, Adam told himself fiercely as he stomped about the place looking for the rascal. He wasn't going to think of that sunlit day so long ago and yet so near. The happiness he had felt. The knowledge, certain within his chest, that he would never cease to feel that joy.

The joy that had slipped away with her life.

"Such a wonderful wedding—"

"—beautiful bride—"

"—such a surprise, her reappearance . . ."

Adam snorted as he marched out of a dining room where guests were picking at delicacies laid out on silver platters and into a ballroom where it appeared everyone who was anyone— including Lady Romeril, worse luck—was dancing.

"—no idea Lady Genevieve could be found—" someone was saying just to his left. "To think, after all these years . . ."

Adam glowered at the gathered horde of well-wishers. *If anyone had truly been worried about Lady Genevieve Cotton-Powell's disappearance,* he could not help but think, *they should have done something about it.* The daughter of the Earl of Armstrong was a beauty, and apparently had brains in her, too, which was not half bad. But she wasn't anything compared to—

Stop it, Adam thought darkly. *All you're going to do is upset yourself. You mustn't—*

"Ah, Your Grace, what an unusual sight," came the sly voice of Lady Romeril. "I can't recall the last time I saw you in public."

Try as he might, Adam was not quite able to force his face into a smile as he turned to the older woman.

"Lady Romeril," he said stiffly. "The Duke of Chetnole is an old friend of mine, and I would not miss his wedding—"

"An old friend? That's interesting," Lady Romeril said, interrupting him with an imperious brow. "He is a spy, as it turns out—I am sure you have seen, it is in all the papers. And you did not know?"

Her beady eye raked over him as though it were possible to sense a spy just by looking.

That you actually could, Adam wasn't about to tell her. You could spot the Frenchie spies a mile off, if you knew what you were looking for. But he wasn't likely to admit that to one of the most daunting women in the *ton.*

"Chetnole kept secrets from all of us," Adam said as blithely as possible. "And now, if you will excuse—"

"So you yourself are not a spy?" Lady Romeril pressed. Did she think he would admit to such a thing in the middle of the Chetnole ballroom? "Because you are intimate friends, aren't you? You wouldn't happen to have used your little trips to France for—"

A movement out of the corner of his eye. For years, Adam had been able to keep good track of anyone moving in his peripheral vision, and with relief, he saw this was the very man he had been looking for.

Moses Warwick, the Duke of Chetnole. And his bride.

"—a few of us suspected, of course, and I thought to myself, I can just ask—"

Adam nodded, hardly aware what Lady Romeril was saying.

His heart had lurched, his stomach risen in growing nausea, and despite himself he could not look away.

Moses and Lady Genevieve. Jenny, as she had been introduced to him. They were walking arm in arm, their laughter just audible, their obvious mutual affection nearly tangible even across the room.

It was a punch to the gut. Adam had known it would be hard. Known his body reacted with pain whenever he saw a couple that much in love. Knew it would remind him of what he'd lost. Knew he would not be able to stop thinking about—

But he mustn't.

He couldn't stay here. Not now he had seen Chetnole all loved up and distracted by his bride. He would come back another day. After their honeymoon, perhaps.

Then he would ask Chetnole if he had any further memories of the traitor in their midst.

"Your Grace?"

Adam blinked. Lady Romeril was examining him with a critical eye, and with a sinking feeling he remembered that he was supposed to be listening to what she was saying.

Oh, blast.

"Your Grace, I have an inkling you have been otherwise distracted," Lady Romeril said with pursed lips. "Am I correct?"

Flattery, then. It was the only way to extricate himself. "As ever, Lady Romeril, you are correct—you must allow me to wish the happy couple my felicitations."

"But Gilroyd—Gilroyd, wait!"

Adam did not wait. He was unaccustomed to heeding the shouts of ladies at the best of times, and Lady Romeril surely only wished to regale him with some nonsense about how the whole of Society now knew him to be a spy.

They couldn't possibly know. They could guess, and they may well be right.

But Adam had been careful all his adult life to keep his role as

Duke of Gilroyd in Society separate from his service to the Crown. He wasn't about to upset that balance now.

But he hadn't been precisely truthful with Lady Romeril. Wishing the Chetnoles well was something he should do, but Adam could not do it now.

Not with his heart pumping pain through every inch of his body. Not with the awful and beautiful memories of his own wedding driving him to abstraction. Not with the knowledge he would never be happy again.

Adam stormed out of the ballroom and into the hall. "Greatcoat."

The word had been snapped at a footman who immediately disappeared into the cloakroom.

Any minute now, he would be out of here—out of this nightmare of recollections and wishes and—

"Well, we're alone now," came a gentleman's voice, spoken low yet echoing across the expanse of the hallway. "And that means—Gilroyd, leaving so soon?"

Adam sighed. *Of course.* He couldn't actually just leave, could he? No, he had to be accosted by the very man who had made the last few weeks so difficult.

Moses Warwick, Duke of Chetnole, was smiling.

Of course he was, Adam thought bitterly, though he tried to return it. The man had just met and married the woman of his dreams and then left the service of the Crown because his face had become too notorious to be useful. All he'd have to worry about the rest of his days was siring heirs and not getting into too much mischief. As for him—

"You're not leaving?" asked Chetnole with concern across his face.

His bride had remained by the door, though Adam saw she was looking over at them curiously.

And well she might. Adam knew what sort of reputation he had. The reputation he'd had ever since Louisa's death, at least.

"I have business to attend to," Adam said shortly. "Business you can no longer attend to."

He had not intended it as a harsh reproof, however much it sounded like one, even to his own ears. Even so, he was unsurprised to see Chetnole did not take it as such. *Water off a duck's back, any criticism of this man*, Adam could not help but think begrudgingly. *It was a skill.*

"Yes, I am sorry about that," said Chetnole quietly, and he did look a little awkward. "I had hoped my career of service would have been longer than this."

Adam nodded. "And the traitor? I had hoped after you fully recovered from your fever, you would have more memories returning. The person who is betraying us—you truly cannot recall?"

"The memory is gone, I think," Chetnole sighed heavily, looking genuinely worried. "I know I left France with a purpose, and it was important or else I would not have left. But what it was—"

"No matter," shrugged Adam, conscious his friend's bride was looking over with great interest. "We'll work it out, Snee and I. If I go to France at all."

Of course he was returning to France. He knew it, Chetnole knew it, and he knew Chetnole knew it. And Chetnole probably knew *that*.

Adam forced himself not to sigh. All the spying, and lies, and cleverness. It took a toll after a while.

"You should get married again," said Chetnole unexpectedly, in a soft, almost kind, voice. "It's no good to hide yourself away and—"

"You don't know what you're talking about," Adam said stiffly, his chest tightening as he frantically pushed aside memories of Louisa. *He would not think of her, he would not.* "Go back to your new wife, Chetnole, and leave me to my grief."

"Marriage is an excellent tonic," his friend said, clasping Adam's arm with his hand.

Chetnole had crossed a line.

Adam wrenched his arm free, boiling anger bubbling over. *Had the idiot no sympathy?* Could he even begin to imagine what it was to love a woman and then to lose her? How could he be so cavalier about finding another wife, as though perfect women grew on trees?

"You know the vow I've taken—you know I'll never marry again," Adam said darkly. "Go and enjoy your bride, Chetnole. I'll take over the real business of spying and danger."

Without waiting to see whether his friend would attempt an apology—an idiotic one, Adam was certain—he grabbed the greatcoat offered by the silent footman and marched out of the house.

Every footstep along the street seemed to crash up Adam's leg, juddering his chest, making it difficult to breathe.

The cheek of the man! The arrogance! He found a woman two months ago and now Chetnole was the expert on women—on weddings?

Irritation and pain tightened around Adam's heart, his chest heaving as he tried to take in enough air. It was infuriating. It was galling. It was painful to the extreme, and the worst of it was, the man simply had no idea he was being so enraging!

Thankfully, Adam did not have to expend much thought on the direction his feet were taking him. He knew the streets of London well enough. In dire situations, he had made his way across it in such darkness, he may as well have been blindfolded.

And so while his mind and heart raged with the injustice of it all, Adam's feet took him, in an indirect route just in case there was a blighter attempting to follow him, back to his London townhouse in Mayfair.

Home. That was what he needed. Some peace and quiet at home before he went to see Snee to discuss what needed to be done about this apparent traitor in their midst.

Adam nodded at his butler as the servant immediately appeared to take his greatcoat—though he had not even bothered to put it on, having simply left it hanging uselessly over his arm.

"Your Grace."

"Dawson," Adam said distractedly, trying to force the image of Chetnole's disappointed face from his mind. "Post?"

"A . . . delivery has been made, Your Grace, but—"

"Where is it, man?" He was not surprised when his butler raised a single imperious eyebrow at his brusque treatment. "Apologies. But where is it?"

A delivery sounded like something interesting—something important. Something he should see at the earliest opportunity.

Dawson cleared his throat. "Justice Snee is waiting for you in the library, Your Grace, but—"

"That's not a delivery, man," muttered Adam, all thought of good manners disappearing as he strode across the hall. "It's only Snee."

Which in truth, was probably a little unfeeling. The man had, after all, dedicated the better part of the last decade of his life to fighting against crime and, more recently, working with a select number of dukes in their attempts to make England a safer place.

Adam was not even sure how many of them there were. Penshaw, of course, and Martock apparently. Chetnole, definitely, and Chantmarle if the rumors were to be believed. Which, knowing him, they probably were.

Each of them worked hard in their own ways to keep England safe. Some in France, some in England, but all of them connected by this man.

Mr. Snee, as he preferred to be called, rose swiftly from an armchair in the library. "Your Grace! Your butler said I should take a seat. I did not intend any disrespect when I—"

"Yes, yes, of course," Adam said, waving a hand nonchalantly at the man who slowly regained his seat. "You have been fed and watered?"

He winced to hear himself speak with such a cavalier attitude. When had he stopped caring about the polite niceties that the world valued? When had rudeness become the order of the day, and not genuine hospitality?

You know when, a dark voice at the back of his mind pointed out. *When you lost—*

Don't even think about her, Adam thought darkly, walking over to the fire and prodding it, entirely unnecessarily, with a poker. The less he thought about her, the less painful it would be. Wasn't that how it worked?

"You went to the wedding, then?"

Adam sighed, resting a hand on the mantelpiece and leaning against it. There was little you could get around old Snee. Oh, he played the fool at times. The bumbling little judge, a magistrate who didn't know what was going on.

It was all an act. Adam was almost certain he was one of the few people Snee did not play it on. He knew better than to attempt to fool the Duke of Gilroyd.

"Yes," Adam said testily.

"You shouldn't have gone," said Snee with a sigh. "You knew it was only going to upset you."

Adam's fingers tightened on the mantelpiece, but he said nothing.

Because Snee was right. Yet, as much as he hated weddings, still he could not help himself. They drew him like a moth to a flame. The agony there was exquisite, but just for a moment, a mere heartbeat, it was like being back there with her again. *Louisa.* As though the rest of their lives stretched out before them, unchanging, ever growing in love—

"You fool."

Adam's head snapped up. "I don't need a lecture from you, Snee."

"You need something," said the man, unruffled by the duke's rudeness. "A partner."

It was all Adam could do not to snarl in response, the idea was so ridiculous. As it was, he swallowed twice before saying in an undertone, "I don't need a partner."

It had been a foolish idea the first time, Adam wanted to say, *and look where that got us. Look what it destroyed!*

"I think you do," Snee said, his voice unrelentingly composed.

"I think you've been tying yourself in knots these last few years, Gilroyd, and you've got sloppy. Slow. Idiotic—"

"I am not idiotic!" snarled Adam, taking a step toward the seated man.

Even in the heat of his anger, he could see he was being ridiculous—but he could not help himself. His temper had always been something he had guarded fiercely, knowing how foolish he would look if the damned thing escaped.

Like this.

Snee was unfazed. "You know you work better with someone at your side, Gilroyd. Why do you think I paired you with Louisa in the first place?"

Breathing heavily, hands clenched into fists, Adam stood just a few feet from the magistrate and tried not to think about that moment.

A partner, Snee had called her. A woman who had given service to the Crown, just as he had, and who needed an additional pair of hands on her next mission. Adam hadn't even thought to be outraged that he was the spare pair of hands, that the mission had belonged to her.

He'd been too transfixed. Her beauty. That clever, knowing smile. The way she—

"You have to let her go."

Adam's throat was knotted so tight, he wondered how he was able to speak. "Don't you dare speak of her."

"Louisa would never want you to—"

"You didn't know my wife like I did," Adam growled, pacing away from the irritating man and standing by the window, looking out at the bustling London street. "No one did."

No one could understand, either. Oh, Chetnole thought he did. Sedley had tried. Even Wincham had had a go at speaking to him, not that he'd been much help. *And Snee was the worst, always looking at the bigger picture,* Adam thought wretchedly. None of them could know—really know, what it was like to lose someone. For your better half to slip through your fingers, and before you know it—

"It was your fault." The words had slipped from his tongue before he could stop them. Not that he would take them back, now they were spoken. It was the truth.

When Adam turned on his heel to glare at Snee, the man was staring back calmly. "I wouldn't go that far."

"It was your idea to push the mission in France longer than we agreed," Adam said, every word dull in his mouth. "Yours, not mine. And Louisa—"

"She died a hero's death," Snee said quietly.

"She died before her time, and you know it," said Adam, his voice breaking. *Damn it, he wasn't going to let Snee see how much this got to him.* He was a consummate professional. He could go back to grieving Louisa in his own time. "And I don't want a partner."

"Well, I did not actually ask for your opinion in this matter," said Snee smoothly. "And I think you'll find the partner I have selected for you has just as much desire for vengeance against the Glasshand Gang as you do."

Now that was interesting. Adam narrowed his eyes. "I . . . I don't wish vengeance upon the Glasshand Gang. Not personally."

Well, it was mostly true.

Snee seemed to know what he was thinking. "Of course you don't. A figure of speech."

They fell into silence as Adam's mind whirled.

It was completely impossible, of course. After what had happened last time, there was no chance he would accept a partner. The man, whoever he was, wouldn't be able to keep up. He would be lazy. Or ignorant. Or worse of all, consider himself lucky to be chosen and therefore require constant encouragement.

Adam breathed out slowly. He'd be slowed down by a partner, and Snee knew it.

So why had the man made the suggestion at all?

"Yates deserves a partner who can be trusted, and this mission requires two people," Snee said quietly. "I wouldn't ask,

Gilroyd, if it weren't essential."

"Essential? I have no wish for a partner, no need for one, and if you think you're going to encumber me with a man who cannot complete his own mission—"

"This mission requires a pair," Snee said, cutting across him and drawing out his pipe, a distinctive one with a dragon holding the bulb. "Trust me."

Adam snorted, but said nothing.

Yates. It wasn't a name he recognized, but that wasn't saying much. Snee had a network far deeper and darker than anything he could have created. That was why rooting out the traitor Chetnole had heard about was proving to be so difficult. Why, Snee had spent the last three weeks trying to hunt him down, all to no avail.

And he had vowed to serve the Crown, hadn't he?

Adam sighed heavily as he met Snee's eye. "Just one mission?"

"There's only one that requires a partner," Snee said, nodding. "English soil, likely only a few weeks. You'll be back here, rid of Yates, before you know it."

Shoulders slumping, Adam nodded wearily. "Fine. Send him along when—"

"Actually, I brought Yates with me," Snee said smoothly.

Adam glared. "Of course you did."

"Ring the bell, will you?" asked Snee innocently.

As provoking as it was to be given orders in one's own house, Adam nonetheless stepped over to the bellpull by the fireplace and gave it a tug.

A door opened.

"Finally," said a woman with almost white blonde hair and a knowing smile. "I never thought it would take so long to persuade him, Mr. Snee."

CHAPTER TWO

RY AS SHE might, Dottie Yates could not quite force her heartbeat to slow.

"You're being ridiculous," she murmured under her breath as she stepped closer to the door between the drawing room and the library. "Just—just stay calm."

Stay calm. It was a simple enough directive, and one she had given to a number of people over the years. Dottie knew her quiet, firm, and authoritative manner worked. At least, it worked on other people.

There were voices in the library, but the door between them was closed and it was impossible to hear what they were saying.

Well, impossible at the moment. Dottie did not subscribe to the belief that anything was truly impossible, not once one had put one's mind to it. *Her* mind usually found a solution within a minute.

And it was not so difficult to crack open the door. The whole house was decrepit, but thankfully the inhabitants of the room did not hear the creak of the hinges as she pushed the door—just an inch. An inch would be enough.

From her vantage point, her eye close to the gap, Dottie could see much of the library. There was Mr. Snee, the man who had recruited her in the first place. He was sitting in what appeared to be a most comfortable armchair. He was looking lazily at a gentleman standing before him.

The man had his back to Dottie, but she did not need to see his face to know him. That was Adam Seymour, Duke of Gilroyd.

She'd heard the rumors. Most of them had to be false, she was certain. One man could not be that dark, that bold, that bitter. Though she had to admit, he certainly sounded angry . . .

"Essential? I have no wish for a partner, no need for one, and if you think you're going to encumber me with . . ." The voice became muffled, the exact words getting lost. ". . . cannot . . . own mission . . ."

Dottie swallowed. That she needed another person was unfortunate, but she was not going to permit this duke, no matter how bitter or angry he was, to get in the way of her mission.

"There's only one that requires a partner," Snee was saying inside the library "English soil, likely only a few weeks. You'll be back here, rid of Yates, before you know it."

Yes, a few weeks and it would all be over, Dottie thought, her gaze flickering to the back of the gentleman on whom her plans depended. His shoulders were slumped, and his head was hanging low. The Duke of Gilroyd did not seem pleased with the idea of working a short and easy mission with a woman like her.

She bristled. *Was working with her truly that terrible?*

He was speaking now. "Fine. Send . . . when—"

"Actually, I brought Yates with me," Snee interrupted him with the well-practiced art of the magistrate.

Dottie had to hand it to him, it was well done. The duke muttered a reply she didn't catch, but his tone sounded bitter.

"Ring the bell, will you?"

Dottie hurriedly stepped back from the door. That was the agreed upon signal. Snee had said it would take a few minutes to persuade the man, but as soon as she heard the bell, to go right on in.

Heart hammering and hating herself for getting so worked up, Dottie smoothed the skirts of her gown and held her head high.

She was Dottie Yates. She had completed more missions than most gentlemen in Snee's employ and performed better. She had never met a gentleman she could not woo, a lady she could not befriend, or a servant she could not bribe.

There was nothing to fear.

The Duke of Gilroyd rang the bell.

Dottie created a confident smile as she opened the door fully and beheld the two gentlemen. "Finally. I never thought it would take so long to persuade him, Mr. Snee."

She had intended her words to be light and cheerful. Other gentlemen would have beamed at her sudden presence, perhaps chuckled at her jest. They would have bowed, asked Mr. Snee for an introduction, and been clay in her hands within the hour. Maybe two hours at the outside edge.

It was therefore with great surprise that Dottie watched the tall gentleman turn, glare, and snap, "What do you want?"

Dottie's eyes widened. "I may ask you the same thing."

"How did you get in my—never mind. Be off with you," the Duke of Gilroyd said in a snappish, almost exasperated tone. "I would have thought Dawson would be here by now, Snee, with your Mr. Yates. What have you done with him?"

Dottie's mouth fell open.

He—he was expecting a man? How on earth would that help, given the mission that they were to undertake together?

Her ego prickled. He truly had not heard of her? Dottie Yates, one of the most elegant and impressive operatives for the Crown?

True, her last assignment had been rather trivial. Watching over the Lady Margaret Everleigh at a house party had hardly called on the great variety of her skills. Even so, she had kept the woman safe. In the main.

"This," Mr. Snee said delicately, "is Miss Yates. Your new partner, Gilroyd."

Dottie hastily closed her mouth and curtsied. Well, he was a duke. If they were going to work together, it wouldn't hurt to start off on the right foot.

Not that starting off on the right foot appeared to be a concern of his. In a show of great injustice, and more than a little rudeness, the Duke of Gilroyd was staring in uncomplimentary amazement.

"This is your Yates?" he said, distrust painted across his brow. "You honestly think I will work with a woman?"

Dottie tried her best not to bristle, but it was most unfair. Why, the man hardly had a sterling reputation! She'd heard tell that one of his previous partners had been killed in action!

Not that she would be so rude as to point that out. Still. She had never lost someone. She had always succeeded in her missions. Whatever this man's reticence, *she* was the experienced one with a perfect record.

"I know my value, and it is far greater than it appears you would credit," Dottie said with more composure than she felt. "And though you may not wish to partner with me, Your Grace—"

"I'll partner with you when hell freezes over," snarled the Duke of Gilroyd. "What in God's name did you think you were doing?"

This last question appeared to have been shot at Mr. Snee, who was still sitting serenely in his armchair.

Dottie hid a smile. There was something about Mr. Snee. No matter what the situation, she had never seen the man ruffled. Bumbling and easily impressed he may sometimes appear, but she wasn't fooled. Mr. Snee was a clever man, and he used his bumbling guise to get by.

And she wouldn't let him take the fall for what had been none of his fault.

"It was my idea to find a partner for this mission," Dottie said to the Duke of Gilroyd, who appeared determined not to look at her. "It requires—"

"I doubt you have any idea what a mission truly needs, though I thank you for your service," the Duke of Gilroyd snapped. He turned back to Mr. Snee, utterly ignoring Dottie's outrage. "You think you can just slip in a girl to—"

"Excuse me!" Dottie said hotly. "I am not a *girl*. I am four and twenty—"

"And I am sure you cut a very nice figure in a ball and play cards exquisitely," said the Duke of Gilroyd, rolling his eyes.

Perhaps if he had not rolled his eyes, Dottie would not have been so furious. As it was, it was enraging to be treated so. This may be a ducal library, and this—this fool may be a duke, but he certainly didn't know the first thing about good manners!

"Don't you dare speak down to me as though I have no comprehension of what is required," Dottie shot back, striding toward him and stopping just before the astonished Duke of Gilroyd. "I have served on many missions and I—"

"Please, Miss Yates, do not concern yourself," Mr. Snee interjected as Dottie's blood boiled. "I can speak with His Grace, and—"

"I can defend myself," Dottie cut across him hotly.

Honestly! How on earth did men manage to convince themselves that they ruled the world, when it could not be clearer that they had no idea what they were doing? Every household in the country was managed, run, and kept going by women. Great amounts of industry were performed by women. Women were birthing the next generation, a far more dangerous mission than most given out by Mr. Snee!

And this man, this Duke of Gilroyd, thought he had the right to lecture her about what she could and could not do? What she was *able* to do?

And now the Duke of Gilroyd was laughing. *Laughing! At her!*

"Of course you can't defend yourself, do not speak nonsense, Miss Yates," he was saying. "You are not a man, you cannot—"

Dottie did not think. Her instincts had been honed precisely so thought would not be necessary in moments that required swift action, but the trouble was, she wasn't often faced with a duke.

And so when she lunged forward, pulling a hidden knife from

her belt and halting just as she brought it to his throat, her other hand clasping the back of his neck, she ran purely on instinct.

But then the instinct ran out.

Dottie tried to take a deep breath, but it was difficult. He was so—so much taller, broader than she had first thought. There was a strength in him that she had seen but not quite understood. And now she had her hands around him, her chest pressed against his own, and . . .

Even swallowing did not remove the sudden giddiness. Dottie swayed, ever so slightly, and tried not to breathe in the heady musk that the Duke of Gilroyd emanated.

Dear God, he was intoxicating!

She needed to step back—yet Dottie would not do so until he had admitted, once and for all, that she could defend herself.

The Duke of Gilroyd glanced down toward the knife pressed against his throat. He wouldn't be able to see it at that angle, but he could certainly feel it. "Dear God."

"That's enough, Miss Yates," said Mr. Snee lazily. "I am sure His Grace is not impressed by such displays."

"I think His Grace is," said the Duke of Gilroyd slowly. "Bloody hell, woman, where did you come from?"

It was rather startling for Dottie to realize she was breathing quite heavily. And so was the Duke of Gilroyd. In fact, their heaving chests appeared to be breathing in sync. As though . . . as though . . .

Dottie stepped back, slipping her knife back into her gown's bodice.

Just in time, she could not help but think. Lord in his Heaven, she had never known herself to be so taken in by a gentleman. Heavens, it was magnetic, the effect he had. Did he know? Had the Duke of Gilroyd any idea what impact he was surely having on any woman who got within six inches of him?

Dottie swallowed. *Not that she would be getting within six inches of him again. Obviously.*

"How dare you?" the Duke of Gilroyd continued, though in

rather a more conversational tone than an outraged one. "You know, you could have cut me."

Dottie grinned. "I could have done far more than that."

"Well then, why don't you?" he snapped, stepping forward.

Hating herself, Dottie took a step back. She couldn't be that close to him again, not yet. She still needed to clear her head from the last time.

The small smirk on the Duke of Gilroyd's face proved he knew she would be accepting his challenge. *Oh, blast it all to hell,* Dottie thought bitterly. She was not one to have her head turned by a handsome face. And it wasn't his face that was the problem. It was his . . . himself. The power he exuded, the confidence with which he had stood, accepting the blade against his throat.

As though . . . as though being hurt by her was in some way an honor. As though he was far more interested in seeing what she would do next than protecting himself.

As though he had nothing much to live for.

"If you wish to be harmed, Your Grace, that can be seen to," said Dottie sweetly.

Though what she would do if he dared her further, she did not quite know. This was all going wrong. She had been determined, once Mr. Snee had revealed who he thought her perfect partner would be, to win over the Duke of Gilroyd with her charm, skills, and abilities. Holding a knife against his throat and bitterly arguing about whether she should even be there had not been part of the plan.

This was the trouble with being a lady in a gentleman's world. Dottie had known it the minute she had agreed to join Mr. Snee's collection of servants to the Crown. There would always be those who thought she did not belong, no matter how much she proved otherwise.

And there was a glint in the Duke of Gilroyd's eye that told Dottie he was another one of those people, a gentleman who refused to accept that a woman could serve, that she could form and carry out a plan, that she could know what to do with a knife.

In short, a man who refused to accept that a woman could be trusted.

"You wouldn't dare to hurt me," opined the idiotic Duke of Gilroyd. "You're just—"

Dottie moved swiftly, but sadly, not swiftly enough.

She did not quite know how he had done it, but Mr. Snee had suddenly risen from his chair and placed himself between them, hands raised.

"Now then," said Mr. Snee quietly. "I did not bring Miss Yates here for you and her to have a fight, Your Grace."

"She said—"

"I know what she said, and she was within her rights to say it," Mr. Snee said with a knowing look. "And I am within my rights to say this: The two of you need to calm down and think for a moment. Don't react. Think."

Dottie was breathing heavily again, something she hated. How dare the man have this effect on her! How could she be so weak, so foolish, as to be taken in by a few good looks and, admittedly, a dazzlingly delicious aroma?

She would have to do far better than that once she and the Duke of Gilroyd were out on their mission. Assuming she had not tired of him first, of course.

"You don't have to protect her, Snee," the Duke of Gilroyd was saying. "I wasn't going to actually hurt her."

Dottie was pleased to see Mr. Snee laugh at that. "It wasn't her I was worried about, Gilroyd."

Her satisfaction increased as she watched the Duke of Gilroyd's eyes widen. "You mean—"

"She could have taken your head off in three different ways before you even thought how to defend yourself," said Mr. Snee with a glance at Dottie. "If I were you, I wouldn't risk it."

Dottie held up her head boldly and grinned as the Duke of Gilroyd's gaze met hers.

There. It wasn't the resounding endorsement from Mr. Snee that she had hoped for, but it was certainly better than nothing.

And it was true. Although Dottie had never killed in the field—she had never had to. There were other ways of threatening a man which made it far easier to get information, then she was on her way.

"Fine," the Duke of Gilroyd snapped, lifting his hands in mock surrender and stepping back.

Slowly, Mr. Snee lowered his own hands and stepped back to his armchair. "Now I know neither of you were expecting—"

"You said a partner," the Duke of Gilroyd interrupted almost immediately. "I thought you meant—"

"You were the one who assumed I was speaking of a gentleman," Mr. Snee pointed out as Dottie continued to beam. "I said nothing of the identity of Yates. Nothing whatsoever."

The look of ire the Duke of Gilroyd shot her was potent. If Dottie had not been prepared for it, she may have been genuinely hurt by it. But several months of service—and being around tiresome gentlemen who did not believe she could be of any use—had hardened Dottie's skin.

She gave a delicate curtsy to the duke. "At your service, Y'Grace."

The man snorted. "I doubt that."

"I don't suggest this partnership for the good of your health, Gilroyd, but the good of the country," interjected Mr. Snee, and there was a sharp edge to his voice Dottie had never heard. "You must—"

"No one gets to tell me 'must,' not after—. You know my feelings on this matter, Snee," the Duke of Gilroyd said darkly, walking away from them to stare out the window.

Dottie watched him curiously. Oh, she was accustomed to gentlemen throwing a temper tantrum because they did not wish to work with a lady. It was why she had accepted the Duke of Dulverton's plea to keep an eye on his sister just a few months ago. A fortnight in a country house watching a duke's sister to ensure she didn't get into trouble? Practically a holiday.

Except for the violent attack, of course. But Dottie could

hardly have predicted that.

Yet this was different, somehow. The Duke of Gilroyd was not merely against her, from what she could tell. He seemed to have difficulty with the very idea of having a partner.

The arrogance. What, did he think he could always act perfectly alone, without any help?

"—know how I feel about partners," he was saying in a low, pained voice. "I will not have one, Snee. Particularly . . . particularly a woman."

Dottie bristled. One day, the world would no longer care whether it was a gentleman or a lady completing a task. They would just care that the task was done and done well.

If she could push the world closer to that reality, then she would have achieved something. And that meant convincing this arrogant Duke of Gilroyd that she was worth it.

Infuriating man.

"I believe a woman can be just as good as a man when it comes to serving England and the Crown," Dottie said clearly. "You may disagree, Your Grace—"

"You can assume whatever you like of me," came his testy reply.

But Dottie was not going to give up. She would make the man see. "A few weeks, and we won't even be going out of England. You'll be back here ready to be miserable on your own before you know it."

The Duke of Gilroyd glanced over his shoulder with a glower. "I never said—"

"Gilroyd," said Mr. Snee quietly, "it really is an important mission."

Dottie glanced between the two of them. How far back these two gentlemen went, she did not know. But there was evidently a trust between them that went beyond anything she could imagine.

She watched as the duke met Mr. Snee's eyes. Something unspoken passed between them.

Then the Duke of Gilroyd sighed. "Fine. Miss Yates, was it? I'll give you a trial, heaven help me."

Dottie nodded curtly, and wondered what on earth she was getting herself into. "And I will give you one."

CHAPTER THREE

3 November 1811

ADAM GLARED ACROSS the breakfast table and swallowed the first three complaints he wished to voice.

Firstly, she had been late that morning. How difficult was it to hear a gong? It wasn't as though breakfast was particularly early. Nine o'clock in the morning was late for breakfast, in his book.

Secondly, she—*Miss Yates* was poorly dressed. Scandalously so.

Not that he was staring. Not much. But the gown she had chosen was far too memorable. Someone serving the Crown should know better. It was outrageous to wear a gown that was that tight around the bust and so . . . so low. At the bust.

Damn it.

And thirdly, Miss Yates was otherwise proving to be the perfect houseguest.

Wait a moment. Was he supposed to be annoyed about that?

"What excellent soft-boiled eggs," Miss Yates said blithely, cracking into her second one. "You must send my regards and compliments to your cook."

Adam glared. Compliments to his cook, indeed. As though

having a cook who could boil eggs was something to make a fuss about!

Even if they were good.

"Fine," he said shortly, glaring at his toast and marmalade.

This was all Snee's idea, of course. *The cad.*

"Why doesn't Miss Yates stay with you for a few days, Gilroyd?" the magistrate had said just as he had been leaving Gilroyd House after saddling him with a new partner. "Give you both time to learn a little about each other. It'll be important for the mission."

And before Adam had been able to point out just how ridiculous that would be, how irritating, how much scandal would be thrown up by having a woman—*a woman!*—move into the place, the indefatigable Miss Yates had stepped in.

"What an excellent idea, Mr. Snee," she'd said brightly. "I'll have my things brought over directly."

A man should decide who lived in his house, Adam thought darkly as he poured another cup of tea. A man shouldn't be maneuvered into having a . . . a woman about the place.

Despite his better judgment, he looked up again.

Miss Yates was serenely eating her soft-boiled egg the way a child would. She'd cut her toast into long strips and was dipping each one into the egg, covering it with runny yellow yolk.

It looked delicious. It reminded Adam of how he'd delighted in having soft-boiled eggs on a Sunday morning as a boy.

Dear God, was he getting jealous of the way the woman was eating eggs?

"Are you enjoying your stay, Miss Yates?" Adam asked, as icily as he could manage.

That was the important thing. Distance had to be maintained at all times, both literal and metaphorical. The last thing Adam needed was for this young miss to think he had any real interest in her.

Dear God, the way she had pressed herself against him: the sense of her breasts against his chest, her breathing, light and fluttered, the warmth of her fingers at his neck—

The very last thing he needed was for her to come that close to him again.

"Not particularly, Your Grace," said Miss Yates with a wide smile. "No, I do not think I can describe my stay as enjoyable at all. To date."

Fury flared in Adam's stomach, but he did his best to rein it in. There was no point in permitting his emotions to get the better of him. Allowing Miss Yates to get the better of him.

For this was all a game, wasn't it? A strange sort of game to play with a duke, to be sure, but a game, nonetheless. She was trying to make a point here, and if he was foolish he would let her.

Adam forced a smile. "Oh dear."

"Yes, you are a remarkably poor host," Miss Yates continued, as though they were discussing the weather. "I will admit, I have never been so uncomfortably welcomed."

Swallowing hard, Adam forced himself not to respond immediately.

There was no point giving Miss Yates precisely what she wanted, which was an argument. No, he wasn't so foolish as to fall into that trap.

Probably. He could not deny, at least to himself, that annoyance was fast becoming his primary feeling whenever he was around Miss Yates. She seemed to draw something out of him that he thought had been bred out of the Seymour line.

Petulance.

It was most irritating. But Adam knew he only had himself to blame. If he had been able to convince Snee he did not need a partner—and would certainly never acquiesce to a female partner again—he wouldn't be in this mess.

As it was . . .

"You're not very polite, you know," Miss Yates continued conversationally, a gleam of mischief in her eye. "Probably no one has told you, you being a duke and all. But you *are* a gentleman, and I was rather under the impression that gentlemen were supposed to be good hosts. That they should actually try to make their guests feel welcome, at the very least."

Adam took a deep, slow breath.

How dare she be right? Though it galled Adam to admit it, even in the privacy of his own mind, he had not been a good host to Miss Yates, and she was right to call him out on it.

Even if it was infuriating in the extreme.

"You are . . . you are correct, Miss Yates." *Dear Lord, why was that so hard to say?* "I hope I can be a better host until you return to . . . to wherever it is you live."

Strange. Now Adam came to think about it, Miss Yates had stayed with him all of yesterday and he knew no more about her now than when she had stepped into his library with old Snee. He had barely asked her a thing.

He was slacking.

"So tell me," he said bracingly. "How did you fall in with Snee?"

"There's no need to say it like that, as though I seduced him into my bed, then put him to work by finagling my way into the homes of dukes," Miss Yates said lightly, though there was a steel in her gaze Adam did not like.

"I did not mean it like—"

"Didn't you?" she said quietly.

Adam hesitated. *Well, not consciously. Not entirely.* "I just—"

"I don't know why you hate me so much, Your Grace," Miss Yates said in a tone she might use to ask a haberdasher whether the blue ribbon would be coming in next week. "I have never met you before, as far as I can tell, and all the people I have cheated and betrayed were French."

He tried another smile. "Very clever, Miss Yates."

"Yes, I am," she said quietly. "Cleverer than you, I dare say."

How did the woman expect him to be polite and calm and all the other gentlemanly attributes Adam despised if she was going to say such things?

Besides, he did not hate her, though he was not surprised it was coming across that way. He had never been particularly good at sharing his emotions.

That had all changed with Louisa. For a short time.

The sudden shock of pain was akin, Adam presumed, to being struck by lightning. It certainly seemed to fry him from top to toe, the abrupt jolt in his chest pausing his heartbeat.

It started again—as it always did—but every thump was agony.

He was not going to think about Louisa. Thinking of his wife would only lead to sorrow, and Adam had experienced enough of that to last a lifetime.

"Your Grace?" Miss Yates was saying. "Are you quite well?"

Her voice seemed to be coming from a long way away. There was another woman's voice in his ears now, one he knew and loved dearly. He had not loved it as he should have done—as he would come to do—when they had first met, of course.

That had been a completely different conversation with Snee—in the garden, here in London. They had been discussing infiltrating a home, and as a maid brought out a cup of tea, Adam had been saying something foolish, as usual.

"—never be able to do it."

And Snee had lifted an eyebrow and said, "You don't think I know of anyone who can easily infiltrate a house?"

Adam had shaken his head as he took the tea from the maid. "No, and—"

"Your money or your life," a voice had said.

It had lilted. That was what Adam remembered most. The voice had a musical quality he had never heard in another and wasn't likely to again. There had been a knife pressed into his chest, and all he could think in that moment was: who was this maid?

Snee had been laughing. Adam had turned, slowly, to look at the maid who had only moments ago been handing him a teacup.

She'd had dark hair, almost black. Her eyes had glittered with satisfaction, and the knife—

The knife was a teaspoon.

Adam's laughter had joined Snee's. Laughter around Louisa had felt easy. Everything had felt easy. He had congratulated Snee on his idea, for using a woman pretending to be a maid was an excellent idea and would surely come in useful during their upcoming mission.

"Oh, don't thank me," Snee had replied with a nod of his head. "Praise Miss Louisa Taylor. It was her idea."

And that was Adam's first inkling that the woman he would partner with on that particular job, and for all others, was unlike any woman he had ever known. Beautiful and charming and clever—everything, in short, that he wanted.

And nothing like this Miss Yates at all.

"Your Grace?"

Adam blinked, then shook his head as though ridding his ears of water.

It was easy enough to fall into daydreams when you were alone, he chastised himself silently. It was the height of bad manners to do so when you were supposed to be entertaining.

Not that he'd put in much effort at entertaining Miss Yates.

"Are you quite well?" Miss Yates asked again, concern spread across her face. "You . . . well, you sort of drifted off for a moment there."

Adam's jaw tightened. "Just thinking."

"Happy thoughts, I presume," she said softly.

How dare she look at him like—like she could begin to guess what he was thinking? Adam straightened in his seat and reached for his teacup.

He looked down into it, and his mind replaced it again with a teacup from another time, held out by a woman who would become so dear to him—

"I suppose we should talk about the mission."

"The mission?" The idiotic words had fallen from his lips before Adam could stop them, and he cringed the moment they were said.

Was he trying to make himself look the complete fool? Why had he said something so ludicrous?

"Are you sure you're well—?"

"Yes, the mission," Adam said sternly, as though it had been Miss Yates, and not himself, who had sounded so foolish. "After all, I think it only right and fair that I get a good idea of how I will have to be looking after you."

It was evidently the wrong thing to say—though Adam could not for the life of him understand why she should react so strongly. At his words, Miss Yates had swelled, her breasts—*her chest*, Adam corrected as heat flushed through him—puffed out with indignation.

"You looking after me?" she repeated, a glower in her eyes. "I think it far more likely that I'll be looking after you!"

This was an argument, Adam knew, that would be easy to slip into. It would give him the excuse to rattle off a few frustrations, and Miss Yates he was sure would enjoy throwing back a few ideas of her own. They would get increasingly annoyed, one of them would say something to truly hurt the other, and one would storm off.

And then it would be even harder to get through the next few weeks and complete this mission. Whatever it was.

No, it was time to prove his breeding and gentility, Adam knew with a sinking heart. He would have to be the bigger man. It was not as though Miss Yates—

"I apologize, Your Grace," she said with a sigh.

Adam stared. "I beg your pardon?"

He must have misheard her. Even in the couple of days he had spent in her presence, he was certain Miss Yates was not the sort to apologize.

Still, her cheeks were red and her eyes defiant. Perhaps he had heard correctly.

"I should not be picking fights with you, even if you do make it far too easy," said Miss Yates, almost undoing the conciliatory work of her remarks with her tone. "We should focus on the mission and nothing else. Not how unsuited we are, not how irritating you clearly find me, and not how priggish I find you."

Adam's mouth fell open. *Of all the outrageous, thoughtless, rude—*

"So, the mission is a simple one," said Miss Yates, placing her elbows on the table in a most uncouth manner and placing her head on her folded hands. "I would have thought it would even be simple enough for you to understand."

And this was her idea of not picking a fight?

It took a great deal of effort, reserves of patience Adam had not even known he had, but he managed it. He nodded and said not a word.

A flash of triumph and something else flickered across Miss Yates' face. Was she purposefully attempting to goad him into another speech that would further embarrass him? Or was she impressed at how he had managed to restrain himself?

And why did impressing Miss Yates suddenly seem so damned important?

"Simple?" he prompted.

Miss Yates nodded. "You would have heard of the Glasshand Gang, I suppose."

Adam snorted, leaning back in his chair. "I do not think there is a soul in London who has not heard about them! No matter how many of their members are found and taken to justice, there always appear to be more of them."

"They are a canker," said Miss Yates darkly.

"Now on that, we agree," said Adam, trying not to think of poor Sedley. Losing a father—and a brother—to that notorious gang must have been awful. The man never spoke of it, but that in itself was enough to show the depth of pain he experienced. "But I thought Snee had given up on chasing after the Glasshand Gang?"

"Mr. Snee," Miss Yates said in a reproving voice, "had. But I did not. I came across some information in a . . . a conversation, shall we say, with a young man."

It was all Adam could do to keep his face placid.

A conversation. Well, he had not inquired about Miss Yates through any of his contacts, presuming she would tell him enough about herself that mattered as time went on. And now she had. Though perhaps not in the way she would think.

A strange sense of disappointment curled around his heart.

Why, he did not know, but the knowledge that Miss Yates had already used her body to get information, like a common harlot, was rather a setback.

Because you wanted to be the first to touch that skin, give her pleasure.

The thought passed through his mind like a bullet. Immediately, Adam felt sick, nausea churning his stomach. Was he truly so base and animalistic as that? Was one moment with a pretty woman enough to turn his head?

Was he ready to betray the memory of his beloved wife, just for a blonde who—

"—and that's how I think we'll do it," Miss Yates finished.

Adam stared. He hadn't really taken in that she was even still speaking. Lord, he was going to be left in the water if he didn't shape up soon.

Perhaps Chetnole had been right. Perhaps he was losing his touch, getting old.

Old? He wasn't even forty yet!

"You disagree," Miss Yates said calmly. "You think there is a better way?"

Hesitating only a moment, Adam said as confidently as he could manage, "Probably. But I'll humor you."

"You blackguard," she shot back, far more directly than he could have guessed. "You weren't even listening."

"Listening? I most certainly—"

But his bluster did not convince the woman on the opposite side of the breakfast table. "Go on, then. Tell me the plan."

Fury rattled up Adam's back and shoulder blades, settling in his temples. But he had been caught out, and he would have to admit it. Even if it did grind his jaw.

"Fine," he snapped, finally pushed beyond all endurance. "I wasn't listening. But that doesn't mean—"

"Do you think bringing the Glasshand Gang to its knees is important?" Miss Yates demanded swiftly.

He needed no time to think about that. "Of course. They are England's greatest enemy, save for the French, and the damned bastards are on our own shores. The Glasshand Gang must be ended—"

"And that is precisely what this mission will accomplish, if you do what I say and keep a level head," said Miss Yates. "Honestly! The number of times I am told it is ladies who get emotional, and yet men—"

"I am sure the men you work with are very happy to have their reason taken from them," said Adam darkly. "And once I can prove I could perform this mission without you—"

"It was my informant, and my mission," Miss Yates said hotly, and Adam was rather delighted to see that he had finally got under the woman's skin. "Mr. Snee is sure the answers lie in Brighton, but it is my mission, Gilroyd."

Time for a dose of her own medicine.

"You do not have a monopoly on insight and intelligence at this table, Miss Yates," Adam said slowly, weighing every word carefully and enjoying how each one landed on the young lady. "You may have worked for Snee before, but I can tell you now, you have already made several mistakes today that in the field would have been deadly."

Miss Yates arched an eyebrow. "Indeed?"

Adam leaned back, lifting a hand so that he could visibly count on his fingers. He was going to enjoy this. "You did not check under the table for a knife, or in your food for poison. You swiftly sat here without even thinking of—"

"This is supposed to be a safe house," Miss Yates shot back. "With my new partner and his servants. If I distrust you, what is the point in proceeding?"

It was an excellent point, damn her. "Care and due diligence are vital skills for a—"

"You cannot expect me to test everything I eat for—"

"I can if you want to stay alive long enough to complain about it," said Adam testily. "There are three exits to this room, none of which you checked. Two pairs of curtains behind which anyone could be standing. You're wearing a gown—"

"What, my gown has offended you, too?" Miss Yates laughed dryly. "You think a gown could end a mission?"

Adam rolled his eyes. "Think, woman! That print is obvious, easily recognized. You could be tracked, watched, kidnapped even just because your gown demarks you as someone swiftly spotted!"

She could sense the truth in his words, he could tell. Two pink dots had appeared on Miss Yates' cheeks. It was irritating in the extreme that they only improved her complexion.

"I perhaps have a few things to learn," said Miss Yates quietly. "But you have made mistakes, too."

"I have not—"

"You didn't even notice that your newspaper isn't here, as it usually is," she said with a wry grin. "I took it. Along with the three letters you were sent. I intended to read them and place them on tomorrow's breakfast table. You would never have known."

Adam's face fell.

Dear God. She was good.

"We only have to trust each other," said Miss Yates quietly as she rose, "not like each other."

She had swept out of the breakfast room before Adam could say anything. Not that he would. The fact that he was starting to respect her was certainly not something Miss Yates needed to know.

CHAPTER FOUR

4 November 1811

ONLY WHEN DOTTIE scrunched her eyes could she make out the handwriting.

Her own handwriting. Really, she needed to improve her penmanship if she wanted to be able to read her own notes.

Curled up in an armchair in the impressive, yet dusty, Gilroyd drawing room, Dottie brought her notebook to her face and attempted to make out what she had written only days ago.

Glasshand Gang nt crful—notes in paper? Why now? Why nt send msgs straight to source?

Dottie sighed. Well, at least that made sense. It was bizarre that the Glasshand Gang appeared to be sending messages through the obituaries of the London newspapers, particularly when she was almost certain they had an impressive network of informants across the country. Why on earth would they need to put secret messages somewhere as public as that?

She turned a page and continued reading. The room remained silent, save for the crackling of the fire she was sat beside and the gentle ticking of a grandfather clock on the other side of the room.

Well, the company here may not be up to scratch, but the

rooms were lovely. Far warmer than her rooms with Miss Clarke, who had reluctantly offered Dottie the use of one of her rooms at her Governess Bureau. Business was tricky at the moment, apparently, and Miss Clarke could use the additional income. It had been quite a wrench to give it up, but Dottie could hardly justify asking Mr. Snee for the money to keep it when she was staying here.

Her gaze darted about the room. An Axminster rug, several paintings on the walls that looked tremendously expensive, and the lazy sort of wealth a duke never noticed. A marble and ivory chess set atop a board in the corner. A few books, leatherbound and exquisitely edged in gold leaf.

Just the sort of accoutrements a duke would have.

Dottie forced her attention back to her notebook. None of the finery His Grace enjoyed was going to help her with this mission. As far as she could tell, His Grace wasn't going to help her on this mission at all. Worse luck.

Her eye was caught by another note she had made to herself, this time at a diagonal in the margin of a page.

Traitor?

Dottie swallowed. *It was only a rumor*, she told herself firmly. The Duke of Chetnole's sudden reappearance in London was swiftly mirrored by a rumor within her circles that there was a traitor in their midst. Someone spilling secrets to the Glasshand Gang, to the French, to anyone they set themselves against.

She'd heard nothing more, discounted it immediately. Mr. Snee would surely not be so swiftly taken in and allow a traitor to remain at work.

She turned another page.

The pvln. Prinny? Danger to royals?

Dottie bit her lip. She'd spent the last day or two attempting to get everything ready for the mission His Grumpiness and she would be undertaking, but the more she read back her own notes, the more underprepared she felt.

It was a foolish idea, of course. It had come to her in the

middle of the night, as all her foolish ideas did, but this one had appeared to have merit. When she had suggested to Mr. Snee that she and a gentleman undertake it, he had been all for it. He'd even shared information from his informants that pointed to Brighton. Of course. Why hadn't she thought of that?

And she needed to concentrate. Needed to read through her notes and be absolutely certain she was prepared for any eventuality. Even if she was constantly distracted by—

"You could try sitting in a more ladylike manner," came a cold, dry voice as the door to the hallway opened. "Put some effort into pretending to be a lady."

Dottie stiffened, though she attempted to keep her expression light and her smile broad as she rolled her eyes. She would not let him see just how easily he got to her. She wouldn't.

"That is uppermost in your mind, is it?" she asked placidly as the Duke of Gilroyd walked into the drawing room. "A critique on how I am sitting?"

Really, it was a strange thing to pick at—but then she had been entirely silent, so perhaps her host had run out of things to complain about.

And it was rather unsettling to have the Duke of Gilroyd close the door behind him and glare, taking in the way her feet were curled under her, the hem of her gown drifting to the carpet.

How did he do it? How did he look at her like . . . like she were an intruder? As though this armchair were reserved for another?

As far as Dottie could see, the Duke of Gilroyd did not entertain. Certainly, no one had come to the house during her admittedly short visit. He had sent no post, received few letters. She'd bribed a footman, so she was absolutely sure on that score.

"It is not a ladylike way to sit," the Duke of Gilroyd repeated stiffly.

"Well, I suppose I should be grateful that you have run out of other ways to criticize me," said Dottie nonchalantly, tucking her feet even deeper under her to make it absolutely clear she was not going to acquiesce to his criticisms.

She met his dark gaze and immediately wished she had not.

Not because the Duke of Gilroyd was not pleasant to look at. That was part of the problem. Whenever the man was in the room, Dottie could feel herself being conscious of his presence. How he looked. Where he was looking.

She found herself, in short, wishing he would look at her.

It was naught but foolishness. *Foolishness and loneliness*, Dottie thought darkly. If she were not so constantly working alone, having to rely on idiots like Marnion to provide her with information, then perhaps she would not be so . . . so taken with him.

The Duke of Gilroyd, that was.

Unfortunately, she could no longer deny to herself that she found the man attractive. Try as she might, Dottie could find no fault in his complexion, no error in his frame—nothing but charm itself in his physique.

His strong, bold physique. One which she had comprehended in a most unladylike manner within minutes of meeting him. A moment indelibly marked in her mind, visiting her in dreams . . .

Dottie cleared her throat. Noticing a gentleman was attractive was no crime. Dwelling on it, however, was a little scandalous.

She needed to focus on something important. Like impressing him.

Not because he was the Duke of Gilroyd, she thought hastily as the man stepped across the room and settled on the sofa opposite, lounging as only a nobleman could. Not because he was devastatingly handsome and clearly far wittier than the average boor on the street.

No, Dottie needed to impress him because she needed him to trust her. That was the only way this mission could work. He may not be intending to help as he ought, but he needed to.

Besides, it was vexing that he didn't admire her already. It had never taken this much work to achieve it before.

"You don't have to be so annoyed," Dottie said calmly—or at least, as calmly as she could manage. *Did he hear the quaver?* "It's not as though I have done anything wrong yet."

And she never did. Oh, there were a few occasions when she could have acted more swiftly. But no one had died.

Yet despite her words, the Duke of Gilroyd glared. "I want my letters back."

Oh, yes. Dottie had quite forgotten about that. Well, perhaps if she had been in his shoes, she would be a tad miffed her private correspondence had been taken. It had made her smile, for a moment, seeing the shock on the duke's face when she'd pointed out that he hadn't even noticed they were missing.

She'd completely forgotten that she'd stormed out of the breakfast room before even thinking about returning them.

"You want your letters back?" Dottie said sweetly. "I bet you do."

Her heart was racing. It was most unaccountable, after deciding not to be drawn in by him in the slightest. Why she gained such a thrill at teasing the Duke of Gilroyd, Dottie did not know. It was unfathomable. Enjoyable.

No, not enjoyable. She shouldn't be enjoying herself. They needed to be scheming!

Together, Dottie thought. *Not against each other.*

"The jest is all very well, Miss Yates, but I truly do need those letters," said the Duke of Gilroyd curtly. "One of them could be of the utmost importance."

Dottie nodded. "Yes, I suppose one is."

It was a tease, that was all. Though she had spoken boldly yesterday at breakfast, Dottie would consider it the height of incivility to actually read the man's letters. She may work as a spy, something few men accepted without a struggle, but she was not totally without honor.

Apparently, the Duke of Gilroyd did not know that. All the color had drained from his face. "You have read—you wouldn't dare!"

"No, I didn't," Dottie admitted. She hated ceding the ground, but his good opinion of her character was far more important than holding fast. Even if that was a strange thing to desire. "But I suppose one day won't make that much difference when it comes to reading them."

"I need them," snapped the Duke of Gilroyd, his temper plainly frayed.

"And I needed to make a point," said Dottie steadily, forcing herself to hold his gaze. "One day you will trust me, Your Grace. For now, I'll take respect."

He met her eye far more boldly than a gentleman should look at a lady. Dottie tried to ignore the tingle of something she did not quite understand rushing up her spine.

Honestly, the way he was looking at her . . . it was probably a good thing there were a few feet between them.

And suddenly, that space had gone. The duke had risen swiftly from the sofa, stepped over the rug, and was now standing right before her, his hand outstretched.

"The letters," he said quietly. "Please."

A shiver of anticipation sparked in Dottie's heart. Would he grab her, perhaps, if she did not immediately hand them over? And why did the thought of him laying hands on her give her not a sense of disgust, but a thrill of delight?

She swallowed, trying to push aside the thought, but it kept returning. She had been close to him once, and Dottie had rather enjoyed it. Had he? Did he wish to touch her again just as much as she wished he would?

The thoughts were shocking. Outrageous. Disgraceful. Immoral.

Dottie had never felt that way about a gentleman before. How incredibly inconvenient.

"My letters," the Duke of Gilroyd repeated, his voice a low burr.

Without taking her gaze from his, heart thumping and resisting all temptations to rise and see just how far this man could be pushed, Dottie reached down the front of her bodice.

The man's eyes widened in shock, and Dottie reveled in the way she could so swiftly confuse him. Oh, it was delightful, to use a few of the feminine wiles she had to get a rise out of a man.

This man, in particular.

"Wh-What . . ." muttered the Duke of Gilroyd.

Dottie could hear the desire in his voice. Even if he did not know he had revealed it, the man found her pleasing.

And that was enough. For today.

"Here you go," said Dottie sweetly, pulling out the three letters she had secreted in her bodice and handing them over to him.

The Duke of Gilroyd took them automatically, but he evidently did not have complete control over his tongue for he said thickly, "They . . . they're warm."

So were Dottie's cheeks. Perhaps she had crossed a line, even if she had not intended to. It was rather wild of her to have done such a thing. The trouble was, she was being rewarded by the Duke of Gilroyd clearly thinking about her breasts.

Unbidden, her back arched. Dottie was horrified at the way her instincts had taken over, but the rest of her was delighted with the way the gentleman's gaze dropped to her breasts, his cheeks coloring, his lips parting—

"Thank you," snapped the Duke of Gilroyd. And he turned away.

Only then did Dottie realize she had been holding her breath. The desperate need for air overcame her, and she gasped as though she had been underwater for several minutes.

If her companion noticed, he did not say anything. He had immediately dropped back onto the sofa and was ripping open the letters she had handed him.

Dottie swallowed her disappointment.

And what had she been hoping for? A kiss? An admission of affection? The revelation he was superbly impressed by her and would happily follow her into the mission and obey her every instruction?

She was being foolish. She was falling into the same trap she had seen countless men do—starting to feel . . . something.

Dottie straightened and returned to her notebook. Missions had been ruined for less, lives lost. If she was serious about tracking and capturing leaders of the Glasshand Gang once and for all, she had to stop thinking about the delectable duke opposite her, and start thinking more about her mission.

"I don't suppose my newspaper from yesterday is down there too, is it?"

Dottie smiled at the gruff question uttered by the duke without looking up. "No. It's not."

She pulled it out from behind her, slowly unfolded it in her lap, and started to read it.

Even looking at the printed page, she could see the Duke of Gilroyd out of the corner of her eye. He looked incandescent with rage.

Excellent, Dottie thought as she slowly turned a page. *That was precisely how she wanted—*

"There it is," she breathed.

She couldn't have hoped for better. Right there, before the world, the Glasshand Gang had made their next mistake. Hopefully, it would be their last.

"Where what is?" came the bad-tempered question from the Duke of Gilroyd.

"Here—another clue about the Glasshand Gang's intentions," Dottie said excitedly, prodding at the paper as though he could see it. "That makes six I've spotted this fortnight!"

The duke nodded, still reading his letters. "Right."

What reaction she had hoped for, she couldn't have said. But certainly more than that. It was most ungracious of him not to recognize she had done something impressive. After all, people across England had been attempting to find and decipher clues left by the Glasshand Gang. Was the man not impressed at all that she had done it?

"Tell me," said the Duke of Gilroyd airily without looking up, "how do you know?"

Perhaps not so nonchalant after all. "I've been keeping a track of the obituaries—"

"The obituaries?"

It was a strange response. Dottie nodded. "Every week three Mr. Smiths die, always the same age, always the same location. The clues are in the short description underneath. It's surely impossible for three Mr. Smiths to die absolutely every week, even though it is a common surname. The same age? The same days each week? The probability is astronomical."

Her heart was racing, but this time it was not the Duke of Gilroyd's presence making it beat so fast. No, this was the thrill of the chase. She was getting closer and closer to the Glasshand Gang. She would find them.

"You cannot possibly recall all the details," came her host's irritable reply.

Dottie rolled her eyes. "I don't have to. We've created this wonderful technology, you see? It's called writing things down."

She waved the notebook, trying not to feel too triumphant.

Well, it was a bit of a coup, wasn't it? Just when she had been hoping she was sufficiently prepared for the mission, the Glasshand Gang had left another piece of evidence that she was on the right track.

"You shouldn't leave that thing laying around, you know."

Dottie blinked. "Of course I would never—as if I would do such a thing!"

The mere thought . . .

"Besides, you should be congratulating me," she continued. "Anyone else would praise me for having worked out such a thing!"

"And is that what you want? Praise?" The Duke of Gilroyd fixed her eyes with his dark ones. It was as though he had pinned her to the sofa.

Dottie tried not to show just what an effect he had on her.

Oh, this was a man who could raise armies and take over nations if he wished. He had a way of speaking to people, even after aggravating them for days on end. Dottie knew she would find it difficult not to follow him anywhere, if he but asked her to. And she wouldn't be alone in that, either. This man had a presence, something intangible she couldn't describe.

Did he even know how potent he was?

"Praise would be nice. For a change," Dottie found herself saying.

She hated that she'd said it the moment the Duke of Gilroyd snorted. "Figures. I told Snee a hundred times if I told him once: We can't have women in the service of the Crown. Not anymore."

Dottie bristled. "And why—"

"Because ladies think too much about themselves," said the duke darkly. "Too much about appearances, too much about consequences. They—when one of them—it's just not a good idea."

One of them?

Dottie frowned, attempting to decipher what the gentleman before her was truly saying underneath all the words. It sounded to her as though there had been a woman, a specific woman, who had hurt the Duke of Gilroyd. Who perhaps . . . had betrayed him?

"There's talk," Dottie said boldly, "of a traitor in our midst." Was that rumor not quite as dismissible as she'd first assumed?

"Really?" said the duke, not bothering to look up as he spoke. "How fascinating."

Scowling, Dottie looked back at her notebook and continued reviewing her scribbles. Or at least, that was what she pretended to do for the next hour. Not a single word she had written seeped into her brain, however, for it was far too distracted.

There most certainly had to be a traitor working with Snee and Martock and the others if the Duke of Gilroyd was so offhand about it. Much as she hated to admit it for consideration, a traitor would explain many of the strange happenings that had occurred of late.

And if he was so swift to divert her from conversation about it . . . perhaps he was the very traitor they had been searching for.

CHAPTER FIVE

5 November 1811

S HE WAS DOING it on purpose.

Adam was almost sure. They had been sitting sedately in the library for almost two hours, at her insistence. Miss Yates had said there was something important she had to tell him.

Well, that was to say Dawson had said Miss Yates had said there was something important she had to tell him.

The nerve of her, using one of his own servants to relay a message of any significance!

Nevertheless, Adam had left his comfortable smoking room, the portrait of Louisa hanging over the fireplace as though she were a guardian angel, and he had entered the library. And what had he found?

Miss Yates. Reading.

"Dawson said—" he began.

Began being the key word. The moment the initial words were out of his mouth, Miss Yates had raised a finger to her lips.

"Shhhh!" she'd said severely, as though he had disturbed the quiet of a nursery where children were sleeping.

Adam had looked around. There was no one there. Just Miss Yates tucked up as she always was, feet underneath her, a book in her lap. The fire was blazing, there were a few candles dotted about the place as the afternoon had already drawn in . . .

And that was it.

He had been unable to prevent the frown that furrowed his brow. "My butler said—"

"I said shhhhh," Miss Yates said sternly as she deigned to look at him. "And I said so advisedly. Sit there. Be patient."

Her cursory glance had indicated the armchair opposite was where she required him to be, and Adam had sat. In poor grace, admittedly. With a growling irritation that turned his stomach into acid, but still. He sat.

And sat. And sat.

From his position in the library, he had an excellent view of the longcase clock his father had purchased, saying the style would absolutely be coming back into fashion. Adam wasn't so sure about that. The wood was far too light, the ornamentation too garish.

It did, however, tell the time with admirable precision, so Adam had been perfectly aware of each minute ticking by, the pendulum swinging in an almost hypnotic manner. Minutes passed. A quarter of an hour. Half an hour. An hour.

Try as he might, Adam could not prevent his gaze from flicking over, once in a while, to the person whose fault it was that he was sitting here in silence as she delicately turned a page every now and again.

Miss Yates.

She had been living in Gilroyd House for four days, yet in a way he was absolutely none the wiser when it came to understanding her character. The woman gave little away, which was impressive. None of his servants had been able to wheedle anything out of her, worse luck, and she'd dropped no hints as to her parentage, history, or doings with Snee or others.

Adam's gaze searched her face, as though the rosebud mouth, light blue eyes, and white-blonde hair could speak of her past.

This Miss Yates, what did she want? Oh, the Glasshand Gang brought to justice, of course, but she was not unique in that regard. And yet she was, somehow, unique.

Adam cleared his throat.

Miss Yates looked up. "Shhh—"

"I didn't say anything!" he protested, hating he had so easily fallen into her trap.

There was a dancing look of glee in Miss Yates' eyes as she hushed him again, then looked once more at her book.

By the time the grandfather clock chimed the next hour, Adam had had enough. This was his house. His library. His damned book!

He rose, his blood roaring in his ears. "Miss Yates, you appear to be under the delusion you can do or say anything to me, and in my own house! Well, let me disabuse you of that misunderstanding. You—"

"Finally," said Miss Yates in clipped tones, shutting the book and beaming. "I was beginning to wonder how long it would take."

Adam's mouth remained open, hot air scalding his lungs, but the fire itself summarily extinguished by the woman before him.

Finally? What on earth did she mean?

As though she could hear the question, Miss Yates' eyes glittered. "I was interested to discover just how long it would take for your temper to boil over and for you to start speaking to me as an equal rather than as a lady. I make that . . . goodness, almost one hundred and fifteen minutes, don't you?"

Adam stared, mouth still gaping.

She was . . . she was toying with him? Teasing him, trying to find out how long it was until his temper exploded? Had any man ever put up with such a woman?

"I admit myself relieved. This book is exceedingly dull," Miss Yates added as she dropped it onto the console table beside her. "Now. I believe you wish to know the details about the mission we shall be undertaking?"

It took all of Adam's self-control not to throw the blasted

woman out of his house and send for Snee to explain himself. That had always been one of the most challenging parts of serving the Crown—remembering that in these matters, it was Snee who was the superior and he, the Duke of Gilroyd, was nothing more than a servant.

She had played him, and played him well. Now it was time—for the moment—to appear to eat humble pie.

Adam had never acquired a taste for it.

Smiling painfully, he lowered himself into the armchair he had so recently vacated. "The mission, yes. Naturally, I would like to know more about it. Everything, to be honest, Miss Yates."

"I thought you'd never ask," Miss Yates said sweetly.

A bubble of rage threatened to surface, but Adam managed to swallow it. She knew perfectly well he had been asking for details about the mission ever since she had arrived at his home, unceremoniously helped herself to a guest bedchamber, and decided to live here.

Never ask, indeed!

Miss Yates was surely the most irritating, the most infuriating—

"And I think we'd do a lot better if we lose the formality, don't you?" Miss Yates was saying. "It's tiresome, continuously calling you the Duke of Gilroyd or Your Grace. What is your first name?"

She spoke as though she had not a care in the world—as though they had been born equals!

Adam bit down his initial response, that he would permit but one woman to call him by his first name, and she certainly did not qualify. But that would open old wounds, perhaps even lead to a conversation about . . . about Louisa.

He couldn't allow that.

Damn and blast it, but he was going to simply answer her, wasn't he?

"Adam," he said curtly.

"Dorothy, but I never go by that. I prefer Dottie," said Miss Yates.

Dottie. Yes, it suited her. Warmth settled in his shoulders, releasing some of the tension. Dottie.

"Now, Adam—you don't have to wince like that, it's not the end of the world," Miss Yates—Dottie—added, waving her hands as she spoke. "Hasn't anyone called you Adam before?"

Adam met her gaze. *Yes*, he wanted to say. *My wife. My beautiful, elegant, intelligent, wife. And she died. And now I'm stuck with you, and you could die, and it'll be all my fault again.*

"Rarely."

"You will have to get used to it," Dottie said firmly, leaning to pick up the poker and give the fire a good seeing to. "It will need to be as easy as breathing, for the mission to work."

Adam frowned. *For the mission to work?*

How did he have the misfortune to be partnered with the most annoying woman Snee could find?

"So, the Glasshand Gang," Dottie said, leaning back in her armchair.

He nodded curtly. "Liars. Thieves. Blackmailers. Robbers. Murderers."

"A succinct and accurate summary," she conceded. "They are a menace. Fighting them is like fighting the French on two fronts, heaven forbid. We need to end them."

It was nothing Adam hadn't heard before. "A great deal has been done and will continue to be done. Sedley—"

"Sedley is too close to the Glasshand Gang, and you know it," Dottie said sharply, her teasing air gone. "His brother is a part of them, their father dead at the Glasshand Gang's hands. No, Sedley is useful, but he is incautious, headstrong. He goes for the hands, the feet, the moving parts of the Gang. We need to go for the head."

Adam permitted himself a slight incline of his own.

Well, that was interesting. It was an assessment he had never heard before, and he could not deny the veracity of her insight. For too long had they fought against the actions of the Glasshand Gang. Perhaps now it was time to attack its thoughts, its plans.

"The leaders, then?"

Dottie nodded. "I've been tracking down—or at least, attempting to track down—the leaders for a while. They are cautious, as is to be expected, but they are also arrogant, weak-minded. They presume upon their own strength."

Had he ever heard a woman speak like this? With precision, as though drawing out a battle plan? This Dottie Yates, she was sharp. Sharper than he had expected.

"I saw one, once."

Now that was interesting. Adam sat up straight. "I'm sorry, you saw—"

"Just a glimpse. In the dark, gaslight flickering, but yes," said Dottie darkly. "If I hadn't been interrupted by a flower seller that I am almost certain was in the Glasshand Gang's employ, I would have rushed over and had a better look. He was a gentleman."

Adam's eyes widened. "You couldn't possibly know—"

"I know what I saw, and the man was wearing an elegantly tailored suit and a beaver fur top hat, smoking a pipe," Dottie said calmly. "We're dealing with someone far cleverer than most people believe."

He sat back in his seat as he tried to take in this new information. A gentleman at the head of the Glasshand Gang? Someone educated, well-connected—perhaps he knew the snake in their midst from university, Society, somewhere else . . .

"And they are using Brighton," she was continuing, "as a connection point to pass their messages. Everyone assumed it was happening in London or Bath—Chantmarle had hoped to find something of them in Edinburgh."

Adam snorted. Chantmarle was an idiot, with no better use than to be sent out on foolish missions. And now he was married—

"That's what I thought," Dottie said with a smile. "But by tracking their messages in the obituaries, and with insight shared from Mr. Snee's sources, I've narrowed it down to Brighton."

His stomach clenched again at the word "obituaries".

Adam knew it was foolish. He knew it was over a year ago now and that others would deem him ridiculous to have been so greatly affected. But they hadn't written their own wife's obituary . . .

"Adam?"

He winced again, then cursed himself silently for having such a visceral reaction to having his name spoken.

It was the strangest thing. He had been named, presumably lovingly, by his parents. They likely as not spent time on choosing that name. And yet as soon as he was a man, he was Gilroyd. No one had said the word "Adam" to him for years, save for Louisa. And now . . . no one.

No one except Miss Yates. *Dottie. Blast it.*

"Dottie," Adam said, as calmly as he could manage. "I have an aversion to Brighton."

"Then I think this an excellent opportunity to cure you of it," Dottie said lightly, as though his opinions mattered very little. "We will be there in a few days."

He could not help it. Adam groaned. "But I would much rather—"

"Oh, I am sorry, I seem to have misunderstood," said Dottie, a gleam in her eye. "I was under the impression we served the Crown, did what was required, and did not complain. Or do I have that wrong?"

It was on the tip of Adam's tongue to point out he was the duke here, this was his house, and by rights he should be the one in charge of the mission—a mission she shouldn't even be on. She had been foisted on him by Snee, and he had been backed into a corner and forced to take her. And she thought she could lecture him?

"I would guard that tongue of yours, Miss Yates—"

"Or what?" she shot back. "What will you do to it if I don't?"

Christ in his Heaven, did she know what that sounded like? Adam had never been one for visiting courtesans—he'd had Louisa, and when he then didn't, he'd wanted to be alone. But he was no fool. He knew what realm of pleasures was out there, and Miss Yates must also, considering her past.

So why was she flushing so darkly at her own words? "I-I mean—what I meant to say was—"

"Brighton," Adam said heavily. The sooner this rigmarole of a conversation was over, the better. "So, we are for Brighton. Fine. I'll have Dawson pack a trunk for me, you can bring whatever you wish, and—"

"I'm afraid Dawson will have to pack a trunk for me, too," Dottie said lightly, shifting on her armchair and briefly flashing a bit of ankle.

Adam's heart contracted, just lightly, just once. *A coincidence.* "For you? Why—"

"Because we are not just going to Brighton," said Dottie, her voice teasing. "We will be going as a married couple. Undercover. As husband and wife."

It took a moment for the words to sink into Adam's mind. Then the only syllable that he could utter forced its way from his mouth.

"No."

"Mr. Snee said you'd take it like this," said Dottie, her shoulders slumping with obvious disappointment. "I told him you were far braver than that."

Adam bristled. *Braver?* He *was* brave, and just because he didn't want to gallivant about the place pretending this snippet was his wife did not mean he had no courage! Why, it would be a brave man indeed to put up with Miss Yates'—

Wait a minute. Had he thought himself into a corner?

"It's the only way we can spend sufficient time together and move in separate circles without rousing suspicion," Dottie was saying, as though she suggested a pretend marriage of convenience with a duke every day of the week. "I can speak with the ladies, discover anything of interest—the leaders of the Glasshand Gang must have wives, I presume—"

"I wouldn't bet on it," said Adam through gritted teeth. "Too much bother, women."

Snee had known all about this, too, he thought darkly. No wonder the man had such a spring in his step when he had left here last week. It was too bad of the man to put him in this awful position again.

Not that anything like that was going to actually happen again, Adam told himself firmly, glaring at the woman opposite. Miss Dottie Yates could not be more perfectly designed to antagonize him to the point of fury. No chance of falling in love and marrying his partner this time.

"You're going to say that there must be another way," said Dottie with a wry look.

Tension sparked along Adam's collarbones. "Well, there must—"

"Why must there?" she shot back before he'd even had a chance to speak though in truth he hardly knew what other way he could suggest. "This is the swiftest and easiest way to pass unnoticed. The Brighton Season is in full flow, there'll be invitations aplenty."

Adam groaned again. She wasn't wrong. "Lady Romeril threatened—I mean, promised to invite me to one of her Brighton balls."

"There you go then!" Dottie said, pointing a finger as though she had proven her point beyond all reasonable doubt. "And that will only be the first invitation the Duke of Gilroyd will receive!"

"You really think Lady Romeril is connected to the Glasshand Gang?" Adam couldn't help his mirth.

She was living in fairyland. What on earth did she think he was going to find, the Glasshand Gang members wearing badges that said "villain" in the middle of a dance set?

Then something else Dottie had said clicked into place.

Adam rose to his feet, glaring at the woman who looked so innocent. "Oh, no—no!"

"You don't like the plan?"

"You said—invitation for the Duke of Gilroyd? You think I'm

going to go undercover but with my actual name? Telling the world that you are my wife?"

She was deranged, completely unhinged. Adam stared, hardly able to believe the audacity of the woman. She could not be of any great family—there was no wealth there if her gowns were any indication. And she wanted to parade about Brighton pretending to be his wife?

"Why can you not be my mistress?" he asked hopefully. "No commitment, no actual vows . . ." Yes, that might be a way around creating this absurd connection.

Dottie frowned. "Strange. That was actually my original plan."

Relief swept through him. "Excellent! Far easier for you to pretend to be my mistress, no vows or legal complications—"

"Yes, but that's also the trouble, isn't it?" she mused. "A mistress is easier to get rid of in the end, I agree, but much harder for one to attend balls and dinners and card parties with, don't you see? If I was your mistress—your pretend mistress, obviously— then I wouldn't be able to go everywhere with you. I considered pretending to be your sister, but you don't have a sister, do you?"

Adam's mind raced. *Quick, man, think of something—anything that doesn't involve her pretending to be your wife!* "I could have a sister. A half-sister, maybe, an illegitimate one, that would explain why no one had ever heard of—"

"Hmmm. One who had never entered Society, never even been heard of, suddenly appearing?" Dottie was shaking her head. "I think that's less believable than the wife."

This was all going wrong. The trouble was, Adam was still struggling to think of a better idea than a fake wife.

A terrible thought struck him.

"You don't . . ." Adam swallowed as he paced away. "You don't actually want to . . . to marry me, do you?"

Her snort of derision came rather more quickly than could be considered complimentary.

"You think I want to marry you?" Dottie said, mirth in her

tone. "Marry a man who doesn't even have the good manners to ensure a maid is sent to a woman's room? Who hasn't asked her a single personal question in the four days she has been here, and doesn't hesitate to grab any opportunity to vex her?"

Adam turned on the spot and met the bold gaze of Miss Dottie Yates.

She was impossible. Beautiful, yes. Intriguing, fine. But impossible.

Thank God she had no pretentions on his title. Or his person. *That was the sensation sweeping through his heart at this moment,* Adam told himself. *Relief. Most definitely.*

"I don't want to use my real name," he said woodenly.

"This may have passed you by, Your Gracefulness, but you are a duke. It's rare that one of your number can pass by unnoticed," Dottie pointed out.

"Penshaw—"

"Penshaw was not moving about in Society, he was undercover with a gang of ruffians in the illegal boxing rings," Dottie said swiftly.

Adam blinked. *Now that was interesting.* "I . . . I did not know anyone else knew—"

"Mr. Snee and I have worked together for a long time," came the calm and rather amused reply of the woman still curled up in the armchair. "Who do you think organized his lodgings? Who established his cover? Who ensured that Wincham found passage home? Who argued with the Oxford lot to make them take Caelfall back?"

Adam stared.

No. It wasn't possible—it had been Snee who had done all those things. Snee who orchestrated their lives, made sure of . . .

But then, he was a magistrate. He surely had a great number of things on his mind, court cases that pressed on his time, responsibilities that made it challenging to give everything he was to the dukes working for him.

And so Miss Yates appears. A woman of no birth, but genteel

enough to meander through any social circle. Pleasant, and clearly able to please . . . but not noteworthy enough to raise suspicion.

"Dear God," Adam breathed.

Dottie inclined her head. "So, we are agreed?"

Agreed? Definitely not.

"I made a vow . . ." Adam swallowed. *Damn, but he never thought he'd actually tell this to anyone, beyond a few close friends.* Chetnole. Martock. Maybe Penshaw, he couldn't remember.

But a woman?

"I made a vow never to marry again. It is not well known, but it is no secret." *Why was his throat so dry?* "I cannot just arrive at Brighton with a wife—"

"That is most inconvenient," she said dryly.

A flicker of anger again down his temple. "I did not take your wishes into consideration, believe it or not."

"No, that much is clear," said Dottie with a laugh. "How about this, then? We divorce."

Adam blinked. Now she had truly lost the plot. "Are you quite well? We're not going to get married!"

"I am perfectly well, thank you," said Dottie serenely. "And you don't actually have to marry me, haven't you been listening? We pretend we were married a week ago, we solve this problem, and then you can tell those who care that we got divorced or, better yet, that the marriage was annulled. I'm sure Mr. Snee could help make the legal side of things seem realistic. Then it's just an unconsummated marriage that was rushed, you've seen the light, error of your ways, et cetera—and you don't want to marry again, so you don't have to concern yourself that you'll drop in the marriage mart."

Adam wanted to sneer, but she had a point. Sister or mistress, neither role would get her into every room, on every invitation. Wife was the only role—and as he was hardly concerned about improving his marital reputation in the future . . .

"This is how I see it," Dottie said, interrupting his thoughts once again. "You have no wish to marry. Fine. I don't want to marry you. We arrive at Brighton with me as your wife, we find the leaders of the Glasshand Gang, all hurrahs and celebrations. You return to your life, saying that I am at your country estate, or whatever you please, just until the pretend divorce or annulment can be arranged to suitably end our pretend marriage. Then I slip back into London and work with Mr. Snee on our next assignment. Do you see?"

Adam scowled, but he did see. It was rather clever.

Only about a thousand things could go wrong.

"I'm not convinced," he said, partly for his own benefit. He had to hold the line—he couldn't have this woman beating him!

"Heavens, I don't know why," Dottie said smoothly. "It is common knowledge amongst those seeking them that there are four leaders of the Glasshand Gang, yes?"

Adam glared. How dare she speak to him like this, in his own home! Like he was some sort of fool! "Yes," he grunted.

Dottie nodded, ignoring his poor attitude. "Three are clearly common men, one of whom has been captured. But one is a gentleman. He mixes with the right people, perhaps at the height of Society."

"And how do you—"

"Anyone with half a brain could work it out," she snapped, finally past her patience with him. "The hits they make, the burglaries! The way they know things about houses—"

"They could have infiltrated the servants," Adam pointed out, though his heart wasn't particularly in it. Besides, he agreed with her rebuttal.

"It goes deeper than that, and you know it." Dottie took a deep breath. "If there's even a chance that the traitor to the Crown and this Glasshand Gang have worked together—"

"No," he breathed.

It was a terrible thought. The Glasshand Gang were a terror, and a traitor would be a disaster—but the two working hand in hand?

"I could be wrong," said Dottie, unconvincingly, "but I've been thinking this through quite thoroughly the last couple of days and I don't think I am."

Adam groaned. It all led to the same conclusion. "We have to go to Brighton and spot a gentleman who is betraying us?"

"It's not a nice mission," she said severely.

He sighed. "They never are."

And that wasn't the worst of it. Oh, no. The worst of it was that Adam knew it would swiftly become completely intolerable to be in Miss Yates' presence.

"You'll have to improve your game if you're to become my wife," he snapped, exhaustion with this conversation threatening to overwhelm him. "How to stand beside me, not argue with me, never contradict me, never distract—"

"My goodness, Adam," said Dottie, slowly rising. "What do you mean, distract?"

Adam actually bit his tongue.

If only Louisa were here. It wasn't the first time he had wished it, but right now, he could do with her quick wit, her ability to act as a buffer between himself and the world.

"You'll need weeks of lessons," he said curtly, entirely ignoring her statement.

Dottie shrugged as she made her way to the door. "Oh, I'll just make it up as I go along. You seem to."

And it was that comment that pushed him beyond all reasonable conversation. "You can't just—"

"Watch me," said Dottie over her shoulder, her blue eyes gleaming. "Now, I'm hungry. Shall I ring the dinner gong, get our servants moving?"

CHAPTER SIX

7 November 1811

DOTTIE SMILED AS best she could. "How absolutely fascinating."

The man on her right beamed. Evidently, he did not notice her sarcasm. That, or perhaps she was getting far better at hiding her disdain. One of the two.

"And that is what I thought!" he exclaimed. "Why the ladies do not always wish to hear every cut and thrust of the hunt, I do not know. How pleasant it is, Your Grace, to meet you!"

Dottie's smile did not waver, but only because she was taking great care that it should not. "How pleasant for both of us."

Pleasant, however, was not a word that she would have honestly used to describe this dinner party. As it was the first invitation that she and Gilroyd had received—calling him Adam still felt wrong, though she continued to do so just to rile him—she'd had no option but to accept.

Now she rather wished they had feigned tiredness. It had been quite a rush to Brighton, after all.

"I don't understand," Gilroyd had said only yesterday, as their coach—his coach—had trundled along the road. "Why are we going to Brighton at such a pace? Should we not wait until—"

"Until the Glasshand Gang decide to switch their location and move somewhere else which will be far harder to find?" Dottie had shaken her head, dropping her gaze to her notebook though the jolting of the carriage made it difficult to read. "No. No, we are for Brighton, and so to Brighton we must go."

She'd never been to Brighton. She'd read about it, however, and Dottie had presumed the sea would be precisely as she had read. But there was something almost unearthly about it that books had not prepared her for. The expanse of blue water, stretching out to the horizon. Nothing to stop it, nothing to hinder its path.

"It's just the sea," Gilroyd had scoffed when he spotted her staring through the window. "It hasn't changed for millennia."

Perhaps it hadn't. But as Dottie had never seen the sea before, it was a sight to marvel at.

The townhouse belonging to the Gilroyd name had been in a far better state of repair than Gilroyd House in London.

"I keep the place spick and span, just in case you do something wild and come down here without a moment's notice," said Mrs. Sharp, the housekeeper who had given Dottie a look to match her name. "And I would have liked to have been informed that you were wed, Your Grace, for I would have—"

"So would I, Mrs. Sharp," Gilroyd had said heavily.

Dottie had been forced to nudge him sharply with an elbow. The heat that fluttered through her chest as she did so was most unaccountable.

"Yet here we are," he had continued with a bright smile that almost looked natural. "And—"

"You have an invitation from Lady Romeril," his housekeeper said with a sniff. "How she knew you were going to be here before I did, I don't know . . ."

Dottie had snatched the invitation from Gilroyd's hand before he'd had a chance to open it. Carefully ignoring Mrs. Sharp's loud sniff, she opened it.

Lady Romeril expects the pleasure of

*the Duke and Duchess of Gilroyd's company
on 7 November at eight o'clock.
Be late at your peril.*

It had been impossible not to laugh. "Be late at your peril?"

"You wanted to meet Lady Romeril," said Gilroyd with a sigh. "Mrs. Sharp, I need a bath, a large meal, and a cigar. In my bedchamber, please."

Dottie's head jerked up from the invitation in her hands. Had he already forgotten—

"Oh, and Her Grace, Dorothy, my delightful duchess, will have a bedchamber of her own," Gilroyd had said bad-temperedly as he marched up the stairs without halting. "Too much of a good thing, you know. See to it, Mrs. Sharp."

He turned a corner upstairs and slammed a door, leaving Dottie alone with the housekeeper.

"Well!" sniffed the servant.

Dottie beamed. "Well."

It had taken . . . oh, almost an hour to charm the older woman with genuine interest in the life of the housekeeper who spent so much time alone in the Brighton house. Within two hours, Mrs. Sharp had promised to find Dottie a suitable gown for the dinner the following evening. Within three hours, Dottie had a large box of chocolates in her bedchamber, an invitation to the kitchen whenever she chose, and a nod that His Grace was remarkably difficult, but everyone got used to him. Eventually.

And so Dottie had arrived at Lady Romeril's Brighton townhouse in a gown far more elegant than anything she'd ever owned, and a sense she was precisely where she needed to be.

A sense which had evaporated the moment she had been seated beside Colonel Markham.

"—and the gut of the race had only just begun!" he said cheerfully, spearing a piece of ham on his fork. "In fact, what I did not know was that the hounds had taken an entirely different route. It was only when I heard the horn . . ."

Dottie tried to nod in all the right places, but in truth, it was hard to know where the right places were. Whenever she thought he needed a little prodding, she made an encouraging noise, though Colonel Markham seemed perfectly able to continue going without much help.

But that still left her utterly trapped beside a complete bore on one side, and on the other . . .

Under her eyelashes, Dottie snuck a glimpse at the gentleman on her left. He was handsome. She could admit it, even if she did not want to. He was eating elegantly, contributing delightfully to the conversation, and not drawing attention at all.

It was infuriating. Adam Gilroyd was not supposed to be so . . . so good at this.

Stranger still, there were a few ladies at the table who kept shooting her looks that, at first, Dottie had not understood. They were not pleasant looks, nor were they friendly. The dinner table was lit with three brilliant candelabras, so she could not be mistaking their expressions. They looked envious.

"So, tell me," Colonel Markham said finally, seeming to guess he had finally lost the full attention of his audience. "You and Gilroyd. Never thought the man would marry again!"

Ah. Dottie's shoulders relaxed as understanding dawned.

Of course—the Duke of Gilroyd was married, for appearance's sake, and the *ton* would have an opinion about it. Roughly half the *ton* apparently did not like this information. That, at the very least, explained why so many ladies continued to surreptitiously glare over their wine glasses.

"Yes, we are married," Dottie said firmly, as though convincing herself of that fact. "Me and Gilroyd. Gilroyd and I. Adam."

Bother. She'd never had any difficulty with grammar before.

"And what a pleasant couple you make," said Colonel Markham cheerfully. "Always good to see a man find a home."

Dottie managed to stop herself from saying that it was Gilroyd who owned the homes, at least three of them at her last count.

It was all rather . . . odd.

Oh, she'd spent sufficient time with gentility, in one way or another, to know their company was pleasant at best, and dull at worst. She knew the right way to eat, speak, incline her head. She'd spent two weeks in the summer at the Sedleys' house party and had not raised any suspicion there at all.

But this was different. There she had been Miss Dorothy Yates. In the main, she could be herself. Even if she had to hide the part of herself that could read other people's letters upside down and from across the breakfast table.

But here? Here, she was Dorothy Seymour, Duchess of Gilroyd. Being Gilroyd's wife was a different matter, and she was rather disconcerted to find that she . . .

She did not like it, Dottie thought firmly as she sipped her wine.

She was not enjoying the envy of others. She did not prefer being addressed as "Your Grace." And she most certainly did not feel a tingle down her arm when Gilroyd had led her into Lady Romeril's dining room.

Absolutely not.

"—just so demoralizing," someone was saying farther down the table. "I thought it would be over by now, and yet the hits just keep on coming."

Dottie's ears pricked. That was strange—she rarely heard anyone in the nobility talk about the war in France. Usually they were far more interested in silly things. Who was that speaking?

"Yes, I quite agree, it is most shocking," said Lady Romeril, their hostess at the head of the table. "Why, my lady's maid told me only last week that she had been unable to buy the right quality silk for less than ten shillings a yard! The audacity of these merchants!"

Shoulders slumping, Dottie reminded herself she should have expected that. The conversation wasn't about the terrible things happening in France. It was about the terrible price to pay for the right kind of silk. Did they not have anything better to worry about? Did the sum of their problems really boil down to something so ridiculous?

Other people worried about how to put food on the table. These people worried about how to put silk on their dressmaker's tabs.

"You are looking indignant," murmured a low voice.

Dottie started, her cheeks flushing as she turned to Gilroyd and found the man far closer than she had thought. He had lowered his head to whisper, which explained the rush of warmth on her shoulder, but not the lurch in her stomach.

Botheration.

"I do not look—"

"When I tell you that you look indignant, it means that on the face of another I would consider the expression one of fury," Gilroyd said, as though they were talking of nothing more important than the weather. "Calm yourself."

The trouble was, Dottie had never taken well to being told to calm herself. "Calm—"

"My duchess would never get herself in such a state over silk," Gilroyd said, his voice so low only she could hear. "She would be far more interested in looking for members of a certain gang than getting herself riled up over the conversation of others."

Dottie took a deep breath and took another mouthful of the delicious ham and carrots on her plate.

Dratted man, he was right. She had permitted herself to get distracted by the fripperies of the occasion and had forgotten—only for a moment—their real purpose in being here.

The Glasshand Gang. Yes, right, that was it.

"You are right," she said under her breath. "Much as it pains me to say it."

She had not intended to say the final words aloud, and Dottie saw Gilroyd smile very briefly before his gaze returned to its neutral stance.

"And have you seen anything?" Gilroyd's breath warmed her

shoulder again. "Do you think Lady Romeril is perhaps a leader of the Glasshand Gang? Or Colonel Markham, or perhaps the Viscount Stulsemere?"

It was most inconvenient to wish to scowl at a man and not be able to because he was pretending to be her husband.

Dottie allowed herself a small frown. "You are teasing me."

"Only a mite," shrugged the duke. "You were in such a rush to get here, so certain your plan would uncover Glasshand Gang leaders scurrying about like rats leaving a sinking ship. And what have we here? A room of nobility, gentility, and utility."

Her gaze took in the only other nobleman there, an Earl of Chester, the ladies and gentlemen seated around them, and the footmen standing by the walls, waiting to be of service.

She could not help it. She smiled. "You never know. A footman could—"

"I doubt a footman would be the leader of the Glasshand Gang, or even *a* leader," came Gilroyd's soft words. "You said you saw a gentleman. They're not here. Admit it."

Dottie shivered—*because of her fury*, she told herself firmly. Not for any other reason. Handsome duke or not, she was not going to be taken in by Gilroyd's charming manners. Manners which, it appeared, he trotted out only in public. She had certainly never benefited from them when they were alone.

"It's only the first night since we arrived," she said quietly. "You cannot expect me to spot him immediately."

"I suppose not," Gilroyd said, his words whispered now into her ear, as though they were sharing some delectable secret between husband and wife. "I expected more from you, though, Dottie Yates."

Dottie swallowed, her chest warming, her heart skipping a beat.

How did he do it? The man was nothing but a tyrant in his London townhouse, and she had grown quite tired of him. But here, in public? The performance took over, and Adam Seymour, Duke of Gilroyd, became almost an entirely different person.

It was perplexing. It was maddening. It was . . . alluring.

Not alluring, Dottie corrected hastily. *Confusing. That was what she meant.*

"You are a fortunate woman."

Dottie blinked. It had not been Gilroyd who had said that—he had turned away, unbeknownst to her, and started speaking to the lady on his other side.

No, it was Colonel Markham who had spoken, and he had a knowing look in his eye as he beheld her. "Very fortunate indeed to have a husband who so clearly adores you."

Dottie stared, then her mind caught up.

You know your husband—the Duke of Gilroyd? The man who infuriates you at every possible moment, making your life impossible as he surprises you at every turn?

That husband?

"Adores me?" she repeated, playing for time.

The man nodded, a twinkle in his eye. "I may not be much of a ladies' man, Your Grace, but I am not blind. I see the way he looks at you. Like he wants to kiss you," he ended with a conspiratorial whisper.

Like he wants to throttle me, Dottie thought privately. "You are too kind."

"I speak as I find," said Colonel Markham. "I know Gilroyd rather well, actually. A familial connection. In fact, that reminds me of a hunt I went on! Only last week, and the weather was something spectacular . . ."

Dottie did not have much opportunity to speak with anyone else at the table until the ladies withdrew. Colonel Markham looked rather sad to lose her company—though why, she could not tell. All she'd done was pretend to listen to his anecdotes and examine the rest of the party with a view to working out whether they were part of the Glasshand Gang.

In truth, not that she would ever admit it to Gilroyd, she was starting to worry. When Dottie had started to plan this mission, she'd been certain that she would recognize the leader of the

Glasshand Gang by sight. It would be obvious. One glance, and she would know.

It was only now that she was in Brighton and in Society, that she realized just how foolish that idea had been.

Know him on sight? The glimpse of the man she'd spotted had been brief, and in the dark. There had been no distinguishing features, no obvious red hair or scar to look for. She was no mind reader, she had no insight into men's souls. And now she was seated in a circle of women talking about gloves and the right way to pin one's hair for the coming London Season, no more the wiser than when she had arrived.

Dottie sighed as the men joined them.

"Ah, Gilroyd, there you are!" Lady Romeril had risen and snatched at Adam's hand, bringing him over to sit on the sofa with his hostess. "Your wife is here, too—and I am most displeased with you, incidentally. No invitation! No note even, to say you were wed!"

Meeting Gilroyd's eye, Dottie prayed he would recall the story they'd agreed upon. It was—

"—all a bit of a rush, Lady Romeril," Gilroyd said smoothly, smiling warmly at Dottie. "We just found we couldn't live without each other and had a small, quiet wedding. Just family."

"You don't have any family," Lady Romeril pointed out irritably.

Dottie stifled a laugh as Gilroyd grinned. "Just so."

"And you! You are quite happy to acquiesce to this slight?" demanded Lady Romeril, turning on Dottie. "Your Grace deserved a wedding full of splendor and jewels!"

It was all Dottie could do not to frown. "Why would I—I mean, I just wished to marry Gilroyd, that was all," she amended hastily. "The wedding itself meant little to me. It is the marriage I am interested in."

Just for a moment, a heart-stopping moment, Gilroyd met her eye and his smile was different. Warmer. Genuine, perhaps, for the first time in their acquaintance.

"Besides," Dottie added, unable to help herself as a mischievous grin slipped across her face. "I am the most perfect wife, I am sure my husband would agree. My husband there could not keep his hands off me. He became so besotted with me, so desperate to become my husband, I had to tell him several times that I would only marry him if he got down on bended knee and begged. We had to marry immediately, otherwise—"

"And that is my wife," Gilroyd said ardently. "Unaffected, truly uninterested in my title and my wealth. She fell in love with me for myself, my person, my character. And being with her brings me a joy I could not have found with another. A joy I could not bear to be without."

Dottie's breath caught in her throat. She had been teasing, but Gilroyd had spoken with such passion, such reverence. There was adoration, to use Colonel Markham's word, in his voice. Something she had never heard in his tone before. Something, in truth, she had rarely heard in any man's voice.

Was it possible . . . surely it was inconceivable that the man had in any way taken to her? She thought him handsome, true, but there was no reason to think . . .

But the way he looked at her. The way he held her gaze, the words he had used.

Well, she had not expected that. It would be a most interesting complication, to extricate herself from him when the mission had ended. Really, Dottie should have foreseen this. Hadn't the young Mr. Marnion fallen head over heels with her in the summer? Had she not had to let him down gently, in the full knowledge he would be brokenhearted?

Though truth be told, she had not expected to break a duke's heart.

"And with that, we sadly must depart," said Gilroyd, standing and offering out a hand to Dottie who took it with surprise. "Lady Romeril, we thank you again for your most kind invitation . . ."

The leaving pleasantries washed over Dottie as she was led to the hallway and her pelisse placed around her shoulders. She was still attempting to take in the astonishing way Gilroyd had looked at her.

Had . . . had he meant anything that he'd said? Was it possible that he could—

The door snapped shut behind them and Gilroyd turned on her, eyes blazing with fury. "Don't you ever talk about me as your husband again."

Dottie started, taking a step back, almost stumbling off the pavement and into the road. "But I—"

"This was your foolish idea and I have lived up to my side of the bargain as much as I am able," Gilroyd snarled, real pain in his features. "But I had a wife, and she was perfect. She did fall in love with me for my person, my character, and she did not have plans to use me as you do."

Dottie stared, horrified. She'd heard mention of a Duchess of Gilroyd but had put that down to a mistake. She'd had no idea Adam—

"And when I lost her, all joy left the world," continued Gilroyd darkly. "You ask much of me, Miss Yates. And I am doing my best. But you had better leave out that sort of talk at the next function we attend, or this 'marriage' will be over sooner than you think."

CHAPTER SEVEN

8 November 1811

HE SHOULD HAVE known from the moment he saw the note. It was scrawled in an untidy hand, had ADAM written at the top, and had been left at the bottom of the stairs on the floor. As though that was a perfectly normal place for a note.

There was only one person in his life, thank goodness, who thought that was a good idea.

Adam sighed. "Dottie Yates."

Leaning to pick up the note, he saw there was actually very little written. And what was there was absolute nonsense.

ADAM

Eating the Head Glasshand Gang spies meeting probably

He glared at the note again, as though by looking at it further, more insight could be provided.

It was certainly addressed to him. Though it had not been signed by anyone, there was no one else who would leave such a ridiculous note laying around. The mention of the Glasshand Gang had to mean it was from Dottie.

So did she want him to meet her somewhere? Why the "probably"—and why was she eating a head?

"Damn it, woman," Adam muttered under his breath. "Eating the head? What on earth does that mean?"

"Your Grace," bowed Dawson on his way through the hallway.

His first instinct was to incline his head briefly to his butler. Adam had insisted on bringing him from London, even though he knew it would rile Mrs. Sharp. The housekeeper liked the idea that she, and only she, could manage the Brighton house.

It was just as Dawson had his hand on the door to the drawing room that Adam wondered. "Dawson?"

His butler paused, turning to face him. "Your Grace."

"Any idea what this could mean?" Adam thrust the note toward him.

This was safe. His butler was not completely aware of all Adam had got up to in the past, but he knew enough to have passed a few notes in his time.

Though now he came to think about it, there was a traitor in their midst.

The thought had flitted through Adam's brain before he could properly dissect it, and it was most alarming. But he couldn't go around accusing fine people like Dawson of being a traitor just because there was one somewhere!

Still, they were losing people, information getting out. So who was it?

Try as he might, Adam could not help but rake his gaze over his servant's face. The servant who had been with him nigh on a decade. Who he would have trusted, before today, with his life . . .

Adam shook his head firmly. No, there was nothing to be gained with that kind of thinking. He had to trust people—at least, until he had a definite reason not to.

Dawson had smiled. "A work of art from your wife, I presume."

Trying to ignore the way his butler had so swiftly agreed to their plan—the only servant who had been given the truth of the situation, in case anyone accidentally let something slip in the market or at a tavern—Adam nodded.

"Hmmm," the butler opined, turning the note over and sighing as he saw there was nothing on the reverse. "Well, it is not a very polite note, but the meaning seems clear enough."

Adam blinked. "It does?"

It was galling to be so easily bested by one's butler, of all people—but then, there was obviously something devious in the note he had not picked up on. Maybe as a duke he simply didn't know the slang. *Yes, that had to be it.*

"Yes," said his butler, evidently confused as to why his master was in turn confused. "She is dining this evening at the King's Head, an inn just a few streets away that has, I am afraid to say, a rather nefarious reputation. She believes the Glasshand Gang will be meeting there and intends to spy on them."

The man spoke with such calm as though it were all so obvious. But it wasn't obvious. Adam could not fathom how the man had come to such an understanding.

"It's all here, Your Grace—"

Snatching the note from his butler's hands, Adam perused it again.

ADAM

Eating the Head Glasshand Gang spies meeting probably

Oh. Well. That did make sense.

If he'd known—or remembered, if he was being completely honest— that inn was so close, he would have been able to work it out, too, Adam thought defensively.

"I knew that," he said aloud.

"Of course you did, Your Grace," said Dawson smoothly.

Adam met his servant's gaze and flushed, cheeks warming, at the knowing look of the older man. "Fine, I didn't," he admitted bad temperedly. "I suppose I shall have to go off and rescue her, then."

Stuffing the note in his pocket, Adam turned to the front

door. After conferring with a few other dukes, Thornfalcone mainly, he had carefully put out feelers to his informants in Brighton. It had taken an extortionate about of money over the years to build the network, but good information had always flowed through it. Now he was thinking on it, one of the serving men at the King's Head was supposed to be one of his own. He'd have to investigate why the man hadn't notified him of meetings of this nature. *Unless he was in their pay too . . .*

"Rescue her, Your Grace?" came his butler's voice blankly. "I did not see anything in the note about rescuing Miss Dottie."

"You wouldn't," Adam said darkly, pulling on a greatcoat and wishing it weren't so cold out there. "But you have forgotten one very important thing."

He pulled on a pair of gloves and rammed his top hat upon his head as his butler said, "I have, Your Grace?"

Adam nodded. "Dottie Yates is unable to prevent herself from irritating me! She may be able to hide this side of her nature somewhere like Lady Romeril's dinner party. But one slip will mean trouble in a place like the Queen's Head."

He had been about to slam the door behind him—making, he thought, rather a good exit.

The impressive moment was spoiled, however, as Dawson called after him helpfully, "The King's Head, Your Grace."

Adam scowled. "I knew that."

He didn't, though. It was an excellent reminder. He would have struggled to find his way there with the incorrect name. As it was, one short conversation and a threepenny coin later, and he was standing outside the King's Head inn.

From the little he could see of the place, Adam had not needed Dawson's insight that the place was one for miscreants and villains. You could see that just by the boarded windows where fists or tankards had broken them. There was roaring laughter coming from the partially open door, and the dark of the evening was broken by the candlelight spilling out.

Adam took a deep breath as he heard someone roar and a

thump that sounded rather like a fist on a table.

"That can't be her, can it?" he said to himself heavily. "For heaven's sake."

If he had been asked, Adam was not sure how he could have explained the fact he had known Dottie was in danger. Though he had known her only a few days, there was something about her that seemed to attract attention.

Oh, she could handle herself—she'd proved she could that day in the library. No woman who could wield a knife as he had seen Dottie do really needed to be worried over. Not exactly. But they were partners, however grudgingly he'd gone along with it. It was his role to protect her and her role to protect him. That was the point. A point she had obviously ignored.

But men . . . weren't the same around her. It was as though they became drunk in her presence, unable to think clearly. He certainly hadn't been able to think clearly since she had marched into his library and into his life.

And so when Adam stepped into the King's Head and saw two men playing fisticuffs, a table overturned with a great many coins and cards on the floor, he was not surprised.

The barfight was starting to grow. Men who had only a moment ago been cheering on the two ruffians were now beginning to fight between themselves. A chair was thrown across the room—Adam carefully sidestepped it—and there were shouts of restraint and encouragement coming from every corner.

And there, trapped by a table and two men circling each other with knives, she was.

Dottie Yates.

Adam's stomach lurched as he saw her white face, her fingers clutching tight onto her tankard.

He was just in time.

Striding past the fighters as though he had every cause to be there, Adam pushed aside a man who had been knocked to the ground and was struggling to get up, and shoved a chair in the path of another man who was rushing to help him. He was able to slip past the two men with knives, neither of whom seemed ready to make the first lunge, and grabbed Dottie's arm.

She jumped, her whole attention having been fixed on the fighting before her. "Adam! What are you—"

"Come on," Adam said roughly. "No time."

But she did not seem to want to move. *Probably afraid of accidentally meeting with a knife or a fist*, he thought. After all her boldness and bravery in the safety of Gilroyd House in London, it seemed Dottie was not accustomed to this kind of thuggery.

Thank God.

It was all Adam could do to keep his heartbeat slow, his breathing calm, as he pulled Dottie out from behind the table and placed her behind him. If anything happened to her—

And a memory, one he had forced down painfully for so long, rose unbidden. Another fight, though this time he was truly outnumbered. And another woman, this time with dark, raven hair, separated from him and taken away.

Another chair flew through the air. Adam ducked, pulling Dottie down toward him, and she cried out at the suddenness.

"We need to keep moving," he shouted in her ear, hoping to goodness she could hear him. *He would control the panic. He would control the fear.* "Follow me—now!"

Ducking and weaving through the ruffians, who were obviously enjoying the fight far more than he had thought possible, Adam half pulled, half dragged the woman behind him.

When they stepped out into the freezing Brighton air, he took in great heaving lungfuls. Anything to get the stench of that place from his nostrils.

Only then did Adam glance at Dottie to see her shaking herself, straightening her back, then most inexplicably . . . glaring at him?

"I had everything under control," she said icily.

Adam's jaw dropped and he turned away immediately, starting to march back to the townhouse. *Of all the ungrateful, idiotic—*

"I could have taken care of myself in there, if I'd had just another moment to think," Dottie insisted, falling in step with him and shivering in the cold. "I was certain, if I could just wait out the fight, I could—"

"You don't just wait out a fight like that, you fool!" Adam snapped, rage coursing through his veins.

Had he expected gratitude? Yes. Had he expected praise for his quick thinking, admiration for the way he had managed to get them both out of there without a scratch? Well, it would have been unlikely but very welcome!

But no, instead he had to be lectured by a woman who had absolutely no idea what she was doing, and seemed more than happy to risk her life for something that was probably nonsense in the first place!

"I was doing fine," Dottie said stubbornly.

Adam halted and she almost walked into him, his cessation of movement was so swift. "Were you? Because as far as I could tell, you were cowering behind a table."

"Cowering!" said Dottie, her cheeks flushed. "I was doing no such—"

"And I don't call getting trapped in the middle of a barfight 'doing fine.' Nor do I think you should have been there in the first place," Adam continued, unable to stop himself, "particularly on your own! Dear God, woman, anything could have happened!"

Anything almost did.

The panic was fading now, but a bitter taste filled his mouth. His shoulders were heaving, his breathing was still ragged, and Adam knew it would take most of the evening to get the sight of Dottie, frightened and huddled behind that table, from his mind.

That a woman should be so vulnerable, and yet purposefully put herself into harm's way—it was enough to drive a man to distraction!

But after what he had seen, what he had suffered . . .

Dottie, however, did not seem in any way altered by his words. She glared fiercely at him, the presence of other people on the dark Brighton street evidently stopping her from speaking openly. But once the couple, arm in arm, turned the corner and the elderly gentleman shuffled into a house, she finally spoke. "I'll have you know—"

"Anything could have happened," Adam said curtly, trying to prevent his hands from clenching into fists. "You took a risk without telling me, without warning me, without giving me the chance to come with you!"

Dottie's eyes widened. When she spoke, her voice was small. "You . . . you would have come with me?"

Probably not, smirked a small voice in the back of Adam's head.

Because truthfully, if she had come to him that afternoon and asked him to accompany her to a place called the King's Head, all in the hope of overhearing a meeting of people whose faces they didn't even know . . .

No, he would not have gone with her.

"Maybe not," Adam conceded, hating how she could draw the truth from him so easily. "But I could have stopped you going—"

"Aha!" Dottie's whole face was instantly animated. "So, that's the truth! You think yourself superior to me and don't believe that I can contribute just as much as you! Or are you in fact the traitor, trying to throw me off the scent?"

"Superior?" Adam repeated in amazement. "Traitor?"

Did she know nothing? Had she never taken in what had happened to Wincham, to Caelfall, and surely dozens of other men who had risked everything to serve their country? Did she not understand what was at stake? Did she not realize this wasn't a competition, a story where the "good guys" always won, and the "bad guys" always lost by the last page?

"This is real life, Dottie, not some game that you happen to be playing," Adam said quietly. "There are no winners, not really. Just people who live long enough to see the result of it all, and you're not guaranteed that. No one is."

"What are you talking about?" Dottie asked.

He had tried to be as direct as possible, but it was difficult to convey what he meant. *And why would she understand,* Adam thought darkly. Hopefully she had never experienced pain and loss the way he had or the grief that dogged him.

No, Dottie Yates knew nothing of such things.

She had taken a step closer to him as she spoke. Her increased proximity spurred Adam to turn away and continue walking. He had to get back. Had to get away from her. Dottie's presence, it did something to him. Something that confused him, that pained him. It was far too much like—

"We are only pretending to be husband and wife, you know," came Dottie's quiet voice as she kept pace with him along the quiet Brighton streets. "Nothing is going to happen. It was just a brawl."

Adam's chest was tight and he could hardly shift it to take another breath. And he desperately needed another breath. The weight of Louisa's loss was bearing down on him so hard, the air was being squeezed from his lungs.

Because that was what she had said, wasn't it?

"Nothing's going to happen," smiled Louisa, his wife, the woman he loved. "It's just an exchange. The inn is perfectly safe—known for being neutral. We'll fit right in. Nothing is going to happen."

But then something had. And he had been alone ever since.

They turned a corner onto the street where his townhouse stood, and Adam swallowed the panic that rose once again as he thought about how swiftly his life had changed.

He was not going to lose himself to this fear. He had mastered it and would master it every time it rose and attempted to take over his life. Adam was determined not to get lost in the past . . . arguably, as he had been doing.

She . . . Louisa—she would not have wanted that. She would have wanted him to keep living. He would have to try harder.

Tears welled and threatened to fall from his eyes as Adam and Dottie walked in silence along the street. Tears he had never permitted to fall. Tears for a woman he had fallen swiftly in love with, then lost so soon.

He could not go back and save Louisa. But he could, if she would let him, try to prevent Dottie Yates from allowing herself to be killed in the present. And that was all he could hope for.

"Nothing happened," said Dottie quietly.

A sudden warmth on his arm. She had placed her hand upon it. The warmth seeped through his greatcoat and into his skin, a strange tingling crawling up his arm.

Her words echoed in his mind. *"Nothing happened."*

"I am just glad nothing did," he said stiffly.

If Adam had hoped Dottie would drop the topic, he was to be disappointed. As they stepped up to his townhouse, Dawson opened the door with a worried expression.

"Your Grace—I was starting to get worried. His Grace said—"

"Yes, I am sure I can guess at what His Grace said," Dottie said smartly, removing her pelisse and handing it to the butler.

"It's just that I found—"

Adam groaned. In his butler's hands was a very familiar notebook. "Where on earth did you find that?"

Dottie snatched up the notebook, cheeks a burning red. "It doesn't matter, the point is—"

"The point is that you left it laying around so that anyone could find it!" Adam snarled, pouring all his frustration into his words. "No offence, Dawson."

The butler cleared his throat awkwardly. "No offence taken, Your G—"

"Will you give us a moment, Dawson?"

Adam bristled. "You don't get to order—"

"It was a request, not an order," Dottie said quietly. "And it is up to Dawson to decide whether he wishes to acquiesce. Dawson?"

He could not blame the man. Adam was not sure what he would have done in such a circumstance, but he was half certain he would not have been able to stare down this blonde woman when she had that glint of steel in her eye.

Dawson met Adam's gaze with an apologetic look. "As it happens, Your Grace, I am needed in the kitchens, and—"

"Oh, begone with you," snapped Adam, pulling a hand through his hair. *The sooner this was over with, the better.*

The moment the door closed behind Dawson, Dottie rounded on him. "Well, now that you've ruined my evening—"

"Don't start with that again," Adam said, pique rising in his chest.

"—I think we should go to the drawing room and run through the plan for tomorrow," Dottie continued doggedly. "Perhaps . . . perhaps it's time that we started to work together."

Her eyes were warm as they met his. Adam could see that though she seemed unable to express it, she was sorry that she had caused him such concern. Sorry he'd been forced into the King's Head, forced through the brawl, forced to help her out.

Just not sorry enough to say it.

"No," Adam said stiffly.

The light faded in Dottie's eyes. "N-No?"

No, he wouldn't get pulled into this trap again. He wouldn't allow himself to feel something for a partner, particularly not a woman. He'd walked down that path before and it had ended. Badly. He didn't want to live in the past anymore, but that did not mean he could not learn from it.

Adam shook his head and walked past Dottie to the staircase. "No. Make whatever plans you want, Dottie. I'll get you into the right drawing rooms, sort your entrance into the world of the nobility where you are so sure the Glasshand Gang is hiding. But don't expect me to dance to your tune. Not any longer."

"But you need to know—"

"I'll wing it," Adam said darkly, reaching the top of the stairs. "Good night."

CHAPTER EIGHT

9 November 1811

W HEN DOTTIE DESCENDED for breakfast the following morning, she had three things carefully considered and agreed on in her mind.

Firstly, no more adventures without Adam.

He was clearly upset at being left behind, Dottie thought as she wandered across the hallway and into the deserted breakfast room. That was why they had argued last night, and that was easily remedied. No more disappearing off without him. Fine.

Secondly, no more concocting plans without Adam.

It probably wasn't fair, on reflection, to draw up new plans and ideas without discussing them with him. He was right to be piqued, and he hadn't been shy about expressing it. He'd had not a civil word for her the moment they entered the house, and when she had suggested talking through her plans for today, he had glowered and marched upstairs.

Well, she wouldn't be allowing that to continue inasmuch as she could change it. They were here for one purpose, and that was to catch the Glasshand Gang at their own game.

And thirdly, she was going to be charm itself.

It wouldn't be hard. Dottie had used her charm on and off

throughout her life and it was a pleasant enough way to get by. There had been moments at Gilroyd House and at Lady Romeril's dinner when she rather thought Adam was the same in that.

So with all the best intentions in the world, Dottie sat patiently at the breakfast table and waited.

And waited.

The only noise in the room after twenty minutes was the gurgle of her starving stomach. *Perhaps*, Dottie thought as she glanced at the sideboard where platters of delicacies lay, *she would be forgiven for helping herself before the master of the house came down.*

After all, she was hungry. And she wasn't actually his wife . . .

A strange sort of fluttering in her stomach. Dottie put a hand to it, but the sensation did not go away.

Just hunger, she thought, glancing once again at the platters. That was all. The feeling certainly did not have anything to do with a certain gentleman . . .

The moment she rose from her seat, unable to placate her growling stomach any longer, the door opened.

"I see you couldn't wait for me."

Dottie dropped immediately into her chair, hoping to goodness her face wasn't red. "I waited for—"

"Not for me, clearly," said Adam brightly as he picked up the silver platters from the sideboard and started placing them haphazardly on the breakfast table. "Come on, eat up."

She couldn't help it. She stared.

Where was the irritable and outraged gentleman she had seen last night? Where was the duke who required everything to be done a certain way? Where was the man who had saved her, begrudgingly it seemed, from a brawl she had absolutely— probably—had under control?

Dottie blinked. Adam was now sitting opposite, piling food onto his plate and not giving her a single glance.

He also wasn't wearing a cravat.

Once she noticed it, it was impossible not to stare. Adam

wasn't a particularly stylish man, but dukes never needed to be. They were fashionable just by being.

But he had always been properly dressed. And now he was most improperly dressed. In fact, with the top of his shirt undone and open, Dottie could see—

She swallowed, refusing to believe the heat searing through her heart could have anything to do with the sight of wiry hair poking out at the top of Adam's shirt.

Finding a man attractive was no crime, of course. As long as it wasn't the man who was supposed to be pretending to be your husband and was constantly infuriating you at the most inopportune times.

"You . . . breakfast," Dottie said weakly.

How could she lose her self-control so quickly? Why did the sight of the man have such an effect on her?

"Yes, breakfast," Adam said cheerfully. "I always thought it was rather ridiculous Mrs. Sharp and Dawson put all the food over there, there's almost never a footman around in my Brighton house. Far easier to place it all on the table and help ourselves, don't you think?"

He smiled, either somehow unaware of or, more likely, enjoying her discomfort.

Because she was discomforted. Though Dottie would not admit it, it was befuddling, him speaking to her like this. After his high dudgeon yesterday, she had expected a pointed silence, not . . . not this cheerfulness, this willingness to bend.

"I used to eat like this as a child," Dottie found herself saying.

"I believe it is common outside of nobility," said Adam, placing a sausage on her plate and gesturing at the rest of the platters. "Eat. We've got a busy day ahead of us."

"We . . . we do?" Dottie asked faintly.

This was most provoking. She was supposed to be the one in charge—it was her plan, her mission! Her idea to bring the Duke of Gilroyd, her suggestion to Mr. Snee that it would all work perfectly.

And now this pretentious duke, who declared he could not allow anything to happen to her, then disappeared at not even seven o'clock in the evening, was telling her they had a busy day ahead of them?

"We do," she said firmly, trying to rally.

It did not work. There was still a tightness in her chest, and her traitorous heart skipped a beat as Adam looked up, grinned, and said, "We do."

How—how dare he!

Dottie did not come here to have her emotions toyed with like this! *Not that they were,* she thought hastily.

And not that he was. Because Adam Seymour, Duke of Gilroyd, was plainly only being polite. Perhaps he had gone upstairs last night, felt foolish, and determined to be a better host and better partner in the morning. Perhaps she hadn't been the only one kept up late, trying to think of new resolutions.

"I did not think you would wish to attend the Earl of Chester's card party this evening," Dottie said quietly, picking up two fried eggs with her fork and awkwardly dragging them across the bacon platter onto her plate.

Really, the whole thing was a lot easier with footmen . . .

"And that is where you are wrong," said Adam firmly. "If you are correct—and I have seen no evidence to suggest the contrary," he said, catching a glimpse of her expression. "If you are correct, I say, then I think it best that we accept as many invitations as possible. Any opportunity could be the one in which we discover this leader of the Glasshand Gang."

Dottie blinked.

That was . . . well, precisely what she had wanted to hear from him. How strange. She had prepared herself for an unpleasant conversation—or at the very least, to slowly acclimatize themselves to the fact that working together was not a natural state for the pair of them, however necessary it was.

But instead, Adam was the one insisting on it.

"Because you want to find the Glasshand Gang," she said

slowly, taking a mouthful of bacon and eggs.

Adam's gaze did not falter. "Because I think this whole exercise—the two of us here, pretending to be husband and wife—is ridiculous. And the sooner I can return to London—and you can go back to where you came from—the better."

Dottie's heart sank.

Well, she didn't know what she had hoped for. Succeed or fail, the end of the mission would result in exactly that. It was not as though this was all concocted as a trick to make the Duke of Gilroyd fall in love with her. Other ladies may have used this sort of situation for just such a thing, but not her.

Fine, it had crossed her mind once. Just the once.

But to hear it so plainly from Adam's very lips—to know he was so disgusted with her presence that he could not wait to be rid of her? That he had so little concern for her that he did not care where she went or what she did afterward?

She had not thought her heart would sink so low.

But it did so only for a moment. Forcing herself to rally, Dottie looked back at Adam. "Then we are agreed. We complete the mission."

"As swiftly as possible."

Dottie winced. "Yes, thank you. You said that."

"I meant no disrespect—"

"I don't honestly see how you could mean anything else, but there it is," Dottie said as brightly as possible. "The Earl of Chester. What do you know of him?"

It was strange, how swiftly time flew when they fell into conversation. He was remarkably astute, this duke, and Dottie forced herself not to look too impressed any time he pointed out something she had not considered or shared a piece of information she'd not got hold of.

And it quickly became obvious that there were conversations going on between Mr. Snee and others she was not a party to. Dottie swallowed her bitterness. Oh, she had known Mr. Snee had not always been completely open with her. She'd only caught him out in a lie once, but that had been enough. Still. It was unpleasant to have the fact she was not in the central circle of spies shoved in her face.

"—agreed then," Adam said, rising suddenly and dropping his napkin on the table. "We will meet in the hall at eight o'clock."

"Y-Yes," Dottie said, hating that her voice faltered. "And—"

But he was gone. And the rest of the day was hers to do with as she wished. Such a shame she had wondered—fine, hoped— that she could spend it with him.

This man. There was something about him. Something in the wildness of his eyes last night, when he had thought her hurt. Something in his charm, the way he could turn it on and off. Something in the darkness of his expression when Adam thought no one was looking.

Dottie had always been drawn to the darkness in people as well as the light. It was becoming clear that Adam had far more darkness than she had first thought.

"But I had a wife, and she was perfect. And when I lost her, all joy left the world . . ."

His words echoed round her mind for the remainder of the day. Restless, unwilling to go walking in the freezing sea breeze yet unable to settle indoors, Dottie moped about the drawing room and wondered where on earth Adam could be.

Surely they could not both be in the house, wondering what the other was up to . . .

By the time the clocks of the house were chiming eight o'clock, Dottie had been ready for an hour, impatient for thirty minutes, and absolutely champing at the bit to be gone for the last five minutes.

And Adam was late.

"You said eight o'clock," Dottie said, not attempting to dim the accusatory tone in her voice when he finally arrived in the hall.

Everything in her seemed to be itching. He had said they would be away at eight o'clock, and it was near a quarter past!

Adam glanced over with a sardonic look. "I did. I am running late."

Dottie tutted under her breath, then stepped to the door. "Come on, then."

They sat in silence in the carriage. She had seen no point in taking a carriage—the Earl of Chester's townhouse was, according to Mrs. Sharp, who was never wrong about these things, not a far walk.

It had surely taken longer to get the horses ready than it would have taken to simply walk there.

But dukes never walked, apparently. That was what Dawson had said, as she had tapped her foot and waited in the hall for the master of the house.

When the carriage pulled up outside the Earl of Chester's, Adam stepped to the pavement, then turned and held out a hand. "My lady."

Dottie swallowed hard as she took his hand, her fingers thankfully protected by her gloves, and stepped out.

He had not left her much room to disembark. Gasping at the sudden closeness, Dottie found her chest pressed against his own, the carriage behind her preventing her from backing away. He was so close, and so potent—surely he knew the effect he had on—

"Keep your eyes and ears open," murmured Adam, his breath warm on her neck. "I don't trust this earl, not as far as I could throw him. He seems far too charming."

Dottie tried to smile. "You don't trust charming people."

His dark gaze flashed. "I've never been given a reason to."

And before she could even think to respond, he was gone.

Not gone. Just stepped away, but the sudden lack of his intense presence was enough to turn Dottie's head giddy. After blinking several times, it was to see her "husband" waiting at the door, an arm offered.

"In your own time," he said gruffly.

Dottie nodded, silently stepping over to him and taking his

arm. What could she say? The man was impossible to anticipate: at first distant and taciturn, then cheerful and jovial, then dark and menacing. Then round she went again on this emotional merry-go-round which did not seem to be showing any signs of slowing.

Who was Adam Seymour, Duke of Gilroyd, really? When all the barriers were taken down, all the frost melted? Was he a good man? A gentle man? Or were the snapshots of rage and bitterness his true nature?

"Ah, the Duke and Duchess of Gilroyd!"

The door was flung open and there stood the Earl of Chester, hands clasped together in apparent delight.

"I never had you down for an elopement, but I did not see anything in the papers—come in, come in, I have tables set up in the drawing room, and you are the last to arrive . . ."

Dottie had known they would be, but she had to admit, there was a small benefit in that. Everyone was already here, which meant she and Adam were introduced most politely by the earl to each of the other guests, and he turned out to be a man who enjoyed a bit of gossip between introductions. All very informative.

"Her debts are racking up far faster than those diamonds would suggest . . ."

"I heard the earl's daughter disowned him, something about a young man . . ."

". . . recently returned from the Continent. What he was doing there, I shudder to think . . ."

Only when Dottie caught Adam's eye did she spot him mouth just four words.

"Late is always best."

Late is always best?

Dottie blinked, the information filling her mind and making sense as she looked about her. She now knew both the name of and a scandalous fact about every single person in the room. And their host, the Earl of Chester, had no chance to whisper anything about them to others.

Late is always best. Of course. She should have known Adam had a greater plan in being half an hour late than mere tardiness or ill-mannered timing. Why he could not have just mentioned that, she did not know.

So, he had done this on purpose. Now they had the perfect scope of the guests and some nuggets of information to dwell on. Perhaps he did know what he was doing, after all.

The evening became a strangely dizzying example of just how little she knew him. The Adam she had spent the last fortnight with would have snapped at Lady Romeril, cut across Mrs. Marnion who was delighted to see Dottie again, and laughed in the Earl of Chester's face when he managed to get hearts and clubs mixed up.

But this Adam did not. He was a revelation.

Charming, beaming smiles, clever quips, laughter and merriment, Adam Seymour, Duke of Gilroyd, swiftly became the heart of the gathering. Drawing in those sitting on the sidelines, even encouraging a wallflower Dottie had never met before into joining in the conversation, it was only as they were saying their goodbyes to their host that she realized what it was settling heavy in her chest.

Envy.

How could the man look at the world with such joy, such equanimity . . . yet never hold a full conversation with her without slipping into an argument?

Her pique was unaccountable, and try as she might, Dottie could not shift it. Not even after accepting the bow of the Earl of Chester and Adam's hand and help into the carriage. The driver's whip snapped. The carriage pulled away.

"You're very quiet."

Dottie tried to smile. "You've done enough talking for the both of us."

Try as she might, bitterness still managed to seep into her words. It was most provoking. She had come into this mission in the secure knowledge that she was a chameleon, able to slot into almost any social circle and be its head within five minutes. Her skills had never let her down before.

But she was a mere amateur compared to this man.

"How do you do it?" Dottie found herself asking, despite her instincts, as the carriage rattled along. "Put on the charm so easily, as though you've been waiting all your life to meet those people."

Adam smiled briefly, but it was gone just as quick. "I have."

Dottie stared. "You cannot possibly tell me—"

"Oh, I've always been able to put it on," he said, shrugging as he turned to look out the window. Dottie tried not to notice the angular line of his jaw, the way his throat bobbed before he spoke again. "Charm is something one can be trained in. I don't know about the other dukes of your acquaintance—"

"None of them are like you."

Heat seared her cheeks. Dottie hoped to goodness the darkness of the evening hid the probable redness of her face.

"I mean—"

"I know what you meant—I think," Adam conceded. He paused before continuing. "They are charming most of the time, and I am careful with my manner. Constructed. Put it on and off again like a coat."

The carriage was warming up, subtly but noticeably enough for Dottie to shift uncomfortably. "Well . . . well, yes. But how do you do it?"

The Duke of Gilroyd shrugged. "I don't like people."

"You don't like—"

"It's all an act, Dottie," he said heavily, turning to meet her gaze once again. "Being a duke, you have to be sociable all the time. Always glad to see people, always delighted with the company you find yourself in, always polite, always, always, always. And I am not one of nature's people pleasers."

Dottie snorted her agreement at that.

"Precisely," Adam said dryly. "So I put it on. With those I am most comfortable with, of course, I don't bother. They get the pure, unadulterated, prickly Gilroyd."

Prickly was the right word. At least, there were prickles of something crawling across Dottie's chest, but she wasn't sure she should be feeling them.

Something like warmth. Or pleasure. Delight in his company, despite all his ill-manners and argumentative nature, and in the strange realization that she had seen the real him.

Had he truly felt comfortable with her?

"I . . . I take my knowledge of your prickly self as a badge of honor, then," Dottie said quietly, the carriage rocking along the cobbled street.

Fire burned in his eyes. Or was it in her chest? Or farther down? "You are rare, Dottie Yates."

"I'm just a—"

"You've put up with my presence for more than a week and you've seen some of the worst of me," he said quietly, his gaze unrelenting. "Not many people could do that."

Dottie swallowed. She was not going to get herself into difficulties. She was not going to misconstrue this as—

"The only downside to this evening, of course, is that we haven't discovered anything more about the Glasshand Gang," Adam said with a sigh, turning to look back at the window.

"True," Dottie said quietly, "but I've learned a lot about you."

CHAPTER NINE

13 November 1811

"THERE IS LATE," Adam said, attempting to keep the ire from his voice, "and then there's *late*. We are *late*."

"I don't know what you are talking about," said Dottie cheerfully, examining her reflection in the large looking glass Dawson had hung in the hallway just the day before. "You are the king of late. And stop tapping."

"I'm not—" Adam stopped talking. He also stopped tapping.

Damn. He hadn't even noticed he was doing it—but then, this woman was enough to push even the most patient man in the world past his endurance.

What could possibly be taking so long? Dottie . . . Miss Yates looked precisely as she did all the time—perfect.

Not perfect, Adam hastily corrected, tugging his gloves tighter on his hands in the hope that it would distract him. Just . . . fine. Beautiful. Good enough for the Viscount Stulsemere's ball.

"Anyone who is anyone is fashionably late to a ball," said Dottie, leaning forward to examine a curl of hair. "Isn't that what they say?"

Why she was spending such time by the looking glass, Adam could not tell. The woman had spent more time than he thought possible with Mrs. Sharp that afternoon, and when the housekeeper had returned downstairs, she had been absolutely beaming. There did not appear to be anything that could please her more than to wait upon Her Grace.

In fact, most of the servants seemed to be of the same opinion.

It was enough to drive one up the wall, Adam thought darkly. Lord sakes, they were his staff! They were supposed to enjoy serving him!

Though now he came to think about it, he wasn't as delightful as Dottie Yates. Nor as pleasing. Nor as grateful.

Adam rammed his top hat on his head and glared over at the woman who was causing him to second guess half of his mannerisms without her even saying a word. It was outrageous!

Worse, he couldn't stop thinking about the conversation they'd had the last time they'd stepped into his carriage. The conversation where he had said too much, and at the same time, perhaps not enough . . .

"You've put up with my presence for more than a week and you've seen some of the worst of me. Not many people could do that."

"We are now officially late for a ball," said Adam in a growl as a clock somewhere about the place chimed nine. "An hour late, in fact. I thought you'd want to be off, finding Glasshand Gang leaders left, right, and center!"

"And I thought you had the right idea when we attended the Earl of Chester's card party," said Dottie serenely, not bothering to turn from the looking glass. "We arrived late—"

"This is a ball, not a card party! The host won't parade us round the guests and introduce us. Our names will be announced upon entry!" Adam's jaw was tightening, and though he knew he was right, he also knew he needed to moderate his frustration. "We should have been there first! Then we could have seen every introduction and—"

Dottie whirled around, panic on her face. "Truly?"

Adam gaped. *What did she mean, truly?* Was that not always

the way things were done at balls? "Yes! You mean to tell me you've attended a ball where they did not do that?"

Her gaze was searching him as though for a secret truth, but he could not have been clearer with her. *What was going on?*

Then a blankness covered Dottie's expression, shutting him out from her thoughts as she said calmly, "I have never attended a ball before."

Despair sank into his chest and settled in his stomach. *Never attended a—*

"Why on earth didn't you say so?" Adam snapped, striding over to the front door and throwing it upon. "We've wasted precious—yes, thank you, Dawson."

The man had rushed forward and taken Dottie's unresisting hand, leading her to the front door.

The Brighton air was blasting cold as Adam stepped into it, but he didn't have time to think. Wrenching open the carriage door, he and Dawson bundled Dottie inside and he followed swiftly.

"Off we go!" Adam said curtly, tapping the roof of the carriage.

It lurched forward at once. Dawson only just had time to slam the carriage door shut before it took off down the street, heading toward their destination.

The destination they should have been at over an hour ago, Adam could not help but think darkly. Oh, Lord, what had he been doing, permitting Dottie—permitting Miss Yates to pull together all the plans? He should have known that—

"You're angry with me," said Dottie quietly.

The woman had no fear in her eyes, which he would not wish to see there of course, but no admission of guilt either. She didn't even look sorry that she had created such a challenge for them.

"I'm frustrated," he admitted.

Well, it was more than he would normally acknowledge, but it was impossible to lie. After spending almost two weeks with the woman, lying felt . . . wrong, somehow.

Even if Miss Dottie Yates was a danger to the mission, a danger to herself—

"It was an honest mistake."

Adam sighed. "And that's why I am not angry. But you have to admit, there are parts of Society I know better than you."

The look in her eye was blank, guarded. "And vice versa."

"I am not contesting that!" Adam swallowed his fury and tried looking out of the window to distract himself from the intoxicating presence of the woman.

Did she know what an effect she had? Surely she had chosen that brilliant green silk gown as a distraction. What, did she hope the Glasshand Gang would all simultaneously propose marriage to her, and—

And a sort of boiling rage rushed through his chest at the very thought. *Dottie Yates, receive the attentions of another? Hell would freeze over first.* Adam blinked. The sensation subsided, though it did not completely dissipate.

Now where had that come from? Since when was he a fierce defender of Miss Yates' honor?

"I just—I've been to Almack's, and danced at house parties, but—"

"It's not the same," Adam said heavily, grateful for the distraction. He looked back at Dottie and momentarily caught a pained look on her face.

His shoulders softened. There was no one in this carriage blaming Dottie more than herself, it appeared. Well, that was all to the good. He needed to work with someone who could hold themselves accountable.

Not that he wanted to work with anyone at all. But if he had to . . .

"I don't even want to go to this damned ball." Adam blinked. *Oh, hell. He'd said that out loud, hadn't he?*

Dottie's expression was now one of curiosity. "You don't? I would have thought—well, all gentlemen wish to attend balls."

"To smoke, drink, gamble, and gawp at pretty women," he said darkly. "I smoke enough as it is, I drink enough as it is, and I have no wish to gamble away my fortune."

Silence settled in the carriage as it lurched around the corner. Evidently his driver was conscious of their lateness. They would be there in a few minutes.

"And . . . and you don't wish to gawp at pretty women?"

"I don't need to go to a ball for that," Adam said without thinking, his gaze meandering down Dottie's nose to her rosebud mouth.

Then every part of him stiffened.

Oh, hell. Oh damn, damn and—

"I don't—oh," said Dottie faintly. Her rosebud mouth was now matched in color by her cheeks. "I . . . you think I am pretty?"

It was a question, and that typically meant that in all good manners Adam would have to answer.

But what on earth was he supposed to say to that? *Yes, you are very pretty? No, you are beautiful? How can you not see—has no one ever told you that?*

Of course they had, Adam reminded himself. She'd bedded men for the cause, hadn't she? Dottie had not precisely told him that, but she'd made it perfectly clear she'd used her feminine charms to advance missions in the past. Why, he was probably just one in a long string of men who had told her that.

Adam clasped his hands in his lap and tried not to think of her. Which was difficult, in a carriage this small. Some parts of him were thinking of her more than others.

"Yes," he said shortly. "Pretty."

For a woman who had played the courtesan, Dottie appeared rather shocked at his words, however few there were, and her flush deepened. It was with great relief that the carriage stopped and Adam was able to fling open a door and step out.

Away from Dottie Yates. Away from her presence. Away from her teasing smiles, her frank apologies, her pretend surprise at being found pretty.

Adam breathed in deeply, lungs sharp with the cold air. Yes, that was it. Remind himself of the pain that was always to be found in that direction. Remind himself of the coldness of his bed now Louisa was gone, the coldness of his heart. How—

"Goodness," said Dottie lightly as she stepped out beside him. "Now this, I could not have expected."

It was overdone, even Adam would admit. But then, the Viscount Stulsemere was always extravagant. It was in his nature.

There were festoons of flowers all along the windows, ledges, and columns outside his home. A myriad of candles, surely at least a thousand, blazed in the dark evening, shimmering light across the street. There were gold streamers interwoven with the flowers that seemed to glitter like real gold, and—was that a pair of white doves in a cage above the door?

"How exquisite!" sighed Dottie loudly.

Adam sighed. *Well, no one was perfect. If she was taken in by such gaudiness, there was no telling—*

"How absolutely lurid," Dottie breathed as she took his arm and smiled through her teeth. "We are being watched."

"We are being—"

Adam would have kept going, but it was difficult to do so. Speaking became a challenge when a beautiful woman was pressing her lips against your own.

It was over in a moment. If he had not been so conscious of her to begin with, Adam could have believed he'd dreamt it.

His body wouldn't. Every inch of him was tingling, on fire, sparking heat he could not understand and could not control. No woman had kissed him since—

Adam caught sight of a man skulking just out of the sparkling light the Viscount's designs created. He was watching them.

Every time he underestimated her, Dottie Yates proved her worth yet again.

Adam gave a miniscule nod and he saw the answering recognition in her eyes. *Dear God, they could make quite a team.*

For this mission only, he thought, the warmth in his chest replaced by fear. He was not going to let what happened to Louisa happen to Dottie. That meant he had to keep his distance.

Keep his distance, and completely forget that kiss.

As predicted, when they entered the ball, a footman announced their names loudly above the chatter of the viscount's ballroom.

"His Grace and Her Grace, Adam and Dorothy Seymour, the Duke and Duchess of Gilroyd!"

Adam winced. He knew precisely the effect this was going to have on the gathering here, and he was not wrong.

"Gilroyd, did he say?"

"Surely not, Gilroyd vowed never to remarry—"

"—standing there with a woman on his arm! An actual woman!"

Try as he might, he could not help his arm tightening. Then quite unexpectedly, there was a squeeze on that very arm.

Blinking as though standing in a dazzling beam of light, Adam saw Dottie give him a small smile.

"This vow everyone keeps talking about," she murmured under her breath as they stepped into the bustling ballroom. "One day, you need to tell me about—"

"Ah, our guests of honor," boomed the cheerful Viscount Stulsemere. "You will of course take the first place in the set?"

Adam's heart sank as he looked over to where the gentleman was pointing.

A set. Eight—no, nine pairs waiting in a line, all eyes turning in expectant interest.

Oh, hell. How had he ever allowed Dottie to convince him that coming to this dratted ball was a good idea?

"You'll have to do it, Gilroyd," came another voice.

Turning, Adam saw old Caelfall. He was still leaning on his stick, but there was a wry look on his face Adam knew well.

"I don't have to do anything," he hissed out of the corner of his mouth.

His old friend laughed, but Adam could not laugh with him.

A traitor in their midst, Chetnole had said. And they still hadn't routed him out. Could it be Caelfall? Was it possible that so longstanding a friend as he could have chosen to take against him? Against them all?

"We'd be delighted to—"

"We would not," hissed Adam, trying to pull Dottie away from the growing crowd. "We—"

But there was nothing for it. He could see that the moment he looked around the room and saw so many eager faces turned in their direction. The ball had to start, and it appeared he had been chosen as the sacrificial lamb.

Well, damn.

"Fine," he said through gritted teeth. "Fine!"

With very bad grace, Adam stomped over to the set, pulling an unresisting Dottie with him. When he deposited her in the line of ladies, it was to see her beaming as he turned to face her alongside the other gentlemen.

"I don't know what you're so happy about," he growled.

Dottie's eyes sparkled. "Don't you?"

She was referring to the mission, Adam tried to tell himself as the music started and he stepped forward to take Dottie's hand. That was all. The mission would surely be easier if they could have a good look at everyone around them—looking for this mystery man Dottie had once seen—and that would be easy if they were in the center of the room.

It certainly wasn't for any reasons like wanting to touch each other, get close, breathe in each other's scent as they turned in the middle of the set, his hand warm on her back.

Adam swallowed. None of those reasons. And yet he was enjoying it, wasn't he? As he paraded Dottie slowly down the set, his palm on the small of her back, his other hand clasping hers, it was impossible not to recognize the rush through his chest.

Desire.

He hadn't felt it in so long. Had thought for a long time that he would never feel it again.

But this was ridiculous—and he was entirely alone in it!

Wasn't he?

Adam's eyes met Dottie's as he turned her in his arms to parade back up the set, and he felt as well as heard the hitch in her breath. Could feel her pulse facing, her hand in his. Saw something in her eye . . .

"Being your wife is making me an object of envy," Dottie breathed lightly, a smile dancing on her face as they separated.

He shrugged, trying to ignore his quickening heartbeat. "I don't know why."

"Don't you?"

"They see a duke with plenty of money," Adam shot back under his breath, though he could not help but smile. "You know the curmudgeon I am."

"Do I?" Dottie said.

Adam tried not to snort in frustration. It was most irritating. The woman never seemed to be the same for two days together. At times stern and bold, at others soft and vulnerable.

And there was this . . . this fire in her, for want of a better word. When the dance brought them together again, Adam could not deny the longing that swept through his heart. A longing to do more than merely take her hands in his or to touch only the appropriate parts of her.

Oh, no. He wanted to touch the most inappropriate—

Noise—loud sound. For an instant, Adam thought it was gunshots and cursed himself for not bringing his own pistol—

But it was only applause. He blinked. The dance was over.

Dottie stepped close, concern on her face. "Adam? You look . . . strange."

Adam swallowed, his mouth dry. He was not in that volley—not again, not ever. He never had to go back there. "I just . . . I thought . . ."

Damn it, why couldn't his tongue obey?

A small hand slipped into his own. "Come on. Let's get some

air."

The Viscount Stulsemere's ballroom had the most splendid view of the sea. The wind was less here, too, the balconies overlooking the waves protected by pillars with a wall on the north side.

As the door behind them closed, Adam leaned on the balustrade and hung his head, breathing in deeply.

He was not there. He was free and alive, and he should be grateful. He should—

"Adam?" came Dottie's nervous voice. "Are . . . are you quite well?"

Adam turned around and did what he knew he should not do as instinct overpowered reason. Pulling an unresisting Dottie toward him, Adam crushed his lips on hers, desperately searching for a repeat of the momentary thrill she'd given him before they'd entered the ball.

And dear God, what a repeat. This kiss was longer, deeper, more passionate than the first, and a tingling, aching desire rushed through Adam's body like a wildfire.

Oh, this was wonderful. All the desire, the need he'd felt whenever he was with Dottie while remaining unable to explain it, unable to understand it—it didn't need to be explained. As his tongue teased along her lip, meeting hers in a cascade of unadulterated pleasure, Adam knew he just had to feel it. Lose himself in these sensations. Not think, just feel.

She craved it too—she must do, for Dottie had tilted her head and parted her lips, letting him in, encouraging him with hands, hands which were reaching for his neck and—

She pulled his cravat.

Adam dropped her immediately as though she were made of hot coals. Just like Louisa—how in God's name had she known? Lifting his hands to straighten his hair, he turned and looked out at sea as though she were not there.

His pulse roared in his ears. Dear God, his actions repulsed him now. How could he have done such a thing? How could he betray her memory?

"A-Adam?"

The cascading waves of pleasure were gone now. All Adam was left with was regret. Regret he had kissed her. Regret he had given her hope. Regret he had not kissed her longer.

Christ in his Heaven, but he was in trouble.

"Adam?" A hand was placed on his shoulder.

Adam shrugged it off as he turned to glare at Dottie. She hadn't done anything wrong, and the confusion in her gaze was well warranted—but he couldn't permit that to ever happen again. *God, he was a cad.*

"That should never have happened," he snapped.

Dottie's eyes widened in pain, and shock, her hands moving as she spoke. "I—I didn't . . . you were the one to kiss me!"

"May God forgive me," Adam growled, stepping around her.

The balcony door snapped shut behind him and the roar of the ball engulfed him—but it wasn't enough to remove the guilt from his discomforted heart.

CHAPTER TEN

16 November 1811

> *Leader one: male, at least 40s. Dark hair (NB: how dark is dark?).*
>   ~~*Unmarried*~~ *married with a son*
> *Leader two: male, at least 50s—though could be older. Graying hair*
>   *(how much?). Known to be in London as of August 1811 (why*
>   *no more recent info?)*
> *Leader three: spoken of, but never seen*
> *Leader four:*

Dottie sighed, pushing back her long hair behind her ears. She really should pin it up—the servants could come in at any moment to light the fire in the drawing room grate, and here she was, in her nightgown and a dressing gown she had found in the bedchamber she'd been given. She hadn't even combed her hair, let alone pinned it up. And it was getting far too long.

In short, she was a state.

But it was nothing in comparison to the state of her mind. That was racing with thoughts she could not capture and ideas she could not articulate. Her notebook, in her lap, was filled with half-written notes and half-considered suggestions.

Trail one of them

Mail coach? Speak to Sedley, must have seen more than he thought
Edinburgh, Brighton, London—what do they have in common?
     Coast? ~~*Population size?*~~ *Popularity?*

Dottie carefully drew a circle and segmented it as she tried to think of the mission.

Her mission. She had been the one to ask Mr. Snee for this, and he had been gracious enough to give it to her. Was she now truly going to throw away that trust merely because a man—

"That should never have happened."

"I—I didn't . . . you were the one to kiss me!"

Dottie swallowed. *It was just a kiss*, she told herself fiercely. *Just a kiss.*

Just the most intense, romantic moment she had ever experienced. Just the most toe-tingling, heart-stopping, passionate kiss anyone had ever experienced. Just a sudden rush of closeness and longing and need—

Which had been stopped.

She couldn't forget the look in Adam's eyes. Pained, almost angry. As though she had done something awful.

Tucking her feet closer to her in the freezing room, Dottie sighed heavily, her breath turning to fog in the cold air.

She should be focused on the Glasshand Gang, she thought firmly. They were wreaking havoc, and she was one of the few who could bring their leaders to justice.

So why did she think it more important to daydream about a certain duke?

"Adam," Dottie breathed quietly.

"Yes?" came a voice as the door behind her opened.

Dottie stiffened, then turned hastily in her armchair to see Adam Seymour, Duke of Gilroyd, step into the room.

He was more dressed than she was—but only just. His breeches were buttoned and so was his shirt, but there was no cravat around his neck, no waistcoat nor jacket. There was a strange look on his face she had never seen before, and his presence had warmed the room.

Or at least, it had warmed her.

You are being ridiculous, Dottie thought as she hoped her cheeks weren't pinking. *He is a duke and has made some sort of silly vow about never marrying. And he's a bore! You don't even like him!*

Well, that was a lie. She couldn't even try to think it for more than a few seconds.

It seemed impossible not to like Adam Seymour. Even though he did not wish for her good opinion, he had it. Here was a man who had served his country faithfully, in spite of loss, in spite of grief. Who pushed away the world but still wanted to save it. Who, after a few complaints, had treated her as an equal: shouted at her, criticized her, and berated her, yes, but as an equal. As he would have done a man.

Despite herself, despite the way he had looked at her after their kiss, she liked him.

"May I come in?" Adam asked awkwardly.

Dottie blinked. *Why on earth was the Duke of Gilroyd asking permission from her to come into his own drawing room? It was bizarre!*

"Errh," she said.

Errh? Was that truly all she could manage?

"You shouldn't be sitting here," Adam said stiffly.

She shouldn't be sitting here? Even just sitting in a chair she was doing something wrong, now? Well, she couldn't see that she was causing any harm, unless you counted the wear and tear on the armchair, and that was hardly—

"Not without a fire," he continued. "Here."

He stepped across the room without another word and dropped to the grate. Without looking at her, Adam started to lay a fire.

Dottie stared. They had returned to his townhouse last night in silence. Adam hadn't even met her eye as they were rocked by his carriage, and when Dawson had opened the door, the duke had stormed past him and off toward his study.

She hadn't cried herself to sleep. Not really. But she had wept, all alone in the small bedchamber. Everything seemed to have gone wrong—and after they were almost growing civil with each other—and she couldn't understand what she'd done.

It was most jarring to Dottie's sense of self. She had never— she was not the sort of woman who just went around kissing gentlemen! He had, after all, been her first—

"You must be freezing."

Dottie swallowed. Adam's voice was sharp, his tone angry. But not at her. With her, perhaps. It was a difference that was hard to articulate.

"I'm not—"

"Don't tell me you're not cold, I can see you shivering," said the man darkly.

Heat seared her cheeks. *He wasn't even looking. How could the duke possibly—*

"What are you reading?"

Still, Adam had not turned to her. Dottie would have to remember this. His peripheral vision must be flawless. That, or he had taken a far closer look at her when he had entered the room than she had thought.

Dottie glanced at her notebook and simultaneously took in the scandalous way she was attired.

Oh, botheration. She hadn't thought she would see anyone when she traipsed downstairs before it had got light. And now—

"I said, what are you reading?" Adam lit a match, holding it under the kindling he had carefully stacked. "Something interesting?"

Dottie snapped her notebook shut. "Just my notes."

"Notes?"

"On the mission. On the Glasshand Gang, on most things that I have been doing the last few years," she said quietly, heart hammering in her chest.

If he asked to see it, she'd have to refuse. Then what would happen? Would he wrench it from her? Clasp his hands over her own as he tried to take it? Would she rise, and find herself pressed against him as they struggled over the—

Dottie shook her head. Dear Lord, she had never been one for passing fancies—and that was far more than passing. *What had gotten into her?*

"It's early to be studying, isn't it?" Adam said quietly as he dropped into the armchair opposite.

His eyebrow was raised but there was a look of genuine interest in his face. And something else. Some uneasiness perhaps.

Oh, Adam had always held himself aloof, his irascibility notwithstanding. Dottie had presumed that was simply ingrained in him, part and parcel of being a duke. Perhaps he was different with those from the same class as him, the same breeding, the right sort of family. Just not with her.

Yet this was still different somehow. His voice was softer, warmer. And that look—

"You're examining me."

Dottie immediately dropped her gaze to her notebook. "No, I'm not."

The denial was ridiculous. She could hear the foolishness, so Adam had certainly heard it. But how did he expect her to just sit and talk to him after what had happened last night? After what they had shared—after he had looked at her like she had poisoned him, as though she had done something most awful?

"May God forgive me."

"I have offended you."

Dottie looked up, but only for a moment. There was such anguish on Adam's face, she could barely bring herself to look at him. No, her notebook's cover was far too interesting.

"You have not offended me," she said to her book, surprised at her voice's hoarseness.

And it was, in the main, true. Though technically, according to the standards of the *ton*, he had. A gentleman should not go around kissing ladies he was not engaged or married to. Although she supposed Society did consider them married. Even so, it was rather scandalous to kiss in public.

But though Society's morals and expectations were quite clear, Dottie had not felt violated. Quite the contrary. She'd felt desired, wanted, needed in a way she had never felt before. It had been intoxicating.

Not for long, but it had.

And she had enjoyed it. Oh, Dottie would never admit that shameful fact to anyone, least of all the man who had given her such a sumptuously delectable kiss. Though the fire was now crackling, warming the drawing room, it was something else that was warming her: the memory of a kiss that, according to Adam, should never have happened.

But how was she supposed to forget it?

"I-I suppose we were just caught up in—in the charade," Dottie blurted out.

Adam's face was a picture of interest. "The charade."

"Yes. You know," she continued awkwardly. "Pretending . . . pretending to be husband and wife. It was a good idea," Dottie added fiercely. "Even if . . . even if it has had a few complications I could not have expected."

Like how I am starting to find myself looking forward to every moment of your company, she did not say. *Or how I cried last night when you looked at me so angrily, though I do not know what I did wrong. Or how, when I close my eyes now, the only person I can ever imagine kissing me again . . . is you.*

"Not expected," Adam said gruffly. "That's not the half of it."

Dottie breathed a laugh and was relieved to see that the corners of his lips turned up.

And he was a rather handsome gentleman, wasn't he? Dottie could not be blamed, surely, for enjoying his caresses, even if they had been brief.

"Dottie Yates," said Adam quietly. "I have a confession."

Her notebook slipped to the floor, but Dottie did not give it a second thought. Not with such fascinating words tripping from Adam's lips.

A confession? What on earth could he mean?

Her curiosity swelled as she saw the discomfort on the man's face. It must be a truly dire confession for him to be so tongue-tied. This was a man, after all, who was a duke. He had been bred, raised, taught to believe that he was the most important and most splendid man in any room he was in. Yet Dottie had never seen him so unsure.

And a thought, unwelcome and unbidden yet impossible to ignore, crept into her mind.

A confession . . .

No. It could not be possible that he was the traitor, could it?

Dottie's heart thumped wildly in her chest, so loudly she was certain Adam could hear it. It had been Adam and the Duke of Chetnole who had been so sure there was a traitor in the group. They had been the ones to tell Mr. Snee, who put everyone on their guard!

And yet . . . was that, perhaps, a ruse?

Mind whirling, Dottie stared at the man who had given her a first kiss but could also have been working for years against the very things she had been protecting: honor, safety, civility. loyalty.

Could Adam Seymour, Duke of Gilroyd, be the traitor they were all looking for?

Adam sighed heavily, shaking his head. "I don't really know how to start."

Dottie licked her lips, trying desperately to think of a way to encourage him to open up. *If she could hear his confession . . .*

"You can tell me anything, Adam. You can trust me."

His gaze met hers and her breath hitched in her throat. The way he looked at her—as though he was desperate for absolution. As though this secret, whatever it was, had been weighing on him for some time. Surely, that could only mean . . .

"You asked, yesterday," Adam said stiffly. "About the vow I have taken. The vow never to get married."

Dottie's shoulders slumped, though she tried to hide the fact she was so instantly filled with disappointment.

He wasn't the traitor, then. Of course he wasn't—that had been a foolish thing to think. The Duke of Gilroyd, the traitor? You may as well say Mr. Snee was the ringleader of the Glasshand Gang and have done with it!

"Oh. Oh, your vow," she said, trying to maintain interest in her voice. "Yes."

"No doubt you think me foolish for bringing it up," Adam said quietly, gaze drifting to the fire. "But I think it will explain my more . . . well, uncouth behavior from last night."

Heat scalded Dottie's cheeks again. "Oh."

She could not think what else to say, but apparently she did not need to. After taking a deep breath, Adam launched into a speech which seemed to have been rehearsed. Apparently she had not been the only one lying awake last night.

"You may not know this," he said softly. "But I was married, once."

"Yes, I—"

"This will be a lot easier on me if you don't interrupt me," Adam said, pain tinging his words. "If . . . if you don't mind."

Dottie stared, unable to hide her curiosity any longer. *What could he possibly have to tell her about his wife, of all people, that was so difficult?*

"Of course," she said aloud. "I will let you speak."

Adam nodded curtly, then looked back at the fire again as though it would be easier to tell the tale without looking at her. Which Dottie supposed was not quite the compliment it could have been.

"I was married. L-Louisa was her name, and she was . . . beautiful, clever, intelligent, charming." Adam blew out a dry laugh. "All the things I'm not, I suppose."

Dottie smiled but managed to hold her tongue, though her heart was sinking. Truly, was this the punishment she was to receive after allowing herself to be kissed by Adam last night? Forced to sit through a monologue about his wife?

"She died."

Though she waited for what felt like over a minute, it appeared Adam had nothing else to say.

"I . . . yes, you mentioned that," Dottie said quietly.

Adam blinked, lost in thought, then nodded wearily as he met her gaze. "Did you not wonder how she died?"

Strangely enough, Dottie never had. It was certainly not her business, and as she'd not had to work a Duchess of Gilroyd into her plan for this mission other than herself, she hadn't given it much thought.

She shook her head.

Adam's look became brittle. "Years ago, before you started working with Mr. Snee, he came to my townhouse in London and told me I had to have a partner for my next mission. Someone named Taylor."

Dottie's heart started to sink. *Oh, no . . .*

"And when Mr. Taylor came out to meet me, it was actually a Miss Taylor," Adam said. "Which I suppose you could have guessed at. The mission went well. Exceedingly well. I asked Mr. Snee, delicately of course, to see if there were any other missions that would require a gentleman and a lady—and if there weren't, to make some."

A smile crept across Dottie's face. "You . . . you fell in love."

"Hard, and fast," Adam said with a sigh. "I proposed to Louisa after the second mission."

She nodded. *Oh, it made so much sense now.* "And she accepted you."

"And she soundly rejected me," Adam said, a dry laugh in his throat. "Damned woman, she wanted me to be sure. She came from nothing, you see. No family, no nobility, no wealth. She thought a duke of my stature should—I don't know, find a countess, or something."

"Perhaps she had a point," Dottie said softly.

Her heart was still thundering but it was in anticipation, and not the pleasant kind. There was only one way this story could end.

"I managed to convince her, in the end," Adam said with a laugh. "When we were married, it was a small party. I wasn't interested in splendor. Just her. We had almost three years. Three years of laughter and arguments—"

"Arguments?"

"Louisa was not a woman to take my opinions as gospel," said Adam, a twinkle in his eye. "And then . . . then Mr. Snee sent us to France. An important mission, he said, and for all I know it would have been if we hadn't been ambushed."

Dottie sat a little straighter in her chair. She had known the worst was coming, but—"An ambush?"

"At an inn. We were outnumbered immediately, and I think I knew then it was all about to go to hell." Adam's voice was quiet, seemingly unable to stop himself continuing. "We got separated, Louisa and I. I should have been by her side at all times! Should have known what would happen, but—she got dragged away, out of the place, and I couldn't reach her. I could barely breathe, a man had smacked me in the chest with a musket, and I was bleeding—there was panic everywhere, and I didn't know who had betrayed us . . ."

Finally his voice gave out.

Dottie could not blame him. There was terror in his tone, real fear in his voice, as though he were back in that moment, desperately fighting to get to the woman he loved.

Only then did she see just what an effort it had been for him to enter the King's Head and wrench her from that brawl.

"By the time I got out of there, she had already passed away," said Adam bleakly. "Nothing I could do. Even the best doctor in the world . . . and she was gone. Taken from me. My partner, my wife, my everything . . . gone."

Silence fell between them. Silence, save for the heavy breathing of a duke and the crackling of a fire.

"I am sorry," Dottie breathed.

It wasn't enough—but what words could be? How could she commiserate with a man she was still getting to know, who had suffered perhaps one of the greatest losses life could offer?

Adam nodded briefly. "It wasn't your fault."

"Still, I am sorry," she said quietly. "If I had known—"

"What, you wouldn't have come here?" Adam interrupted, meeting her gaze steadily. "You wouldn't have come on this mission, continued to pursue the Glasshand Gang?"

Dottie swallowed. "I-I wouldn't have suggested I pretend to be your wife."

Perhaps he could sense in her the genuine pain of hearing his words. Or perhaps he was so wrapped up in his own grief he could not tell.

"The worst of it is, sometimes I go days without thinking about her," said Adam quietly. "It's been years. Longer without her than I ever had with Louisa, and sometimes . . . when I'm tired, or my guard is down, or . . . or I have danced with a beautiful woman . . ."

His gaze remained steady, though there appeared to be a slight color in his cheeks.

It was instantly matched by her own. "Oh. I suppose that explains—yesterday, you said—"

"I stand by what I said, though not how I said it," Adam said. "And I should not have kissed you. But, having done so, I shouldn't have shouted at you. Louisa . . . she would want me to go on with my life. Be happy. She would think my vow foolish. Isolating. Rash."

And something akin to hope leapt in Dottie's chest. *Surely he did not mean—*

"But we are partners on a mission together, and that—that sort of thing is only a distraction," Adam said stiffly. "All good things come to an end. Even dukes. And once this mission is over, you'll be able to go back to your life, and I'll go back to mine."

Dottie knew she should agree. That was the smart idea, one that she should have had. Now she knew so much more about Adam and his life, the way he had so tragically lost Louisa, it was certainly what she should suggest. And yet—

"So, will you forgive me, Dottie?" Adam said, his voice breaking as he met her gaze.

Dottie hesitated. *This was only going to get more complicated, and yet how could she deny him?* "There's nothing to forgive."

CHAPTER ELEVEN

19 November 1811

ADAM WATCHED AS another wave slowly crept up the Brighton shore, and then, just as he knew it would, started to flow back toward the sea. "And this is helping?"

"It isn't helping you?" asked Dottie, breathing in deeply and closing her eyes. "Isn't it marvelous?"

He supposed it was at least a better view, and better sounds, than what they had been forced to endure the last few days.

Brighton. In the Season. Adam had thought he'd known what he was getting himself into. It couldn't be as bad as London, he had thought. London was larger.

The trouble was, it appeared there were the same number of people in Brighton as London, so the result was that they were simply far more crushed in. And no one seemed to care much about personal space, either. Why, at the dinner they had attended last night, a woman had attempted to—well, it was not spoken of in polite company. It was certainly not done.

Adam's bottom had never been pinched like that before.

There were others from the *ton* walking up and down the promenade, but only he and Dottie had paused to look out to sea for quite this long. Adam glanced at those passing them. *Could he be the traitor? Could he?*

"You're fretting again."

"I am not fretting," snapped Adam. Then he tried to take a deep breath, forcing the tension from his temples. "Much."

Fretting *was* the right word for it. It felt as though in every room they went into, every bowing gentleman, every smiling face could be the traitor. Could be a leader of the Glasshand Gang. Could be whispering about him behind his back, laughing at him for not keeping to his vow never to remarry.

Though now he came to think about it, perhaps Adam was seeing too much in that.

"Stop fretting and focus on smiling," said Dottie, opening her eyes and beaming. "We're by the seaside!"

Adam snorted. "So?"

Dottie rolled her eyes in that way that always made his stomach lurch. "You truly are privileged if you cannot see the beauty in something like this. It's the sea, Adam!"

It was, indeed, the sea. Perhaps if he had not come to the seaside so much as a child, he could find new wonder in it. But Adam knew what the sea looked like. He was accustomed to the salt in the air and rather hated the squawking of the birds, circling overhead as they waited for a pie seller to drop one of his wares.

It was just . . . the sea.

"I for one am supremely impressed," said Dottie, looking to the horizon. "It just goes on forever. I love it."

A slow realization started to trickle through Adam's mind, and when he spoke, it was in wonder. "Dottie, do you mean to tell me . . . had you never seen the sea before this visit?"

It was unthinkable. Who had not seen the sea?

If the look of shame on her face was anything to go by, the answer was Dottie Yates.

"What of it?" she asked defensively. "Not everyone has a carriage and can just decide to take a holiday almost a hundred miles from their home. Some of us—"

"Have never seen the sea before," Adam finished in amazement.

It did not seem possible. Yet there was no denying the veracity of her statement. Perhaps he had grown too accustomed to always having his own way, doing what he wanted, acting without considering how unusual it was in life to just do what one wished.

Unlike Dottie.

"Try to see it through my eyes," said Dottie, and she moved to his side, tucking into him so his chin hovered above her shoulder. "Try to recall the first time you ever saw the sea."

Adam swallowed. It wasn't imagining the first time he had seen the sea that was the problem. It was *not* imagining the kiss that had sparked something unnamed within him that was the challenge.

"But we are partners on a mission together, and that—that sort of thing is only a distraction. All good things come to an end. Even dukes. And once this mission is over, you'll be able to go back to your life and I'll go back to mine."

He had spoken the truth. He should not have kissed Dottie, but not for the reason that she might think. Was it possible that Dottie believed he had been disappointed in their kiss—that he had not enjoyed it, and so decided against it? He hoped not.

His protestation a few mornings ago that such things would be a distraction to the mission were precisely the truth. He had been distracted. Indeed, he was being distracted now. As the waves rolled up the beach, Adam was painfully aware of Dottie's breathing. The way her neck sloped. That kissable spot just behind her—

Concentrate, man, Adam warned himself. *You're still on a mission—you're meant to be rooting out traitors and finding gang leaders and all that.*

Not seducing young women. Even if they were—

"See, isn't it amazing?" breathed Dottie, real joy in her voice. "I've never known anything like it."

Dragging his eyes away from the beautiful woman, Adam

looked out at the sea.

And for a moment, just a moment, he caught a glimpse of what Dottie was trying to explain.

The sun broke through the clouds. Light scattered from the heavens, refracting and sparkling on the ever-shifting waves. One of them crested, and the sheer movement, the thrill of nature, the sense that everything was connected in a way he could not explain—

Adam blinked. The moment was gone.

But something of the feeling remained, an echo in his chest.

He cleared his throat. "It is rather spectacular."

"Far more spectacular than our time here has been, at any rate," said Dottie darkly, finally turning from the sea and slipping her hand into his arm as though she did that every day.

Adam nodded as they continued to walk along the promenade. "It has been a frustrating mission so far."

Frustrating was putting it mildly. Adam had known the likelihood of them discovering the truth was low. He had readied himself for weeks of tedious socializing, a growing sense of impatience, then in the new year—or perhaps sooner—Dottie would give up and they would traipse back to London.

But even he could not have predicted just how difficult it had been. *Perhaps it was the intoxicating presence of the woman always beside him,* Adam could not help but think.

Being trapped in Brighton was never fun, even at the best of times. But with Dottie Yates . . .

Adam cleared his throat. "At least we are keeping up appearances. Going for a walk like this—it is precisely what a duke and his duchess would do."

Dottie grinned, looking up at him through her eyelashes. "Why do you think I suggested it?"

Stomach lurching, Adam grinned back. "I suppose you did."

That was the difficulty with Dottie. She was more intrusive upon his life than any woman ever had been, and from the start Adam had been quite prepared to be infuriated by her constant presence.

Unfortunately, more and more often, whenever she did make a comment, it was calm, precise, to the point, and absolutely correct.

It was enough to drive a man to Bedlam.

"Though having said that, I have not heard of any talk about us," Dottie continued, her voice low as a pair of arguing gentlemen passed them. "Which I have to say is something of a surprise. I rather thought the return of the Duke of Gilroyd to Society, and with a wife to boot, would have caused more of a stir."

There was a leading tone to her statement which made it sound far more like a question. Adam grunted, unwilling to commit himself to an opinion.

What was he supposed to say? That he, too, had been surprised at the warmth of the welcome he had received, the lack of whispers, despite how out of character his current actions were? Gilroyd had hardly been a common name in Society before his marriage, during it, or after.

His marriage. *God, Louisa.* He hadn't thought of her for days.

Guilt crept around Adam's heart, but it was almost immediately melted like a frost on a warm window. Dottie had squeezed his arm.

Oh, what a tangle this was becoming.

"I suppose the Duke of Gilroyd will always be welcome, wherever he goes," Dottie said lightly, inclining her head to Lady Romeril who was passing by in an open carriage. "Goodness, she must be freezing."

"Anything to see and be seen," Adam said dryly. "I suppose you're right. Gilroyd is a name that opens doors."

"Far quicker than Yates, anyway," she returned with a laugh.

He supposed she was right. Her comment reminded him of something. Or more accurately, reminded him of nothing. How little he knew about Dottie Yates.

Well, now was as good a time as any. They could still keep

their eyes peeled for anyone who looked particularly "dastardly," which was a word Dottie had adopted and Adam had found himself unconsciously picking up, despite himself.

"Tell me," he said quietly.

Dottie glanced up. "Tell you what?"

"About you. Yourself, your history, your past," Adam said, hating how awkward his voice became whenever he spoke to her. *What was wrong with him?* "I know hardly anything about you."

"That's because you haven't asked," she said, a teasing lilt in her voice as the sea breeze picked up. "Oh, I'm freezing! Shall we turn back?"

She had already slipped her hand from his arm and turned around, but Adam hesitated.

Yes, he was cold. But there was an impenetrable warmth in his chest, untouched by the freezing gusts, like a small fire lit by kindling and matches and by a hope and a prayer.

But it was growing.

"I would rather keep talking," Adam said, the words slipping out somewhat against his better judgment.

He swallowed. Showing weakness . . . it was never something he liked to do at the best of times. But this was Dottie. A woman he wanted to, even if he dare not say it, impress. A woman who didn't seem to see him properly, who considered him a means to an end, a stepping stone in her mission.

And yet she had looked at him only last night at dinner and laughed at one of his terrible jokes, and he'd thought—

You're fooling yourself, man, Adam thought sternly. *She doesn't—she wouldn't think of you like that. And you don't want her to, remember?*

"Talking? You mean, you want to hear me talking?" Dottie asked, her eyes dancing.

"Yes," Adam said quietly.

Perhaps she had expected a jest, but she wasn't to receive one. And only when she saw his gaze did her smile fade and her cheeks flush.

Because of the cold wind, Adam reminded himself. His cheeks were surely a similar color, and that was only because of the wind. *Wasn't it?*

"Come on then, we'll head toward home, and I'll tell you all the saucy secrets of my past," said Dottie finally, returning her arm to where it belonged.

Adam almost allowed that stray thought to escape him before he captured it, interrogated it, and imprisoned it. *Where it belonged?* Dottie's hand did *not* belong on his arm. That was, it did, but only because they were pretending to be husband and wife.

Pretending.

"So, where to begin?"

"Start with the sauciness," Adam found himself quipping. "And then work backward."

It brought him such joy to hear her laugh. There was something about Dottie's laugh; she laughed with her whole body, losing herself in the merriment with no thought to how she may look.

It was how laughter was supposed to be.

"Well, I'm afraid I rather gave you the wrong impression there," Dottie said as they walked along the promenade, this time with the sea to the right and home before them. "I have not led nearly as saucy a life as I could have done."

A strange mingling of relief and disappointment clenched around Adam's heart. Relief she had not been as free with herself as he had thought, and disappointment that . . . well, did that not mean she was unlikely to bestow her favors on—?

Now that's enough, Adam thought sternly. *Dottie Yates is not a woman to be trifled with. She's under your protection, you blackguard. And you like her. But that's all it can be.*

"I can't imagine how you managed to get caught up in this sort of life," Adam said. That was it, back to the mission. "I don't know of any other ladies who work with Snee."

"I suppose not, and that's because as far as I know, I'm the only one," said Dottie brightly. "My father would never have approved, of course. Neither would my mother, I think, but she died not long after I was born. Childbed sickness."

Adam sighed. "It takes too many."

"I can't complain though," said Dottie briskly, as though the loss of a parent was not something to concern oneself about. "I have no memory of her, and my father, God rest his soul, was a marvelous man. Truly affectionate and desperate to raise me in the proper way."

"And you ended up here?"

"I know, it was a bit of a disaster," she teased, the wind whipping through her curls, the sunlight sparkling in her hair. "He was a vicar, actually. Very devout, very pious, but also very good. Really good, not just the pretense some men of the church display. The number of times we went without our dinner because there was someone deserving in the village . . ."

Her voice drifted away as her gaze appeared to latch onto something unseen to the human eye.

Adam permitted her a few moments of reflection. It was clear she held great affection for her father, and great respect, too. He must have died, or else would she not have been living with him?

Dottie swiftly confirmed his thoughts. "Losing him came at a terrible cost. One I could not have predicted. A fever—it was all over within a day and he was gone."

Adam's stomach lurched. She too, then, had known grief. "I am sorry."

She met his gaze, and he was surprised to see a glint of steel beneath the sparkling eyes. Or perhaps he wasn't surprised. Nothing Dottie did could entirely shock him now.

"It was only later that I learned he was poisoned, of course," she said so lightly she could almost be talking about the weather. "The Glasshand Gang, as it turned out. Since then, I have pledged to give them no quarter. No more orphans at their hands."

Adam stared, hardly able to take in her words. What the . . .

And the words of Mr. Snee from that fateful day he had been

introduced to Miss Dorothy Yates resounded in his mind.

"I think you'll find the partner I have selected for you has just as much wish for vengeance against the Glasshand Gang as you do."

"So . . ." Adam swallowed. "How did you go from orphan to working against the Glasshand Gang?"

"Well, there I was, two and twenty with not a shilling in the world," Dottie continued, her voice bright and clear once more.

They stepped up from the promenade, Adam trying not to notice how the wind whipped her skirts around her buttocks and gave him a perfect view. He failed.

When he took her arm again on the pavement, it was with a thudding heart. "You were young, to be alone."

"Alone and penniless! Alone without a protector, sibling, uncle, nothing," Dottie said, as though it was a slight challenge she had swiftly overcome. "Too intelligent to be a governess, and too bold for marriage."

Adam could not help but laugh. "What an indictment!"

"My mother's sister told me that," Dottie said, grinning. "She meant well, I think, yet it was a rather startling revelation. I had never thought myself too much of anything."

"Now that I can believe," Adam said darkly.

Their laughter mingled with the growing noise of carriages as they stepped along the pavement. To all the world, they must have appeared to be a happily married couple, elegantly styled and windswept.

Perhaps they were.

Not married, Adam added hastily. But other than that . . . well, they were happy. Being with Dottie made him happy. All their arguments and strife aside, he'd also laughed more in her presence than he had the whole year before combined. Not that that was saying much.

"As I said, I did not have a plethora of options," Dottie was saying as they turned a corner and headed away from the busier street. "It was by chance in fact that I met Mr. Snee, and when he discovered I had quite a knack for being around all people of all classes—"

"Something a vicar's daughter would have," Adam said, realization dawning.

Yes, that was where she undoubtedly got it from. A vicar would visit everyone in the parish, wouldn't he? Rich or poor, titled gentry or poverty-stricken widow, he would see them all. And a widower with a small child could be forgiven for taking that child with him.

Dottie Yates would have learned how to be comfortable anywhere you put her, Adam thought. *And damn it, she was.*

Her smile was brilliant. "Mr. Snee gave me a challenge. I completed it swiftly, and I have worked with him ever since."

With him, Adam noticed. Not *for* him. This was not a woman who liked to be in the employ of another. In debt to another. This Dottie was far more complex than he had initially suspected.

"And Mr. Snee was right, you know."

Adam started, meeting Dottie's eye. "What do you mean?"

There was a most curious expression on the woman's face. They were almost alone, now. Or at least, as alone as anyone could be in public. The street was almost deserted, and Adam was certain he would notice if someone tweaked a lace curtain to have a look at them.

Probably.

"Mr. Snee said you were the perfect partner for me. For this mission," Dottie added hastily, her already pink cheeks darkening. "I met with him the day after I arrived at Gilroyd House. He said you had hidden depths."

Adam snorted. "Did he indeed?"

"He said you were proud, and stuck in your ways, and morose at times—"

"Oh, charming!"

"—*and* he said you were the absolute best in the business," she continued softly. "He said you'd be able to charm me into saying anything. Doing anything. And he was right."

Adam swallowed.

Oh, hell. What on earth did she mean by that?

Because the damned man was speaking the truth—at least, about the Duke of Gilroyd who'd had a duchess by his side. When he'd been happy, he'd happily taken on the world without a second thought. Why wouldn't he?

But losing Louisa had changed that.

And yet the dull empty ache in his heart was gone. It was only now he came to think about it that Adam noticed. That familiar gap . . . it was filled. Filled by what, he was not certain, but it was certainly not hollow anymore.

Adam's gaze met Dottie's. His heart skipped a beat.

"You downplay your power," she said quietly. "But no one else has ever even made me want to share my story. You did."

"I'm just curious, that's all," he tried to say, tendrils of something hot curling around his shoulder blades.

That was it, focus on the way you feel—no, wait! Focus on anything but that!

"Well, I hope your curiosity is sated," Dottie said lightly. "Now. We can turn left here for home, or right for a longer walk. Your choice."

Adam hesitated. A crossroads.

"I am hungry," he said quietly. "I wouldn't say no to some of Mrs. Sharp's pound cake."

"It's a wonder I ever manage to try any," she said with a laugh. "You eat it up so quickly!"

"Anyone not eating Mrs. Sharp's pound cake is a fool," said Adam with amiable reproach. It was so easy, sometimes. So easy to laugh with her.

"Once we're in, I'll have to go and write some of those damned thank you letters," Dottie said with a heavy sigh. "I may not see you again for hours. I'm fairly drowning in the things."

And that decided it.

"Right," said Adam decisively, hardly knowing why he was permitting this foolishness to continue, but knowing he did not yet wish to be parted.

Dottie's fingers tightened on his arm. "A longer walk with . . . with me? Are you sure?"

Not in the slightest. "I am."

CHAPTER TWELVE

22 November 1811

"B UT HOW CAN you be certain—"

"I am absolutely certain," said Dottie firmly, slamming her hand on the table. "It's got to be this one."

Or, perhaps, it didn't. Dottie could hardly distinguish between them anymore. It had been a long morning of debate after all, and she was hardly a fortune teller with a crystal ball. Maybe any of them would do . . .

Adam pinched the bridge of his nose and strode around the dining table. "Let's start from the beginning—"

Dottie groaned. "We've been talking about this for hours, Adam!"

And they had. But the tiredness in her voice was no excuse for talking to him like . . . like that. Directly. As equals. Using his name and glaring with a threatening aura.

Not that he didn't warrant it of course.

Adam gestured at the plethora of invitations strewn across the dining room table. "I just never thought we'd receive so many!"

"You are the Duke of Gilroyd, and as you have pointed out, I am an enigma," Dottie said with a wry look, sweeping a graceful hand as though she were an opera singer on stage. She was rewarded by a small grin on the man's face.

Which absolutely was not the cause of her heart skipping a beat. It most definitely wasn't the reason her stomach lurched. And she wasn't hot. Not in the slightest.

Well. Maybe a little bit.

"Enigma is one word for it."

Dottie shot him a look. It was meant to be disapproving, but somehow it came out differently. A slight flush tinged Adam's cheeks, but he did not look away.

Oh, this was dangerous. Something had shifted between them, she knew, though she could not explain what it was. Some of the ire had melted and it had left . . .

A duke who laughed. A man who teased her sometimes and held her gaze far more often, and when she'd asked for her hat yesterday it had been Adam, not Dawson who had brought it. Placed it on her head. Grazed his fingers down her neck.

"We have to make a decision," Dottie said firmly. *That was it. Stay on topic.* "It simply isn't possible to attend every single one of these, and—"

"But how do we decide?" Adam said wearily, pulling a hand through his hair. "I know you like the Earl of Chester—"

Her gaze faltered, just for a moment. Was there a hint of jealousy in the man's tone? No, surely not. She was hearing something that surely wasn't there.

"—but we have already attended one of his card parties, and a luncheon, and I didn't see anything there that raised alarm," continued Adam. "Do you honestly think his acquaintance includes a leader of the Glasshand Gang?"

Dottie hesitated.

That was the question, wasn't it? She had been so certain she would recognize the shadowy figure she had once caught a glimpse of. She was the one, after all, who had missed her chance to get a better look. It was down to her to make it right again, to prove to Mr. Snee she could do it. To prove that she belonged, in some small way, to this band of gentlemen who were determined to make the world a better place.

Belonged to Adam.

Now where had that thought come from?

"I . . . I did not see anyone at the Earl of Chester's that reminded me of the figure," she admitted quietly, stepping around the table, gaze raking over the invitations.

A dinner party with Mrs. Howarth, afternoon tea with Viscount Braedon, a ball with Lady Romeril, a recital hosted by the Duke of Axwick, a viewing of the latest designs from Paris from the modiste Madame Jacques . . .

And so many of them occurring at the same time. They simply could not attend them all.

"We need to choose something for tomorrow night that will give us the best chance of seeing as much of Brighton Society as possible," Adam said. "And I am certain the Glasshand Gang would send their leaders to the Assembly Rooms."

He placed a finger on a simple white rectangular card. It had been written out to "Their Graces of Gilroyd," which Dottie had thought rather stingy on flourish.

"And I am certain the leaders of the Glasshand Gang would be at Lady Romeril's ball," Dottie said, picking up a different card.

This one was far more ornate. Gold leaf bordered the circular invitation, on which had been inscribed in an elegant hand:

The Lady Romeril

desires and requires the presence of

His Grace, Adam Seymour, Duke of Gilroyd

and

Her Grace, Dorothy Seymour, Duchess of Gilroyd

for the enjoyment of a ball.

Adam snorted. "You just like the lettering."

"I think Lady Romeril is one of the best-connected people in the world, and so she will have a great variety of people at her ball," said Dottie hotly. "And I think the lettering is exquisite!"

She held his gaze, and a heartbeat later the two of them were giggling from opposite sides of the dining table.

When had this become so . . . fun? Dottie had never worked with another on a mission before. It was not something she had ever considered telling Adam—what good could it do?

She had expected resistance. She had expected irritation. She was a woman, and women were not supposed to have ideas or plans or go on missions. That was what the world said, and Dottie knew very few men who were willing to completely ignore it.

And then there was Adam.

"I don't know," said Adam slowly, his laughter subsiding as he glanced between the two invitations. "The Assembly Rooms will have fewer nobility, but we cannot know what social strata the Glasshand Gang has attracted. Poor old Sedley, his brother—"

"The man I saw was well dressed," Dottie said, closing her eyes just briefly so she could step back into the memory. The darkness of the street, the flare of light as someone opened a curtain, the sudden movement of a greatcoat, a light near his face—"The Assembly Rooms attracts the same people every week, whereas a ball has a wider scope of invitations . . . I think Lady Romeril's ball is our best bet."

She could see his uncertainty, the hesitation. She had not yet won the debate, and she was not sure how she could—

"I suppose the Assembly Rooms will have no musicians to-morrow," mused Adam slowly. "Mrs. Sharp said they will only be playing music on Wednesdays."

And Dottie did not know where the thought came from, but it came spilling from her lips before she could stop it. "Well then, if you want the excuse to dance with me, it'll have to be Lady Romeril's ball."

Her eyes widened as she heard her own words.

What on earth was she doing? Adam was not some sort of rake, desperate to get his hands on her—he would surely laugh at such a suggestion, see it as no more than—

"Is that so?" Adam's eyes glittered with something she had never seen before. "Well, now that does change the shape of the matter."

Dottie's breath caught in her throat.

It was impossible to tell whether the man was laughing at her or was serious. There was an impish darkness about him that made Adam almost impossible to read. Whenever he was serious, there still appeared to be a hint of mischief in him. Whenever he appeared to be bright, there was a shadow in his words.

But he was looking at her like . . . like . . .

"Lady Romeril's ball it is," Adam said softly.

Dottie swallowed. She had never believed that would work—it was astonishing, in truth, that he had not laughed her from the dining room. Did that mean he wished to dance with her?

"I'd better send our acceptance to Lady Romeril and our sorrowful regrets to everyone else," Adam said brightly. "I'll see you at dinner—ask Dawson to clear these away, will you?"

And without another word, without even waiting for a response, he strode from the table to the door and out into the hallway.

Dottie hesitated, hardly sure how she was still managing to stand upright. The world seemed to be swaying, or perhaps she was.

How did he have this effect on her?

It was ridiculous. She would have to get a grip on herself if she truly wanted to catch the Glasshand Gang leaders before Christmas. Getting distracted by dukes who blew hot and cold was certainly not the best idea she'd ever had in the world.

Dottie swallowed. Now all she had to do was try not to think about Adam's arms around her as they walked down a set . . .

It was a long day and a half. Somehow, Adam never seemed to be around. Dottie could not prove he was doing it on purpose, of course. There really might have been a disaster in the stables so that he missed luncheon, and an urgent letter from Mr. Snee that needed a response that kept him busy all afternoon. And there may well have been a debate in the gentlemen's club he was a part of that Adam had to attend that evening, but Dottie hated eating alone in that large dining room.

When Adam did not appear at breakfast the next morning, Dottie bit her lip and tried not to think about it as she poured herself a cup of tea.

He was not avoiding her. Probably. Why would he? She had done nothing wrong.

Except use her feminine wiles to encourage him to go to a ball, merely because she wanted to dance with him . . .

It wasn't like that, Dottie thought as she crunched into some toast and delighted in the fresh marmalade she had just spread on it. She truly thought Lady Romeril's ball was the best place to find—

And the dancing wouldn't hurt, interrupted a small voice in the back of her mind.

Dottie cleared her throat as though to dislodge the thought.

There was no sign of Adam all morning. By luncheon, Dottie was no longer sad about the man's absence, but angry.

Well, what did he think he was doing? Was he on a mission without her? Had he decided to follow a trail, or a lead, without informing her?

As the afternoon sun started to fade, Dottie was quite put out. *The nerve of the man!* Why, for all she knew, he'd gone back to London and—

"There you are."

Dottie rose to her feet, anger boiling over immediately. "There I am? Where have you been? You're the one who . . . who . . ."

It was impossible to keep speaking. Adam was standing in the hall door, and he was holding—

A gown.

Not just a gown. A green gown, her favorite color.

And "green" did not do justice to the smoothness of the silk, the elegance of the gold threaded embroidery, the charm of the pattern, the deftness of the skirts, layer upon layer of silks and lace.

"Where," Dottie breathed, stepping forward, "did you get that?"

"I—well, I had it made," Adam said stiffly. "For the ball. Lady Romeril's ball."

Dottie gasped as she reached out and touched the fabric. It was as light as air, as smooth as water. It flowed through her fingers. The cost of such a thing—it did not even bear thinking about.

Her gaze snapped to Adam's face. "You bought this—for Lady Romeril's ball? For me?"

"Well, I thought—I'm not going to wear it, and . . . it's Lady Romeril, and everyone will be . . ." his voice trailed away, though his gaze never left hers. "And I thought: jewels."

Dottie's eyes widened. *No. Surely he hadn't—*

"I didn't think you'd like anything too garish," Adam said quietly, pulling a blue box from his inside pocket. "Here."

Her fingers were trembling. Dottie hoped to goodness the man did not notice as she took the box and opened it to see—

"I thought, pearls," said Adam unnecessarily, as a delicate string of pearls shimmered in the candlelight. "Perfect for you."

Heart hammering in her chest, Dottie stared at the beautiful necklace which surely cost more than everything she owned put together. Then she glanced at the gown, still held in Adam's fingers.

What on earth had possessed him to do such a thing?

"I . . . you did not have to—" Dottie began faintly.

"I know I didn't," said Adam fiercely. "And I wouldn't have if I did not want to. I wanted to, Dottie. For you."

Hearing her name on his lips was intoxicating. It was all Dottie could do not to lean forward and show him, not tell him, just how grateful she was.

"Mrs. Sharp will help you get ready," Adam said, dropping

the gown in her arms and suddenly stepping back. "We should start getting ready."

Dottie blinked, dazzled by the sudden change. "R-Right, I—"

"Be ready in an hour," said Adam shortly before disappearing up the stairs.

An hour did not seem like long enough, but Dottie found it disappeared even more swiftly than she could have predicted. Mrs. Sharp clucked around her, tying her curls in an ornate fashion Dottie had never managed on her own. The pearls sat, light and precious, around her neck. In the folds of the gown, all elegance and refinement, Dottie gazed at her reflection in the looking glass and saw . . .

"The Duchess of Gilroyd," Mrs. Sharp said fondly. "I always knew you'd do us proud, Y'Grace."

Your Grace. Now that was something she'd miss. What fun it was, to play pretend.

"But you'd better hurry—the ball!"

Lady Romeril had indeed, as Dottie had predicted, invited absolutely everyone of note who happened to be in Brighton for this part of their Season. And, it appeared, everyone not of note. The place was absolutely packed.

"I have no idea how we'll manage to see anyone in here," Dottie said in an undertone as they entered, their names ringing out as a footman announced them.

"Just so long as I can dance with you."

Something shivered down Dottie's spine at his words—not just his words, but his looks. He looked at her as though . . . as though she were the only thing worth looking at. As though he had never seen anything, anyone, quite like her.

Which was ridiculous, Dottie thought as she accepted a glass of punch and held tightly onto Adam's arm to prevent them being separated in the crush. There were plenty of people like her. Hundreds. Thousands. There was nothing particularly special about her.

"Ah, Your Graces," said Lady Romeril, sweeping toward

them in a magnificent pink silk dress with more lace at the cuffs than was entirely fashionable. "Delighted to see that of all the places you could have been this evening you chose, of course, my humble little ball."

Dottie grinned. She could not help herself. There was something rather like herself in Lady Romeril. "My darling Lady Romeril, as though we could have borne being apart from your presence."

"Your Grace is too kind," grinned Lady Romeril, plainly delighted at the compliment. "Now as the most elegant people at this little soirée of mine—" the roar of the crowded ballroom rose to such a pitch, she was forced to shout "—will you do me the honor of opening the dancing?"

Dottie looked instinctively at Adam.

"It would be our pleasure," said Adam, inclining his head. "Wouldn't it, Dorothy?"

Warmth suffused Dottie's heart. *Oh, to be looked at like that by this man forever . . .*

"You've managed to nail that one well, my dear," Lady Romeril said in a carrying whisper that was still rather more of a shout in this din. "We never thought anyone would bring Gilroyd back to heel, but you—"

"Music," Dottie said hastily, pulling Adam away from Lady Romeril and toward the center of the ballroom. "Let us have music!"

Anything to ensure he didn't hear anyone saying something like that . . .

"What was Lady Romeril saying?" Adam asked, releasing her arm and standing opposite her as the crowd murmured and other couples came to join them.

Heat burned Dottie's cheeks. "Nothing."

His eyes twinkled as the music began. "It didn't sound like nothing to me."

Thank goodness the music then struck up, for Dottie was at a loss to think what she could possibly say to that. The Duke of

Gilroyd she had first met had been an entirely different creature—or was it more accurate to say, perhaps, that Adam Seymour had returned to the man he had once been?

Troubled as she was by these thoughts, Dottie could not be troubled for long. The music started, Adam stepped forward, and the moment he touched her, she was lost.

Sensual tingling sparked across her skin whenever his hand met her hand, her arm, the small of her back. When she stepped into his arms—as the dance demanded, of course—Dottie's heart skipped a beat. The ache in her chest was lower now, and when he looked deep into her eyes, his hands on her waist, Dottie realized it was longing.

Longing for Adam.

"You look warm," Adam murmured as they promenaded down the dance, her back pressed into his chest. "Almost as though you are enjoying this."

"I . . . I am enjoying this," Dottie breathed. *What was the point in denying it?*

He looked fiercely into her eyes. "And so am I."

And though the dance demanded they turn and return back up the set, for a moment, just a moment, Adam did something she could never have imagined.

He pressed a kiss, soft yet potent, into her shoulder.

There were gasps around the ballroom and no wonder. Dottie could barely tell how she was still managing to follow the steps of the dance. Not just to kiss her in public, but to kiss her at all was a scandalous thing to do, even for a duke and his duchess! And she knew better.

He knew better.

There was a knowing look on Adam's face as he finally released her and bowed. Dottie stared. The music stopped. The dance was over.

And that was when she understood. The sinking realization thudded through her chest, settling in her heart and making it impossible to ignore.

She was in love with Adam Seymour, Duke of Gilroyd.

Dottie swallowed. This was a disaster. Love had not been the point of this mission—if anything, it would be a great detriment! What had Adam said?

"But we are partners on a mission together, and that—that sort of thing is only a distraction."

The last thing they needed was for her foolish, unrequited affection to distract from what they were meant to be doing. And she'd had to go and fall in love with a duke, of all people!

"Come on."

A hand on hers, tingling up her arm, and an ache in her chest Dottie now knew would never melt away.

"We should circulate," smiled Adam, entirely unaware that her sensibilities were crumbling in disaster. "Keep an eye out. Ready?"

Dottie tried to smile, but it was a weak one. They would find the leaders of the Glasshand Gang. And it would be over. They would leave Brighton, return to London, and after a meeting with Mr. Snee, she would never see Adam again.

She had to grasp at every opportunity she had.

"Circulate," Dottie said weakly. "Of course. Anything for the mission."

CHAPTER THIRTEEN

T RY AS HE might, Adam could not quite stifle a yawn as they stepped back into his Brighton townhouse.

"Don't you start," Dottie said darkly, moaning slightly as she slipped off her shoes. "I am this close to collapsing into bed and never getting out of it again."

Adam snorted. "I think Mrs. Sharp would have something to say about that."

"Not for long," she replied, her voice still low.

He grinned as he closed the front door behind them and leaned against it. "Well. Home at last."

It felt like an age since they had last been inside its walls. Lady Romeril's balls were known for being extravagant things, and it had been a while since he had last attended one. He had forgotten she would always hire two sets of musicians so the dancing could continue for hours on end. And that she would bring out a second supper to keep people eating. And that her footmen would mysteriously take over an hour to find the greatcoats and pelisses of her tired guests who only wished to get home . . .

"I thought we'd never make it out of there," said Dottie, pulling off her own pelisse and placing it on the console table by the front door. "I was of half a mind to call out her pretense and ask why we were her prisoners."

Adam snorted as he dropped his greatcoat on top of her pelisse and placed his gloves and top hat upon it. "She still wouldn't have let you go."

"The woman is a maniac!"

"The woman enjoys a good ball and never wants the evening to end," Adam corrected, jerking his head to the drawing room.

It had become their custom this last week or so to have a small nightcap in the evening and discuss the day behind them and the day ahead. Though they had rather slipped into the habit instead of deciding on it, Adam found to his surprise that the thought of not fulfilling the ritual was rather sad, even if it was so late. Or rather, early.

He watched with disappointment as Dottie looked longingly at the staircase. *Well, he could hardly blame her.* It would take her to her own bedchamber, silence, rest, and the chance to put her feet up.

"Just one glass of ginger wine," Dottie said, stepping toward the drawing room. "And none of your debriefing nonsense. I can barely think."

A smile crept across Adam's lips, though it did not last as he turned his mind back to their task of the evening. He followed Dottie into the room, where a fire was dying in the grate, and sighed deeply as he poured each of them a small glass of the fiery wine.

"Nothing," he said, passing Dottie her glass. "I really thought we'd see something of note."

"The whole world seemed to be there, yet I did not recognize the silhouette," said Dottie quietly, sipping her wine. "I cannot believe it."

The despondency in her voice matched what he felt. Adam sat heavily on the sofa beside her instead of in his usual armchair, his feet unable to carry him any farther.

"I really thought Lady Romeril's ball was the right place to go."

He blinked. Dottie looked a little uncomfortable, as though she were to blame in some way for their lack of success that night.

"You were not to know," Adam said quietly. "You made the right choice—the entirety of Brighton attended, or at least anyone who could be described as wearing a gentleman's coat. It wasn't your fault."

"Yet we didn't find anything, or spot anyone," Dottie said wistfully. "You bribed the footmen?"

Adam nodded. He'd never run through one-pound notes quicker, yet there was nothing interesting in the gossip they'd had to tell. "I know far more than I ever wanted to know about the Viscount Stulsemere's gambling habits, and I'll never be able to look Mr. Marnion in the face, but there's been nothing that could be construed as being about the Glasshand Gang."

And it rankled. He'd never had such a disappointing result before.

Here they were in Brighton, far from London and old Snee, and they hadn't found a thing. This mysterious leader of the Glasshand Gang? He was nowhere to be seen. In fact, there didn't seem to have been any Glasshand Gang activity here for weeks now.

Was it possible they had caught wind of their investigation? Had they been sent word of his and Dottie's mission? Were they lying low until the coast was clear, as it were?

"I didn't even notice anything I can write to Mr. Snee about," said Dottie with a sigh, sipping her wine. She tucked her feet under her, a habit Adam had almost ceased to notice. "And I wanted to . . . well."

Pink dots appeared in her cheeks. *Though that could certainly be the ginger wine,* Adam told himself. Not the fact he had put a hand on the sofa and accidently brushed a finger against one of her own.

Most definitely not that.

She wasn't thinking of that sensual dance they had shared. She wasn't dwelling on the fact that the happiest he had been in months was when she was standing in his arms. She hadn't been overcome by desire to the point where she kissed him in public . . .

Adam swallowed. *Damn it.*

"I wanted to find the traitor."

He sat a bit straighter. "I beg your pardon?"

"You heard me well enough," Dottie said with a dry laugh. "I know there's a traitor somewhere in our midst, and I thought— well, they could be a part of the Glasshand Gang! It would make sense, don't you think?"

It was a novel idea, but one Adam could not discount out of hand. Yes, if their traitor was also aligned with the Glasshand Gang, it would certainly explain how the miscreant was so swift at escaping their clutches.

"I thought if I could do both," Dottie was saying, "find the Glasshand Gang leader and identify the traitor, I mean—well, then perhaps I could become a permanent part of Mr. Snee's organization."

Adam snorted. "You give him too much credit. He's just a magistrate."

"He keeps all you dukes in order though, doesn't he?" Dottie pointed out. "He keeps you coming and going, giving you different missions, different objectives."

Now she said it, it was a fair description. Not that Adam liked it. He didn't work *for* anyone. He wasn't part of any organization. Not if he could help it.

"The traitor, whoever he is, is clearly well hidden," he said slowly, "or we would have found him out by now. We tracked down a traitor in Edinburgh with ease—"

"Yes, Chantmarle told me about it," said Dottie quietly.

Adam snorted. "I bet he did. But our traitor, the one in our midst? He has to have been working closely with all of us, and still we haven't spotted him. A duke, a servant, a friend? It's impossible to know."

They sat for a moment in silence, the shifting last embers of the fire the only sound in the room.

Well, that and Adam's heartbeat. He was certain Dottie could hear it, it was thundering so loudly.

Why he had got himself so worked up about this, he did not know. Dottie had made it perfectly clear she had used her body for missions before. But this felt different. There was a modicum of respect between them that Adam had never had with another woman before.

Never before, save once.

Louisa.

The thought was so sharp, so unexpected, he almost jolted to his feet. Dear God, he had not thought of her for days. But now that he was thinking of her, there was no pain there. Regret, certainly, that she had not lived. But no agony. No desperate need to hold himself back from the world merely because she was not in it.

Adam swallowed. *Now that was a first.*

"I cannot put off writing to Mr. Snee any longer," Dottie said softly, breaking the silence as she placed her empty wine glass on a small side table. "I will simply have to tell him we haven't found anything."

It would be a heavy blow to old Snee's ego, Adam thought darkly. But worst of all, it would be the end of this mission.

And a desperate need for them to stay here in Brighton overwhelmed him like a wave upon the shore. Adam's throat tied itself into a knot, his need for Dottie was so strong.

How could they go back to London now? It would be the end of their connection, for her plan had only been accepted by Adam because they would separate at the end of the mission.

The Duchess of Gilroyd, such as she was, would cease to exist.

He was having a harder time lately envisioning their make-believe annulment, but she could retire to the country, or go abroad for her health. And Miss Yates, an entirely different woman, would return to her life.

"But I don't want to."

Adam blinked, his vision sharpening. Dottie had a shy smile. Shy? He'd never seen Dottie Yates shy before. It was not in her nature.

"Why not?" he said, voice hoarse. Clearing his throat, Adam attempted it again. "I mean, why not tell Snee the truth?"

"Because you know what that would mean," Dottie said, her gaze unwavering. "It would mean we would have to leave Brighton, go back to London, stop . . . stop being the Duke and Duchess of Gilroyd."

Try as he might, Adam could not help but see more into this than surely Dottie was meaning. Just because he was an old fool, that did not mean he could presume such things!

"I'll still be the Duke of Gilroyd," he pointed out with what he hoped was a smile.

Dottie's smile faded. "But I will no longer be the Duchess of Gilroyd. And . . . and I'll have to leave you."

Adam's heart leapt at the sorrow in her voice. Was it possible—surely he could not be fooling himself that she felt something for him?

No, they were on a mission together. He'd meant what he'd said, after he'd apologized for kissing Dottie.

"But we are partners on a mission together, and that—that sort of thing is only a distraction. All good things come to an end. Even dukes. And once this mission is over, you'll be able to go back to your life and I'll go back to mine."

This was not the time to rush into anything, he reminded himself. And not just because of Louisa.

Though she had always said, hadn't she, that if something happened to her, she wanted him to go on living?

"I . . ."

"I know I will probably regret this in the morning, but right now, I don't care," said Dottie severely, turning on the sofa to look directly at him. "I don't think—I know I can't go on without saying this."

Adam stared, heart thumping in his chest. *Surely she did not mean—*

"But you . . . you would not want to hear . . . I am sorry, I did not think." Dottie's face was red now. "I am sorry. I should not have said anything."

He did not need her to explain any further. She was thinking of Louisa, of course she was. After their conversation about his wife—which had been a challenge for him—no wonder Dottie thought he would have absolutely no interest in pursuing anything with anyone.

Up until quite recently, she'd have been right.

Adam took a deep breath. It would be strange to say these words aloud, but he had to. Not only for Dottie. But for himself.

"Dottie," he said quietly.

Her gaze immediately darted to his own. "Yes?"

Adam hesitated.

It was late. They'd had a long day. He'd had rather too much ginger wine to be entirely sensible and his desire for Dottie was still making his fingers tingle. And that was before even considering his manhood, which had been half hard ever since she had stepped forward to take his hands in the first dance at Lady Romeril's ball.

Perhaps this was not the right time. Perhaps it would be best if he followed Dottie's instinct and decided to remain silent.

All good things come to an end, he thought bitterly. His time with Louisa had. And now, perhaps, his time with Dottie.

But something warm and defiant in his chest would not release him. He had made a vow, hadn't he, never to marry again? But now it felt foolish, idiotic even, to believe he would spend the rest of his life never meeting any woman who could entice him into happiness again.

What arrogance! What had he been thinking?

"Louisa was a very special woman," Adam said slowly. He saw the awkward pain and disappointment in Dottie's expression, and continued swiftly, "She was. But her being special does not mean I have to be a martyr to her memory."

Dottie's lips parted in astonishment. "What do you—"

"I made a vow, once," he said, shaking his head. "A vow which I thought meant I was honoring her memory. I thought by promising never to marry again, Louisa's memory would always be within me, never tainted or spoiled. I thought it was the only way I could respect what we had. But I was wrong."

Somehow his hand had reached out and found Dottie's. She pulled away, just for a moment, then permitted him to take it.

"But it was making me miserable," he confessed with a laugh. "Precisely what Louisa would have hated, now I come to think of it. I thought I was being noble, but I was being stubborn."

"Yes, I think I've seen something of that characteristic in you, now you come to mention it," Dottie said dryly.

Adam squeezed her hand in silent acknowledgement of her gentle reproof, and his heart skipped a beat when she squeezed back. "What I mean to say is, I thought my life, my very sense of self, would come to an end if I permitted myself to feel anything for anyone. I shut myself away and was determined to do nothing with my life save serve."

Dottie's expression was warm. "And you have served."

"But I have not been happy." He had to make her see, even if she would not reciprocate his feelings. "I have been happy these last few weeks, Dottie."

He saw the bob of her throat, the changing color in her cheeks, and knew beyond a shadow of a doubt how she felt.

But she had not said it.

"Because . . . because you're here, in Brighton," she said quietly. "Because you're working, serving, seeking out justice—"

"Because I'm with you," Adam said simply.

The drawing room fell silent as Dottie stared. All the brashness, the boldness, the determination to have her; all that had faded away.

His gaze flickered over her. The pearls he had agonized over, the gown he had spent several hours arguing about with Madame Jacques, the modiste. The way her hair shone in the dying firelight. The boldness of her eye, even when she felt vulnerable.

"There is still so much of you, Dottie, that I don't know," Adam said slowly. "So much I want to find out about. If you'll let me."

Her gaze fell to their hands, fingers entwined. "So . . . so we can work together better. A-As partners. For this mission."

"So I can stop wondering what it is to kiss you without any possibility of interruption," Adam admitted wryly. "And know."

There had not been a single thought left in his mind after those words. He had no plan after his admission, no next step along the path of this difficult discussion.

Which was why it came as a great relief that Dottie then took charge of the conversation.

Well. If you could call it a conversation.

In a sudden rush of silk, Dottie moved into his arms and kissed him firmly on the lips. Her passion, her ardor, was quickly reciprocated. Adam brought his arms around her, pulling the heavenly woman closer into his embrace. His tongue darted out, teasing open her lips as pleasure swept through him, and Adam moaned as she welcomed him in.

Oh, this was everything. A kiss given freely, greater understanding between them than they had ever shared—and passion, unbridled passion that had swiftly brought Adam's hands down Dottie's back and to her buttocks.

He groaned at the intimacy. She felt wonderful, smelled wonderful, tasted—dear God, he had never tasted anything so sweet.

"I thought you'd never ask," gasped Dottie as the kiss broke, but only for a moment.

Adam worshipped her very lips, plundering her mouth for the exquisiteness of her affection, and was rewarded by her shivering in his arms.

Dear God, if they weren't careful—

"I thought you had no interest in me," Dottie said, ending the kiss but remaining in his arms, eyes searching his for the truth.

And he had to give it to her. Though Adam knew it would be strange, being so open with another woman after all he had shared with Louisa, he knew it was right.

This was right, what was between them.

"I had far too much interest in you, the moment you stepped into my library," Adam confessed with a laugh. "I meant what I said. That kiss, on the balcony—it was far too great a distraction. You are far too great a distraction."

Dottie shifted in his arms and he groaned as his manhood strained against his breeches.

"You are the distraction," Dottie breathed, kissing him briefly on the corner of his mouth. "Do you have any idea how distracting it is to have a grumpy duke—"

"I am not grumpy!"

"You absolutely are, you know you are," she continued, speaking over his protestations. "And yet I still . . . I still care about you, Adam."

Adam tried to breathe out slowly, but it was a great challenge. This night had certainly not gone the way he had expected, but he could hardly complain seated here on the sofa in his drawing room, Dottie in his arms and—

And he had to stop here, didn't he? *He had to be the gentleman and send this delectable lady to bed.*

Adam almost groaned at the very thought. It was most unfair, but there it was. Dottie Yates was a lady, and he was a gentleman. He had to act honorably.

Even if he wanted to push her back on the sofa, push up her skirts, and—

"I suppose now we've got all that out of our system," Dottie said quietly. "You . . . you have no wish to do it again. It's just a distraction, after all."

Adam saw the misunderstanding at once, and took both her hands in his before he said seriously, "Yes, I adore kissing you—"

"Adam!"

"But this is more than that," he continued doggedly. "More

than kissing, more than pleasure, more than all that. This . . . this is something more, Dottie. I can't give it a name, not yet. You'll have to trust me that this will need to be slow for me. But I want you—all of you—and one day, I hope you will trust me enough to—"

"Want me?" said Dottie, cheeks pink but gaze defiant. "Well for goodness sake, Adam. If you want me now, why not have me?"

CHAPTER FOURTEEN

D OTTIE STARED AS Adam spoke the words she had hoped for but never expected to hear.

"Want me?" said Dottie, unable to help herself. He'd said so much and yet so little—and she knew why. He needed encouragement, her encouragement to say more. "Well for goodness sake, Adam. If you want me now, why not have me?"

Heat scalded her face.

She had not intended to speak so boldly! Certainly she had not thought she could say such words aloud, and while nestled in the arms of a duke!

But Adam wasn't a duke. Well, he was—but he did not depend upon the title, leaning on it because he had nothing else in his character to recommend him.

Oh, no. Quite the contrary. There was so much about Adam that drew her in, it was almost a miracle she had not confessed her feelings before now. Though Dottie could not recall when those feelings had first started to permeate her heart, she could not now find a single inch that was not devoted to him.

Devoted to Adam Seymour, Duke of Gilroyd.

"There is still so much of you, Dottie, that I don't know. So much I want to find out about. If you'll let me."

"I know I speak plainly, perhaps too much so," Dottie added in a rush, "but not rashly. And I know I would always regret not speaking so openly if I did not do it now, in this moment."

Still Adam was silent. He was just staring, eyes wide, as though astonished she had been so uncouth.

Dottie's hopes started to fade, and she started to shift awkwardly. She needed to get out of Adam's embrace. Though a moment ago it had been the most at home, the most peaceful she had ever felt, it felt wrong now. If he could not return her affection, if he did not want what she wanted, then it was surely best she remove herself—

"You don't know what you're saying." Adam's voice was dry, almost hoarse. "You don't know what you're suggesting."

Dottie grinned weakly. "I think I do."

He shook his head. "A lady like you—"

"A lady like me has spent enough time in the world to know that few things are certain, and even those can change unexpectedly at times," Dottie said impetuously. "You don't love me."

"Dottie—"

"I am not saying you have to, don't you see?" she continued, barreling forward as though her wits would abandon her if she did not. "I . . . I think something can grow between us. Something truly special."

Adam's smile was faint. "I think so, too."

"Then I do not know why we have to wait for perfect love, or devotion, or whatever you want to call it, before we can enjoy . . ." Dottie swallowed, ". . . each other."

It was a scandalous thing to think, let alone say, but it was out now.

Besides, she meant it. Adam had been married before, lost his wife in a tragic way Dottie could not fathom. Demanding complete and utter devotion from him before they shared in the most delightful lovemaking—what was the point in that?

"I suppose you would be the expert in that," Adam said quietly.

Dottie frowned. "Expert?"

What on earth was he talking about?

Leaning back slightly, Adam released her and it was as though all the warmth had been taken from the room. Dottie gasped, shocked by the sudden change. How had she been this dependent on him for her warmth? When had her center moved so that it was not herself, but Adam that gave her balance?

"You said when we first met that you . . . you came across some information in a 'conversation,' you called it, with a young man," Adam said awkwardly. "I have never asked—it is not my place to ask—but—"

"Adam Seymour!" said Dottie hotly, pulling away from his hold completely and rising from the sofa. "Do you mean to tell me you thought I—that I have in the past, used my . . . *myself?*"

Her mind whirled. That was certainly not what she had said—and most definitely not what she had meant! Did he think her a harlot, then? A courtesan of Mr. Snee's, trotted out whenever it would be useful?

"I thought that was what you meant!" Adam said hastily, rising to his feet, too. "I didn't think—"

"You thought I had given myself!"

"And you haven't?" he said, with a questioning look.

Heat was scalding Dottie's cheeks, but she had to make him understand. She couldn't have him thinking—

"Absolutely not," she said firmly. "I have not—no man has ever . . . I am an innocent."

A smile broke out across his face. "Damn. I almost hoped— well, I thought if you had already . . ."

Dottie looked at her hands. She knew what he meant. That if she had been compromised before, it would be less of a risk for her to permit him to make love to her now.

But wasn't all of life a risk? Wasn't everything she did, every mission, everything undertaken in service to the Crown, a risk?

Why not take a risk that would give *her* something in return?

"I may be untouched until now," she said quietly to her hands, "but that does not mean . . . I want to . . . damn it, Adam, I want you to make love to me!"

And he moved to her so quickly she could barely take in his sudden presence. It was intoxicating, making her head spin, making all decisions she'd made to get to this place the best ones. Because they had brought her to him.

"You are certain?" Adam breathed, pressing his forehead lightly against her own.

Dottie took a deep breath. Certain was a strange word. She had been certain Lady Romeril's ball would be the place to find the Glasshand Gang leader. She had been certain this mission would be over within days, maybe a few short weeks.

And she was certain, in this moment, she wanted to make love to Adam Seymour, Duke of Gilroyd.

But what happened when that certainty disappeared? Faded away like the early morning frost? Swept back on the tide, disappearing over the horizon?

She met Adam's eyes and her heart melted.

She had certainty now. That was enough. It had to be.

"They say all good dukes come to an end," Dottie said, breathing the words. "I'd rather like to be the end of you."

Adam groaned and without another word, crushed his lips against hers. His ardor was exotic, unlike anything she had ever experienced with him. It was as though the beast within had been unchained, the repressed desire he had fought for so long finally free.

And what freedom it was. Dottie gasped in his mouth as Adam's tongue teased more pleasure from her lips than she could ever have imagined. His hands were cupping her buttocks, bringing her closer, and a rough hardness pressed into her hip.

Now that had to be . . .

"You're so beautiful, Dottie," Adam breathed, trailing a line of kisses down her neck as Dottie clutched his shoulders. "Do you trust me?"

Trust him? He could ask her to strip off all her clothes and walk along the Brighton beach, and she would do it.

"Dottie?"

Ah, yes. She probably shouldn't say that aloud. "Y-Yes, Adam. I trust you."

Then Dottie gasped again—there was no other reaction possible, for Adam had captured her lips and was teasing them open once more.

But his hands were not idle. While his left remained on her buttocks, his grip tightening in a way that made red hot flames flare inside her, the other—

Dottie closed her eyes. *Oh, the other . . .*

"You wouldn't believe how long I've wanted to do this," Adam breathed, as his right hand moved under her skirts and between her thighs, stroking, caressing, worshipping. "How long . . ."

"And I've got no idea what you're doing, but I want more," Dottie replied, unsure how she could be this direct, but knowing he deserved it. He deserved all of her. "More of—Adam!"

Eyelashes fluttering, hardly able to keep her eyes open, Dottie clung onto Adam's shoulders as her knees went weak.

And they went weak because his right hand had continued to wander—up her thigh. Higher, and higher, until his finger brushed against her curls.

A shot of desire pumped through her and before she could speak again, before she could ask what he was doing, Adam had gently brushed his thumb over her secret place—and slipped a finger inside her.

"Oh, Adam," moaned Dottie.

There was nothing else to say. How could she even contemplate initiating a conversation while his finger stroked her, slowly at first, but then building to a steady rhythm that was growing a warm ache between her legs?

Her vision dimmed, and the slow moan she had tried to swallow poured from her mouth. "Oh . . . oh, yes, like—like that."

Her breathing was quickening, quickening to the pace of his finger—his fingers. Adam's lips brushed against her mouth as he slipped a second finger into her, joining the first and yet deeper, and Dottie moaned into his mouth, not caring that they could be overheard, not caring that there were servants in the house who may hear them—

All she could focus on was the steady rhythm within her, building her pleasure, stirring it—

"Adam!"

At least, that would have been her cry if Adam had not burned his lips into hers, muffling her cry as ecstasy overwhelmed her. Dottie could hardly see, hardly breathe, the pleasure was so exquisite, roaring through her body like a fire—a blaze that could never be burnt out, his fingers working her, keeping her on this glorious precipice . . .

And it faded. His fingers slowed, his kiss ended, and Dottie slumped into his arms, hardly aware of how she was still managing to stand.

"Dottie?"

Dottie tried to blink, tried to think, but how could she? That was pleasure? That was what others had been enjoying while she had always used her cleverness, her wit, her words?

Dear Lord, she had been missing out . . .

"Dottie?"

She blinked again. This time the view of Adam's face, concerned, swam into view.

"I did not hurt you, did I?"

It was all Dottie could do not to laugh. "Hurt me? Adam, I've never—I didn't know it was possible to . . ."

Her voice faded once again, but Adam's look of concern transformed into one of relief. And, if she was not mistaken, a little pride.

"I thought I'd warm you up before we get any further," he said gently, stroking her cheek with his hand.

Dottie swallowed. *That was a warm-up?*

She was not entirely ignorant. She knew the process, the theory of lovemaking. From the little she had heard from the ladies in her acquaintance who were loose with their tongues, the process did not sound that enjoyable. The man entered the woman, and after a moment, he received his pleasure.

No one had ever mentioned anything like this . . .

"R-Right," Dottie said, wishing her voice was stronger. "And now I suppose it's . . . it's your turn."

It was a shame her slice of pleasure was over, but then, Dottie supposed it was only fair. A moment for her, then a moment for him. If what she'd heard from others was anything to go by, she was fortunate that Adam had thought of her pleasure at all.

But there was a knowing gleam in his eye that suggested to Dottie's quickening heart that her turn might not be entirely over.

"Turn? I suppose you could call it that," Adam said quietly. "But I think first I'd like to see you."

"See me? You can—"

"All of you," he cut across her in almost a growl.

The speed of his words sparked something warm between Dottie's legs again, and a longing to feel such pleasure rushing through her again emboldened her.

All of her? "You first."

Dottie had not intended to speak the words. They had been a momentary thought, a wish to see Adam without the trappings of duke or gentleman.

From what she could see in his sparkling eyes, he was not averse to her demand. "Together."

The rare times Dottie had thought about herself being nude before a gentleman, it had not been like this. She had presumed she would undress somewhere else, in complete privacy, and rush into the bed before the man in question had much time to see.

When she thought about it at all.

It certainly wasn't like this. There was something intensely erotic about standing in a drawing room—where anyone could walk in on them—in front of the dying embers of a fire that nonetheless kept the room warm . . . and slowly taking off her clothes.

And Dottie had the great misfortune of being constantly distracted by Adam.

When his shirt fell to the floor, joining his waistcoat and jacket, she swallowed. "You . . . you are magnificent."

There was no other word for it. Dark hair trailed from his chest to his breeches, promising something her body seemed to recognize, even if her mind had no word for it. His shoulders were broad, his arms strong, and there was a look of dark confidence in Adam's posture as he slowly started to unbutton his breeches.

"And you are still dressed," he pointed out, fingers halted at the last button. "Come on. Time to keep your end of the bargain."

Dottie swallowed. *He was right, of course.* "You'll have to help me."

Hating that she would immediately lose sight of him, she turned around and gestured at the tiny pearl buttons that ran down the length of her gown.

It had taken Mrs. Sharp over ten minutes to button them up. Hopefully, it would not take long for Adam to—

"Adam!" Dottie gasped.

There had been multiple causes for such a gasp, and she hardly knew which one was more responsible for her audible astonishment.

Firstly, Adam had moved close to her. Very close. She could feel the warmth of his chest flowing through her back, feel the rough scraping of his wiry hairs against her arms. Goodness, he was a magnificent specimen.

Secondly, Adam had not undone a button, but merely ripped it off. The pearl had pinged off toward a corner of the room. *Was he truly so desperate for her*, Dottie thought wildly, *that he would rather destroy a beautiful and surely expensive gown just to save time?*

And thirdly, his left hand had moved around to her hip, pulling it sharply backward into him. She could feel the hardness of his manhood pressing into her buttocks.

But it was his left hand immediately leaving her hip and curling over her secret place, through her gown, that had made Dottie breathe his name.

"Adam, you can't—"

"Stop me, if you want to," Adam breathed into her ear, placing a kiss just beneath it that made her shiver. "But I don't think you want me to stop, do you?"

Another pearl button pinged off in a different direction, and at the same time, Adam's finger shifted against her secret place, rubbing against her through the fabric of her gown.

A whimper left Dottie's throat. "N-No."

"Tell me to keep going, then," he breathed in her other ear, another button ripped off, another rub against her secret place that she now knew would lead to ecstasy. "Ask me."

"Please, Adam."

"Please what?"

It was a good thing he was so close behind her, for Dottie was leaning against him, her legs quivering. *Oh, this was too much, and yet she wanted it so badly . . .*

"P-Please rip off my buttons."

Another button fell to the floor, another smooth rub of his finger, and Dottie gasped as the pleasure intensified.

"Please touch me."

Another button, another rub, and this time he did not stop.

"Yes, oh yes, please, Adam. Touch me, ruin the gown, ruin me . . ."

The pressure was building in her once again and Dottie closed her eyes, losing herself in the intensity of the sensations. Her gown was slowly falling apart, but then wasn't she as well? Wasn't everything she knew about herself falling aside so she could give herself, all of herself, to this wonderful man?

"Oh, Adam!"

The last button fell as Dottie exploded in his hands, Adam's fingers working her to ecstasy once again. This time it lasted longer, the glow cascading through her body, and when it finally subsided, she did not have time to turn around before her gown fell to the floor.

"I need you," came Adam's voice hotly. "Take it off—all of it."

Dottie did not need to ask what he meant. With fumbling fingers she untied her stays, wrenched them off, cast aside her undershift, and turned around to see—

Adam. Breeches and boots gone. Manhood erect, tip wet, desperate for her. And his eyes, blazing with desire that for him had been unsated.

"Take me," Dottie breathed.

He did not, apparently, need any greater invitation. With a swiftness and a gentleness Dottie could not have believed unless she herself had experienced it, Adam moved forward and lifted her up into his arms, gently placing her onto the rug that lay before the fire.

"God, you're warmed up for me," he breathed, nestling himself between her legs. "Ready?"

Dottie nodded, though she could hardly tell what she was ready for. All she knew was that she had her hands around Adam's neck, and he felt glorious between her legs, and she ached, still ached, for him.

Adam grinned wickedly. "No, you're not."

She had intended to reply, but there was no breath left in her lungs as she moaned—and she moaned because Adam had guided his manhood gently to the entrance of her secret place and pushed into her.

And into her. Dottie hardly knew how there was enough room for him and yet he kept on going, and every inch of him sparked greater pleasure, pooling into the ache between her legs. Where he met her. Where they became one.

"Dottie," Adam groaned, kissing her harshly.

She accepted the kiss, arching her back and thrusting her hips forward as he slowly left her—but not quite. Soon Adam was building the same rhythm with his manhood as he had with his fingers.

All Dottie could do was hold onto him, his broad shoulders, until the rhythm reached a pace when she could no longer. Her fingers left him, clutched the rug, and as her body once again pulsed with pleasure at a peak she could barely stand, she cried out—

"Adam!"

"Dottie!"

Their voices mingled, no care given to the world, and Dottie rocked against the rug as Adam thrust heavily into her, pouring into her, giving her everything until—

Until he fell into her waiting arms and they lay there, panting, as their pleasure slowly came to an end.

CHAPTER FIFTEEN

24 November 1811

I T WAS NOT in Adam's nature to wake up late.

Get up late, yes. There had been many mornings when he had just lain there, unwilling to get up, unable to fall back to sleep. It was a strange sort of warm cocoon, his large ducal bed in Gilroyd House, and in the last few years it had been increasingly difficult to leave it.

But as he opened his eyes this morning, it was difficult for a different reason.

Adam placed a hand on his chest before he even opened his eyes. Something was different. Changed, within him. The heavy weight had somehow disappeared.

Impossible.

He opened his eyes.

And started. He was not where he was supposed to be—far from it. Instead of seeing the red silk canopy of his bedchamber in the Brighton townhouse, which was what he had expected to see, there was instead . . .

A rather beautiful painted ceiling. *Hang on, he remembered that. He'd seen it recently. Hadn't he?*

Adam blinked. The drawing room ceiling faded, then sharpened into view.

Drawing room ceiling?

He shifted against the mattress but groaned as his elbow hit something far harder. *The floor?*

Adam blinked again, looking around, and the memories of last night rushed back.

"P-Please rip off my buttons."

"Please touch me."

"Yes, oh yes, please, Adam. Touch me, ruin the gown, ruin me . . ."

A slow smile started to creep over Adam's face. Dear God, they hadn't even moved from the rug before the fire. He had lost all control, given in to his wildest and most hedonistic desires . . . and Dottie had come with him.

In more ways than one.

"God, you're warmed up for me. Ready?"

Was it possible it had been a dream? It did seem fantastical, after all—the woman who had brought him here, who was nothing like Louisa and yet had her kindness, allowing him to make love to her?

Yet the memories were so vivid. It was impossible not to think of all those little delectable moments. When she first shivered in his arms. When she lifted her lips to be kissed. When she had claimed her pleasure, demanded it as she grew in boldness . . .

Adam's smile broadened as he took in the abandoned silk green gown beside him, utterly devoid of pearl buttons. Well, perhaps he had gone a little far there, but it had felt wonderful to have that much power over a woman—and for her to give it.

Dottie.

Only as her name filled his mind did Adam look around hurriedly for the woman he cared so deeply about. He had assumed, once he'd recalled last night's adventures, that she would be here beside him.

But though there was space on the rug for another body, there was no Dottie. Only a gap. Far more disappointing.

Adam propped himself on his elbows and looked around.

It was most curious. After sharing such a thing—after giving Dottie her first taste of pleasure—he had thought she would remain. That they could talk, though what Adam would say, he wasn't sure.

Waking without her, utterly alone, felt most dissatisfying after the intense connection he and Dottie had built yesterday. Trust and faith and a new way of appreciating each other . . .

Adam shivered. Many ways of appreciating each other—and with the sense there were more to come.

Dear God, he never thought he could leave the pain of Louisa behind. And in a way, he hadn't. He still felt the lack of her. Sometimes looked for her to tell her something amusing he had heard, or to ask her opinion on something.

But that had faded. The pain had faded, too. All that was left was the love, a delicate shimmer across the world rather than a blazing light that blinded him to all around him.

Though if he spent much time with Dottie, he would certainly find himself blinded . . .

Adam sighed heavily and looked around the room. There was no sign of her. It was as though she had disappeared into thin air.

"—and I told him, lighting the fires is a serious business," came a voice rather too close for comfort. "And he said—arrgh! Your Grace!"

Adam stood hastily at the sudden sight of the chamber maid who had stepped in from the hall.

Which was the wrong decision.

The blanket which had been covering him fell to the floor, and unfortunately he had obviously been warmed up and worn out by Dottie last night, for it did not appear he was wearing any—

The chamber maid's face went pink, then a brilliant red. She swiftly averted her eyes to the elegantly painted ceiling. "Y-Y-Your Grace!"

Adam looked down. Then he swiftly picked up the blanket,

wrapped it around his waist, and said hastily, "My apologies—"

"I-I didn't see anything! At least, I saw something, obviously," babbled the chamber maid, stepping backward and desperately feeling for the door handle, fingers scrabbling against the door. "But I won't tell—no one ever needs to—what are you doing here, Y'Grace?"

It was a very good question. Adam could not recall precisely why he and Dottie had not ventured upstairs after their first bout of lovemaking. Perhaps they were too tired to collect their belongings and clamber up the stairs.

Perhaps, he thought with a grin. *But they hadn't been too tired to—*

"There's no need to look at me like that, Y'Grace!" burbled the maid.

Adam's face fell. "No, no, I wasn't thinking anything like—"

"I should think not!" said the chamber maid, finally finding the door handle and wrenching it open.

She was in such a hurry to leave, she didn't even close the door properly. Adam could hear her rushed footsteps across the hall.

His shoulders slumped and the blanket around him drooped. *Well, he would have to thank God for small mercies. At least it wasn't—*

"My goodness, if you are that behind in laundry, I shall have a word with your valet," said a slightly awkward, but nonetheless defiant voice.

Adam's fingers tightened on his blanket, and he cursed himself for not immediately going upstairs once he had awoken.

Mrs. Sharp was standing in the doorway. "How interesting."

Trying to hold himself upright and hold his housekeeper's gaze as though he weren't standing nude with nothing but a blanket covering his manhood, Adam nodded curtly.

"I had wondered precisely what the duchess meant when she asked me to deliver this note to you when you were . . . how did she put it? 'Suitably dressed,' I think was her phrase," said Mrs. Sharp with an eyebrow raised. "I thought she meant you may have come down without a cravat."

Adam smiled weakly. "Mrs. Sharp. There is a perfectly reasonable explanation for—"

"I am quite sure there is," she said, and a flicker of a smile touched her lips. "I was young once, you know. Not for long, sadly. These things always rush by. But I was young once. And you and Her Grace . . . well, there is clearly a deep affection between you."

Adam stared. *There was?* He wasn't sure if he would have described it that way, but it was rather gratifying to hear his housekeeper say it.

Though this was ridiculous, of course. What he and Dottie had . . . it wasn't affection.

At least, it was affection, Adam thought wildly. But it wasn't love—or at least, he hadn't thought it was. Love had been so uncomplicated with Louisa. With Dottie . . . it was so difficult. Yet it was strong. Powerful. If anything happened to her—

"Your note, Your Grace," Mrs. Sharp said, stepping forward and averting her eyes, as though the blanket may slip at any moment. "And may I suggest a pair of breeches?"

"Yes—yes, I will get some momentarily," said Adam, distracted by the note now in his hand.

A note? From Dottie? Did it explain, perhaps, where she had decided to disappear off to without saying a word to him?

It was difficult not to be piqued, in truth, by her sudden disappearance. After they had bared so much, shared so much, it was strange to wake in a world in which she did not immediately appear.

A door closed. Adam looked up to see his housekeeper had decided to leave him to it.

Placing the note carefully on the sofa, he spent a few quick moments doing what he perhaps should have done as soon as he realized he was downstairs at this early hour. He got dressed.

Doing up his shirt hastily and tucking it into his breeches, Adam sighed. At least now if Dawson were to walk in, he would not have an equally awkward explanation as to what he was doing there.

Now. Dottie's letter.

Settling onto the sofa and groaning—who knew sleeping on a rug could be so injurious to the back?—Adam unfurled the note, which hadn't even been sealed. Well, why would it? It was only his servants here, after all. If he couldn't trust them, he couldn't trust anyone.

Dottie's handwriting was like her. Wild, bold, and clearly in a hurry.

Gilroyd—

Couldn't bear to wake you but had a thought. Just checking something out, will return for luncheon. Don't bother rescuing me—I promise, I won't need it.

Save your strength for later.

Dottie

Adam's grin broadened. Save his strength for later? Now that did bode well.

He could forgive the fact that she had rushed out, evidently without a second thought, to chase up an idea she'd had. It was a part of Dottie's nature, he was starting to learn. Once an idea had popped into her head, it would annoy her to the point of distraction until she'd cleared it up. And besides, it was not that long until luncheon.

Then he would see her again.

Joy soared through him at the mere thought of her, so potent Adam actually placed a hand on his chest as if he might touch it. When had Dottie become so important to him? When had he found it impossible to be without her longer than a morning?

He had thought, those weeks ago when they had first met, that Dottie may slow him down. That the investigation could only be done by a man—or at least, would only be done well by a man.

"This is your Yates? You honestly think I will work with a woman?"

Yet time and time again, Dottie had proven she was just as capable, if not more so, than half the men in his acquaintance. Who could tell what other preconceptions he had which were incorrect? Who knew how many of his ideas Dottie would tear down and remake in her own image?

Adam amused himself for a few minutes by thinking about all the things he could teach Dottie. The list was quite extensive, but he was unable to finish it because the door once again opened.

"Your Grace."

He turned to see Dawson with a small silver platter. Upon it lay a letter—this time, one which had been obviously sealed and sent from a great distance.

Adam's stomach lurched. *Snee?*

"A letter for you, Your Grace," said his butler smoothly, stepping across the room and proffering the platter.

"Thank you, Dawson," Adam said lazily, taking it from him. "By the way, later on this morning, could you have a footman clear up the place?"

His butler's eyebrows rose. "Clear up the place, Your Grace?"

Both he and his master looked about the drawing room.

It was a complete mess. Adam had to admit, he could have taken better care of a few things when he had made love to Dottie against the wall. That painting would have to be reframed, and it was such a shame the little crystal vase on the end of the console table had fallen. Then there were the pearl buttons scattered everywhere. And worse than that, Dottie's green silk gown was still in a heap on the floor by the fireplace.

Adam met Dawson's eye and worked hard not to flush. "As I said. Clear up the place."

His butler inclined his head, though there was a knowing look in his eyes. "The moment you have stepped out of here, Your Grace."

"I'll read my letter first."

"As you wish," said Dawson, bowing low.

Adam purposefully averted his eyes to avoid the possibility of seeing another knowing look. Dawson had been with the family a long time. A very long time. It was rather like being caught by one's parents.

Once the door closed behind him, Adam ripped open the letter. It was indeed from Snee. And it brought bad news.

Gilroyd—

Disappointed. Thought you and Yates would have got something by now. Not calling you back to London until you find the Glasshand Gang leaders in Brighton. Send daily reports. Not impressed.

Snee

Adam raked over the letter again, hoping to find something that was at least a little more encouraging. It was not there.

Disappointed. Not impressed.

It was never pleasant to hear such words, but it was galling to read them now. Had not he and Dottie done precisely what they had agreed? And yet none of their informants had brought any news of note, and the parties and balls they had attended had given them no clues to go on.

It was almost as though the Glasshand Gang leaders weren't even in Brighton . . .

The thought was such a fleeting one, Adam almost didn't pay it any attention. But when his stomach lurched, all his instincts flaring, he realized he may have just worked out the biggest part of the puzzle.

The Glasshand Gang leaders weren't here.

It would make sense. No wonder they could not find them, could see no clues, could hear no hints. It would explain why Dottie had not seen a single gentleman that fit the description of the man she had glimpsed, why none of their informants had anything to share.

Which meant Dottie had been fed a false trail.

Oh, it had been cleverly done. Adam could well recall how proud she was that she had cracked their code in the obituaries of the newspapers.

It was the traitor, the traitor in their midst. It must be. They had laid this false trail for Dottie and got him dragged into it, to boot. *The arrogance. The cheek!*

"It's outrageous," Adam muttered to himself.

It had to be stopped. This couldn't continue—missions going nowhere, misinformation being spread quicker than blinking.

He turned over the letter onto his knee and pulled out a pencil from his breeches' pocket. Time to make a list.

After a few minutes, Adam looked at the list with a sinking heart.

Penshaw. Dulverton. Caelfall. Sedley. Martock. Wincham. Old Hebblethwaite. Chantmarle. Thornfalcone. Ashcott. Chetnole. And himself. *Gilroyd.*

It made for grim reading. Every single one of these gentlemen he had, at one time or another, trusted with his life. He had depended on them for safety, for help, and in some cases, for information.

The idea that any one of these dukes could in some way be a traitor was repugnant.

But it had to be considered. Even if he did not wish to think it, one of these men . . .

And his conversation with Chetnole, when he had brought back news of the treachery in their midst, rose in his mind.

"There's a traitor."

"What did you say?"

"It's just a feeling—a sense I knew that, that's why I was coming back to England. I can't tell you more than that, but—"

"A traitor? Serving the Crown?"

Adam swallowed. *Oh, hell.* This whole time, he'd been so focused on finding the traitor and bringing him to justice that he hadn't even considered . . .

A man. Who said it was a man?

He leaned back into the sofa, feeling the tug of uncertainty at his heart. If it could be a woman, it could be anyone. Mrs. Sharp!

His chuckle rang out in the silent room, but then swiftly disappeared.

Mrs. Sharp. Or . . .

Slowly, hating that he was doing this with every fiber of his body, but knowing he had to consider it, Adam picked up his pencil once more and added a further name to the list.

Yates

Adam almost expected a thunderclap. Something to show how momentous this moment was. Because it couldn't be Dottie, could it? There was no possibility the woman he was starting to care about more deeply than his own self was the traitor. Was there?

"Mr. Snee and I have worked together for a long time. Who do you think organized his lodgings? Who established his cover? Who ensured that Wincham found passage home? Who argued with the Oxford lot to make them take Caelfall back?"

An uncomfortable feeling settled in his chest. But Dottie did have access to so many of them, didn't she? Involved in so many of their lives, working behind the scenes even if they did not know it.

It would not be difficult for her to pass on a piece of information here, ensure a particular warning note wasn't sent to this person—

No. No, it wasn't possible.

Adam shook his head as though he could rid himself of this treacherous thought. He cared about Dottie. He truly cared for her.

But it had been her idea to bring them to Brighton, wasn't it? And if there were no Glasshand Gang members here, then perhaps she had suggested it to draw him away from London. Away from where the miscreants really were.

His stomach lurched so suddenly, Adam thought he might be

sick. And it was Dottie Yates, and no one else, who said they had actually seen the leader of the Glasshand Gang.

Oh, hell.

Adam spent the next two hours pacing about the drawing room, attempting to convince himself, one way or the other. First he would be convinced of her innocence. How could he even consider such a thing? He was a vile person to even think it. Then the pendulum would swing, and he would wonder how he had ever been such a fool as to believe her. She had entirely taken him in, even bedded him! Perhaps he had been getting too close to the truth. Perhaps—

It was the luncheon gong that finally stirred him from his reverie. *Luncheon? Now?*

Adam marched into the hall. "Luncheon?"

"It is one o'clock, Your Grace," said the unfortunate footman who had evidently been given the task of ringing the gong.

Scowling, Adam nodded. And still Dottie wasn't back. Had something gone wrong while she was following a lead on the Glasshand Gang?

Or, and his heart sank, *was it quite the opposite?* Was she meeting with her fellow Glasshand Gang members, informing them that she had finally brought the Duke of Gilroyd under her control?

There was nothing for it. He'd take a horse, ride about Brighton, and find her. Adam could no longer wait.

"Your Grace?" the footman said uncertainly. "Your Grace, luncheon!"

"Hang luncheon," Adam said, grabbing a greatcoat and striding through the hallway to the back corridor.

He'd go straight to the stables, no need to find a hat or gloves. He wasn't looking to socialize, he was looking for—

"Dottie," Adam breathed.

He had wrenched open the door in anger, but that anger had faded when he saw the sight before him.

Dottie. She was wearing a delicate grey gown, perfect for

slipping in somewhere unnoticed. It went beautifully with the navy bonnet that adorned her head, but clashed horribly with the red that splattered her blonde hair.

She was lying on the cobbles.

Adam rushed toward her, somehow aware he was shouting her name, panic pouring through his lungs—and when he reached her he fell down beside her, tried to lift her into his arms . . .

But there was no use. She was cold.

CHAPTER SIXTEEN

30 November 1811

EVERYTHING HURT ALL at once.

Dottie blinked. It was rather a surprise to her that she could. She seemed to be lying deep down at the bottom of a dark well. Everything hurt, but of course it did. If you fell down a well, you would expect everything to—

Light.

Dottie closed her eyes quickly. The light was far too bright, stinging her eyes, making it impossible to see anything but the dazzling brightness.

She could still see the red glow of the light through her eyelids. *Oh, everything hurt . . .*

Eventually the light faded. At least, the red glow did. Slowly, Dottie parted her eyelids.

It was daylight. And there was more of it than she would have expected, considering she was at the bottom of a well. But that . . .

That did not make sense, did it? What would she have been doing anywhere near a well? She was in London, and London didn't need wells, not like in the country. Dottie had never been a one for country pursuits, but she was almost certain—no, definitely certain—

Oh, her head hurt.

Dottie raised a hand and clasped her head. There was something strange about it. The hair on this side, it was gone.

Gone?

She raised her other hand. It was all gone. Her hair, her beautiful hair—it was one of the few things she truly loved about her appearance. As it curled naturally, it had taken her an absolute age to grow it long, and she had been proud of it.

And now someone had cut it. Poorly, too, with little consideration it seemed for the look of the thing.

Who on earth was cutting hair down a well?

Dottie blinked, and for the first time, looked around her.

She was not in a well. She was in a bedchamber. It looked rather resplendent, nothing like the room she had taken in London with Miss Clarke at the Governess Bureau.

The window was wide, framed by rich blue velvet drapes. There was a dressing table opposite the bed with an ornate gold leaf chair, and paintings on the walls that she did not recognize. A bird in flight. A still life of oranges in a silver dish. All the paintings were framed with gold leaf.

There was far too much gold for this to be a place where she belonged, surely?

Dottie tilted her head to take in the rest of the room and a shooting pain exploded through her head. Blinking away the agony, she saw to her left a variety of console tables, all covered with a plethora of jars, bottles, tonics, and what appeared to be bandages.

Bandages? Was someone injured, then? Was she injured?

But that did not explain why she was here. Who had brought her here, and where was it? The view through the window looked like London, but not a part of London she was familiar with.

What on earth . . .

"Good afternoon, Miss Yates," said a quiet voice. "Welcome

back."

Dottie started, but she tried to hold herself still as the pain cleaved her head once more. Slowly, every inch taking a few seconds, she turned her head to the right of the bed.

There was a sofa there, and two armchairs. The armchairs were pulled right to the bed, and one of them was occupied. Occupied by . . . a woman.

Dottie blinked. It was not a woman she recognized. She had chestnut brown hair which fell about her brow in curls, and sharp eyes. Her look was kind, her fingers clasped together tightly above an apron.

The woman smiled briskly. "How do you feel?"

"Feel?" croaked Dottie.

Croaked? She had not thought her voice would be so dry, yet it felt as though she had not drunk a thing for a week.

"Here, have some honey in apple juice," said the woman firmly, as though it was her business to know about such things. "It'll help."

It was impossible to disobey. Partly because Dottie had rarely encountered a woman with such determination in her voice, and partly because the woman had already lifted a glass to her lips, and it was drink or drown.

Dottie spluttered as she drank, but she had to admit, the mixture was delightful for her throat.

When she spoke again, her voice was stronger. So was her resolve. "Who are you—and where on earth am I?"

She had expected panic. Dottie had ever thought if she were kidnapped by a rogue from the Glasshand Gang, she would panic. Even with her skills and experience, there was nothing quite like having your liberty taken from you.

Yet Dottie did not feel panic. She certainly felt sore, though, all over—her head especially. And there was something strange about all this. Something not quite right.

"My name is Jenny Powell," said the woman as she leaned back. "I actually go by another name now, but that's less important now. I'm a doctor."

Dottie stared. "A doctor?"

The woman named Jenny Powell—at least some of the time—returned her question with a glare. "Is that a problem?"

Trying to sit up against her pillows, Dottie considered.

Was it a problem? Well . . . no. She had never seen any reason why a woman could not do most things as well as a man, if not better. It was not as though they had the monopoly on good sense. If anything, the opposite.

It was unusual, to be sure. Dottie had never heard of a lady doctor. But now she came to think about it, that sounded rather fine. It would be far easier to talk about the complexities of the female form to someone who actually knew what she was talking about.

"No problem at all," said Dottie quietly. "Except I have no idea why you're here, or where here is."

She tried to glance about the room again but had to cease immediately as her vision swam. What on earth had happened to her? She'd never been a particularly sick person. She couldn't even remember the last time she'd needed a doctor.

"And who cut my hair?" Dottie added, her hand returning to her head.

Doctor Powell smiled ruefully. "I am afraid that was me. By the time I got to you, so many men had bungled up the healing, I had no choice but to take most of it off to see what I was dealing with. I can assure you, it will grow back."

Dottie nodded slowly, as though that would explain everything. Again, she stopped quickly when her head swam.

"I don't understand," she said slowly. "I was about to meet Mr. Snee—I had an idea . . . for a mission . . ."

It had been an excellent idea. She would have to find Mr. Snee soon, for it was a matter of great importance. He must be told—the secret messages! The obituaries!

"I need to speak to Mr. Snee," Dottie said decidedly. "Where—"

"What date is it, Miss Yates?" asked Doctor Powell gently.

Dottie stared. *What a curious question to ask.* "How . . . how long have I been here?"

"Six days," said the doctor.

Six days? It wasn't possible. What on earth could have happened to her to lay her up here in bed for that long?

"Six days," she repeated.

Doctor Powell nodded. "What day is it, Dottie? What is the date?"

Though her head ached and calendars had never been her forte, Dottie thought about it. It had been the first of November. No, October. November? That seemed more right. So if it had been six days . . .

"The seventh of November," she said confidently.

It was only when she saw the pitying look in Doctor Powell's eyes that something uncertain curled around Dottie's heart.

"It . . . it is the seventh of November, isn't it?"

Doctor Powell hesitated, then shook her head. "No, Miss Yates. I am sorry to tell you that it is the thirtieth of November. It appears the attack has left you with some memory loss. Some quite severe memory less, I am afraid."

Dottie stared.

No. No, it couldn't be. It wasn't possible—an attack? She would remember something that like, wouldn't she? She must.

Slowly, Dottie raised her hand to her head once more. Her hair was cut short, but if she pressed her fingers against the right of her head, just above her ear, there was something else there.

A scar. No, a scab. A wound.

"But I don't . . . I don't remember an attack," Dottie breathed.

Doctor Powell looked genuinely saddened by her words. "That's rather the point, don't you see?"

Dottie's breathing was rapid, yet there did not appear in her mind any great explanation, any idea why it was like this. And she thought it would. Her mind had never let her down before.

But neither had her memory, a small voice at the back of her mind pointed out. *And really, all she had to go on was this woman. Who was this Doctor Powell? She could be lying.*

She could be part of the Glasshand Gang . . .

"Who are you?" Dottie said, perhaps a little more rudely than she had intended. "I don't know you, nor where I am—where have you taken me? Why—"

"It was not I who brought you here, Miss Yates," said Doctor Powell calmly, as though patients shouted at her on a daily basis. "As I said, I am Doctor Powell. I also, just a few weeks ago, married the Duke of Chetnole. I believe you and he work for the same . . . organization, for want of a better word."

Married to the Duke of—

Dottie's shoulders relaxed. Tension drained from her chest and out of her heart. If she was married to old Chetnole, she must be one to be trusted. He was an untrusting sort at the best of times.

"I can see you believe me now," said Doctor Powell wryly.

Dottie smiled warily. "Forgive me. I did not know—"

"And there is no reason why you should," the doctor said firmly. "But now I need to do a few tests, if you do not mind? It is to review your awareness, see how much motor function you have retained after . . ."

The words washed over Dottie and she did not attempt to follow them. This was what she would expect from a doctor. A lot of long words, phrases that did not make sense, and terminology she was almost certain doctors made up just to feel important.

It was as Doctor Powell was carefully examining her eyes that it happened. The sound of a door, the strange sense of movement just beyond her vision, and then Dottie saw him.

A tall man. A dark-haired one, with heavy bags under his eyes and a wan look to his face that suggested he was not sleeping well. Despite that, he was rather handsome, in a sort of aloof way.

A gentleman, Dottie thought as she tried to follow Doctor

Powell's finger as it was moved rapidly before her face. A nobleman, if she was any judge. And she had certainly known her fair share of nobles . . .

"You said," Dottie said quietly as Doctor Powell took her pulse and the strange man sat on the edge of the sofa, a little farther back from the bed. "Just a few minutes ago, you said you were not the one who brought me here. But I still don't know where here is."

She did not imagine it. Doctor Powell glanced over her shoulder, just for a moment, at the man seated silently on the sofa. He nodded.

Doctor Powell turned back to Dottie. "You have been brought to Gilroyd House. His Grace ensured that you were brought here as swiftly as possible—once they were certain it was safe to move you. He sent for me."

Dottie stared. *The Duke of Gilroyd? But that—*

"I was about to meet him," she said eagerly, suddenly recalling and leaning forward, though she was immediately and kindly pushed back by Doctor Powell. "With Mr. Snee, he and I—"

"Yes, you were," said the man quietly.

Dottie looked curiously over. "And who are you?"

She had not intended her words to be rude, but she could see how it would likely seem that way. Yet the man did not frown as she had expected. He would have been quite within his rights, after such a blunt remark, to return that she had no need to speak to him like that.

But he just watched her. There was a smile dancing across his face, as though she had acted in precisely the way he had expected. It made a strange shiver rush through her.

What was going on?

"I think I'll leave you two to talk," said Doctor Powell delicately, rising from the bed. "I'll be back in just over ten minutes, mind. Don't wear her out."

The doctor had stepped lightly around the bed toward the door before Dottie could ask her to stay. But what could she say?

Don't leave me alone with him? She was as much a stranger to the doctor as she was to this man, though in fairness, she at least knew the doctor's name.

As the door clicked behind Doctor Powell, Dottie looked at the strange man with a bold eye.

She had nothing to be ashamed of. If it were true, that she had been attacked and therefore lost her memory, perhaps this was one of Mr. Snee's experts. He had so many and called on them from time to time to help him with a particular problem. Perhaps he—

"My name," said the man slowly, still seated on the sofa, "is Adam Seymour."

Dottie's eyes widened. "Then—then you are—"

"The Duke of Gilroyd," said the man, inclining his head. "We were due to meet on the first of November, though I did not know it at the time."

A strange sort of warmth was suffusing Dottie's heart, but she did not know why. Her voice quavered as she recalled hazily, "Y-Yes. Mr. Snee thought it would be better for me to come along, rather than let you know ahead of time."

"He was right to do so," said the Duke of Gilroyd quietly. "I am not sure I would have wanted to meet you, if I had known you were coming."

Dottie bristled, despite the ache in her head and the exhaustion in her bones.

Well, really! Was that the sort of thing to say to an invalid?

"And yet you don't remember our first meeting, do you?" The Duke of Gilroyd's voice was quiet, but there was something deep and dark repressed in every syllable. "In fact, Doctor Powell tells me it is likely that you will not recall me at all. Is that true? Do you remember anything, Dottie—I beg your pardon, Miss Yates?"

Dottie stared.

Her gaze raked over his face. His eyes, his nose, the curve of his lips in a slight smile. The breadth of his shoulders. The way he held himself, stiff and yet relaxed. Definitely a nobleman.

None of it was familiar.

"No," Dottie said quietly. "I am sorry, Your Grace . . . I have no memory of you."

For a moment, just when she said the words "Your Grace", she thought she saw the man flinch as though she had injured him. But that was surely a trick of the light.

"That's a shame," said the Duke of Gilroyd quietly. "You and I . . . we formed a friendship of sorts, you see. We went to Brighton."

Dottie nodded slowly. "Yes. Yes, that was my plan. To go to Brighton."

"To find the leaders of the Glasshand Gang. And the traitor, if at all possible," said the Duke of Gilroyd steadily, his eyes not leaving her. "You were under the impression that they were the same person. That we could, as it were, kill two birds with one stone."

Dottie swallowed.

There was something about the way the man was looking at her. His voice was heavy with meaning beyond his mere words, meaning he plainly wanted her to understand. But how could she if she had no memory of meeting him? Surely it was impossible to have any meaningful conversation with the man, considering she had no recollection of him whatsoever?

"Do you remember anything of the Glasshand Gang, Miss Yates?" the Duke of Gilroyd asked softly. "Anything at all?"

Dottie hesitated. It was a trick. Somehow, something was wrong here. She could not put her finger on what it was, but this Duke of Gilroyd . . . he was up to something.

Oh, if only she had her memory back! Then she could be sure who to trust, and who to dissemble to. Until she was more certain, she would simply have to plead ignorance. It would not be so difficult, as it was the truth.

"I am sorry, Your Grace, but there really is nothing I can tell you," Dottie said quietly. "I don't remember anything. Not our meeting in London, not going to Brighton together, not—"

"Not falling in love?"

Dottie started.

Falling—falling in love?

He was mad. Mad! Dukes couldn't go around saying that to young ladies!

But there was a look of earnestness on the gentleman's face Dottie had not expected. The Duke of Gilroyd was looking at her closely, as though desperate to spot a hint of recognition in her eyes.

As though . . . as though he really did care.

"I beg your pardon," Dottie said slowly. "I . . . I have no memory of you at all, nor any of your servants, nor your acquaintance in Bath, whoever I fell in love with. With no recollections, how could I remember—"

"I just wondered if you had a feeling about me," said the Duke of Gilroyd softly. "A good feeling, if possible. An instinct, you know, after spending so much time together. It was just a passing thought . . . a hope . . ."

Dottie shifted uncomfortably in the bed. She was alone in a room—in bed no less—with a man who appeared to be declaring his love for her. Was he saying that she had fallen in love with someone in Brighton—surely he could not mean himself? What was going on?

And then all of a sudden, the moment ended. The Duke of Gilroyd rose to his feet, smoothed his jacket, and looked at her benignly.

"I mustn't keep you," he said cheerfully. "Doctor Powell will be here in a moment. Can I get you anything while you are recuperating in my home—anything that will make you feel better?"

Nothing could make her feel better. Her head hurt, she still wasn't entirely sure if she could trust these people, everything was all wrong, and—

And there was something that would make her feel better.

"A pencil, and some paper," Dottie said, an idea striking her. "Something to doodle away the time. I am sure you understand."

For a heartbeat, she was certain he would guess. The Duke of Gilroyd was clearly a smart man, after all. He had to be, all things considered.

But then he smiled and turned to take something out of a drawer of one of the console tables. "Of course."

He placed the paper and pencil near her hand, careful not to touch her, then nodded. "I . . . I hope you are in better health when next I see you, Miss Yates."

"Thank you," Dottie said with as much calm as she could muster.

She waited until he was most definitely gone from the room, then pulled the pencil and paper toward her. She would have to ask Doctor Powell to have this delivered, but of course, there was no reason why the doctor would refuse her. She was only sending a short note to a friend, after all.

With shaking hands, Dottie took a deep breath, and started to write.

Mr. Snee,

I am horrified to learn I have been attacked, and that some of my memory is, for the time, missing. We will have to hope it returns soon.

In the meantime, I wish to tell you something of great importance. I shall have to hope this letter is not intercepted, for if it were to fall into the hands of the Glasshand Gang, we would all be at risk.

I have found the traitor. His name is Adam Seymour, Duke of Gilroyd.

CHAPTER SEVENTEEN

2 December 1811

ADAM PULLED AN exhausted hand through his hair. It had seen better days. When was the last time he'd had a bath? "You're absolutely sure?"

Doctor Powell—though he should probably think of her as the Duchess of Chetnole—sighed. "There are never any guarantees in medicine, Gilroyd, and—"

"But you're sure, aren't you?" he said curtly, leaning back in his chair and fixing the woman with a stern gaze.

Though she hesitated, it was clear Doctor Powell had only one answer to give. "Yes. I don't think she'll regain her memory."

Try as he might, Adam could not prevent the pain of that statement from rippling across his face.

He had been prepared for it. Each day that Dottie had lain asleep upstairs, unwilling, it appeared, to return to consciousness, he had known it became a greater possibility. The blow to her head had been severe, and God knew how long she had been out there by the back door, waiting to be found.

His stomach twisted as nausea rose.

He should have looked for her sooner. She had been unnoticed for hours, by his reckoning. In the darkness of the night when he truly had nothing else to do but rail at the world, Adam would find himself calculating. If she had left at six o'clock, and he had only found her at one o'clock . . .

It was down that path that madness lay. But perhaps that was what he wanted. To lose all his senses and avoid having to face the fact that every time he ventured into that bedchamber, the woman he loved looked back at him with absolutely no recognition whatsoever.

"You cannot blame yourself—"

"Who else do I have to blame?" Adam asked in a voice that cracked. He tried to pull himself together, but it was impossible. *What was the point?* Doctor Powell had already seen him weep. "I should never have permitted her to go alone. If I had been there—"

"From the little I know of Miss Yates, I do not think she would have wished to make you her nursemaid, you or anyone else," Doctor Powell said firmly, stepping over to her bag on the study desk.

Adam sighed. "Maybe."

"It is something I am sure of," she said firmly, pulling something that looked remarkably like a brandy bottle from her bag. "I thought you might not have any."

She thought wrong. "I did not know Chetnole had slipped into smuggling."

Doctor Powell, who had so recently married the Duke of Chetnole, grinned. "He hasn't. But I was in Kent for three years. I know some . . . people."

Adam tried to smile as his study door opened and Chetnole walked in. "I suppose I shouldn't be too startled by that."

"Jenny," said the Duke of Chetnole with warmth in his voice. "I hope you haven't been working too hard . . ."

Averting his eyes, Adam found it impossible to watch the two newlyweds embrace, if only for a moment. It was bad enough to see anyone happy, but to see two people who had so recently found each other, realized their love for each other, and now had the rest of their lives to enjoy it . . .

Try as he might, he could not help his envy.

That should have been him. Him, and Dottie. He knew it, yet Adam could not bring himself to say it. Not when the loss of her, of what they had become to each other, was so recent.

He'd taken to spending an hour or so with Doctor Powell most evenings just before dinner to discuss Dottie's progress. Sometimes there was little to discuss, and sometimes there were more steps backward than forward.

Every day, though, there was something. Adam knew it was ridiculous—that he was being ridiculous. Hearing these reports each day, they did nothing to his ability to actually help her. But perhaps they helped him. Gave him a comforting—if false—sense of power in the midst of his helplessness.

"Chin up, Gilroyd," said Chetnole bracingly, taking a seat without being offered one. "Things will look up—"

"Please don't give me your pitter patter," Adam said darkly, pain leeching into every word. "If you had just lost Jenny—if she looked at you but saw right past you, had no memory of how she had saved you . . . would you want to be told just to smile, and wait for things to look up?"

He met Chetnole's gaze and saw the truth.

"Well, of course not," said his friend quietly.

Adam nodded as Doctor Powell handed him a glass of brandy. "I thought not."

It had been a difficult few days. Mr. Snee had been to see her, as had Chantmarle, Penshaw, Martock . . . and she recognized all of them.

It had taken a great deal of self-restraint from Adam not to march in there and demand, beg, cajole Dottie into recognizing him. It was madness, that she knew them and was nothing to them, and yet she did not know him.

Well. Not precisely nothing. In fact, he'd almost been certain he'd seen Sedley cry, but that could just have been because he was away from his wife. Their newly announced pregnancy had brought a well-needed hint of joy to the gathering at Gilroyd House.

And yet still, despite all Doctor Powell's ministrations, despite even a visit from Doctor Walsingham—who Adam had been informed was a miracle worker—there was little change in Dottie's condition.

She improved only in small ways. Her head did not spin when she sat up now, and Doctor Powell said the scar on her head would barely be noticeable once it had healed fully and her hair had grown back.

Adam swallowed. And yet the memories would not come back. That was clear in Doctor Powell's mind, and according to Doctor Walsingham, it was a fair assessment.

All those moments. Those conversations. The flicker of warmth that had surely spread through both of them when they had danced together. The secrets they had shared, the laughter.

It was all gone.

Gone, at least, in Dottie's mind. In Adam's heart, they would never disappear.

"There are some people who want to see you," Doctor Powell said gently.

Adam scowled. "I don't want to talk to them."

"They have come to support you, man," said Chetnole in a low voice. "The least you could do is see them—"

"The least I could do is put them all up after they arrived without a moment's notice or a thought of warning," Adam snapped, his temper rising. "Which I have done! It may have passed your notice, Chetnole, but I'm stabling four and twenty horses right now around London because my own stables cannot fit them, and my poor kitchen staff have never seen the like of this! The house has never been so full—not since—"

"Not since Louisa," Chetnole said. "Yes, I thought that, too."

Adam opened his mouth, realized he had absolutely no idea what he was going to say, then closed it again.

Damn. But the man was right. Louisa had been one for company, but he never had. It had been her idea whenever they sent invitations, her excitement at having people to stay that invigorated him. Her pleasure in company. Her laughter that had echoed through these corridors.

These walls knew what it was to have a woman in the house who brought joy and laughter. And now the rooms of Gilroyd House were full again, and again it was because of a woman. It could not have happened in much more different circumstances.

"Louisa would never have wanted—"

"Oh, Moses, don't talk rubbish," interrupted his wife with a grin.

Adam stared as he watched the two of them bicker.

"How on earth would you know? You never met Louisa—"

"I know Adam Seymour, Duke of Gilroyd," Doctor Powell said firmly. "And that's enough—"

"Know him? You only met him a few weeks ago! I've known the beast—no offence, Gilroyd—"

"None taken," said Adam, smiling despite himself.

"—known the beast almost all my life! Hardly able to escape each other, our fathers sent us to the same school, we even went to Cambridge at the same—"

"Oh, and you'd like to tell me, as a woman, what a woman would have wanted for her husband?"

"That is a completely different . . ."

Their gentle squabbling washed over Adam, allowing him to slip once more into his own thoughts. He had to admit, it was rather pleasant to watch them. There was no bile in their tones. It couldn't be more obvious that Chetnole thought the world of his wife and would never actually wish to say anything to truly harm or irritate her.

No, this was just the way Chetnole was. Or perhaps it was just the way they were. There was a fiery, intellectual passion in their relationship that Adam had never thought to see anywhere near Chetnole. He had never been much a one for intellect. Yet this Doctor Powell brought it out of him.

Just as Dottie had brought joy out of him.

The thought was fleeting, but Adam could not deny it. After spending so long in mourning, thinking he would never know what it was to feel happy again, Dottie had proven that the right person could change everything.

Change everything . . . then disappear.

"I am sorry, Your Grace . . . I have no memory of you."

Adam's jaw tightened. He was no rake, nor cad. He would not tell Dottie what had happened between them. If she had wished to know, she surely would have asked—and yet she had treated him much like the stranger that, in her eyes, he was. She was always polite, always grateful, particularly when she had discovered it was in his home that she was recuperating. But nothing more than that.

"—well there we go!" said Chetnole triumphantly.

Adam looked up. "You won, then?"

"Won?" Chetnole's eyes were twinkling. "Absolutely not. Against her?"

Doctor Powell was grinning. "The poor man didn't have a chance, but there it is. It's good for his mind to get a little exercise every now and—"

"Jenny!"

"Can't argue with the truth, Moses," she said with a warm smile. "Brandy?"

Adam's stomach lurched as he watched the new Duchess of Chetnole lightly kiss her husband's head as she poured him a glass of brandy.

That was what he had missed—and would now miss again—the most. Not the grand gestures, pleasant as they were. Not the heady, pleasure-seeking tumbling in a bed, wonderful as it was. No, it was the small things. The little moments shared with that person and no other. The sensation that there was nothing grounding you to the earth except that one person.

Something in his expression must have shown the pain he was in. Chetnole flushed and leaned back. Doctor Powell saw the change in her husband, glanced over at Adam, and flushed in turn.

"I—"

"Don't even think of apologizing," Adam said with a heavy sigh, though he tried to smile. "Please. It's . . . it's good to see that there's still some happiness in this world."

He hadn't intended to sound so bitter, and he cringed at the way his words landed. But then, he had been bitter for a great deal of time, hadn't he? It had been Dottie who had lifted him from that darkness, and Dottie's accident—attack—had dropped him straight back into that all too familiar place.

How was he going to live without her?

"She will recover, Gilroyd," said Doctor Powell gently as she sat beside her husband on the sofa.

Adam nodded curtly. "She will. But she won't be my Dottie, will she?"

The two Chetnoles exchanged looks.

"Now, let's try to be plain," said Chetnole slowly. "When you say 'my Dottie,' you mean—"

"I don't think we need to go into details," said Adam awkwardly, determinedly not looking at Doctor Powell. "But yes. We . . . oh, blast it all to hell. We fell in love. I think."

He was not one to talk about such things, never had been. Adam wasn't even sure he had the language for how he felt about Dottie. Love? It wasn't enough. Adoration? Not enough. That feeling you had, as though there wasn't enough air in your lungs whenever you were in her presence, and yet you knew you would die if you left it? What was that feeling called?

"That would explain your . . . your great care for her," said Doctor Powell quietly. "And your desire for her to regain her memory."

Adam swallowed and nodded. There were no other words.

"The Dottie you loved is still there, Gilroyd," continued the doctor in a quiet voice. "But you are not the man she knows. That opportunity, I think, may have passed."

"Jenny!" Chetnole looked genuinely astonished. "How can you say—"

"I think His Grace would prefer truth and honesty, facts and reality, over pretty little platitudes that I could trot out and would mean absolutely nothing," said Doctor Powell calmly, looking over at Adam. "Am I right, Gilroyd?"

It was all Adam could do not to laugh. "I wouldn't turn down a few pretty little platitudes," he admitted, his heart contracting painfully. "But . . . but you're right. I would rather hear the truth."

"Then hear it," said Doctor Powell firmly. "You could spend the next hundred years waiting for that memory to come back. It may return tomorrow—"

"Jenny, you can't tell him—"

"—or it may never return at all," the doctor continued, glaring at her husband. "I know what I'm doing, Moses. I tell you, he needs to hear this."

Adam swallowed as he watched the unspoken interaction between husband and wife. There was such trust between Chetnole and his bride. Such understanding.

It was galling to think that if things had been different, the three of them could have been joined by another bold and intelligent woman. The four of them would be laughing, exchanging stories, perhaps even celebrating the discovery of the traitor within their midst . . .

"Gilroyd."

Adam started. Both Chetnoles were staring, but it had been the wife who had spoken. "Yes?"

"You need to make a decision," Doctor Powell said quietly. "And it's a difficult one. Only you can make it."

There was such seriousness in her gaze, Adam's lungs tightened, just for a moment. *It surely could not be life or death, or she would not be speaking so calmly—could it?*

"Having Miss Yates here. It is a great service to her, and I am glad that you brought her back to London and contacted me,"

Doctor Powell was saying. "You did well. But keeping her here as she recovers . . . that is going to be a burden on you, Gilroyd. Do not lie and pretend it will not be, because I can already see it wearing on you."

"It's not—" Adam began automatically.

"It is wearing on you," Doctor Powell continued with a sharp gleam in her eye. "I have already seen the change in you. If you keep her here, hoping beyond hope that one day she will turn to you with recognition—"

"Jenny," said Chetnole quietly.

She touched his arm but did not look away from Adam. "You know I am right. If you do not intend to tell her, one day, what she was to you, then I think it kinder to let me take her back with me to Chetnole Lacey. Let me care for her there, where you won't have to be burdened by—"

"Dottie is not a burden," Adam said hotly. Fire licked through his veins and anger followed. *The very idea that—*

"Isn't she?" asked Doctor Powell in a steady, gentle voice. "It's tearing you up inside, Gilroyd. I can see it. You'll fall sick if you spend your days trying to care for her and your nights wishing that things could be different."

"And you think that would stop if she were taken away from me?" Adam said, unable to help himself. His voice broke, and though he knew he should censor himself, stop himself from being so vulnerable, he could not prevent the words slipping from his tongue. "You think every day for the rest of my life won't be filled with care for her? Wondering where she is, if she is safe, warm, happy? If she is being treated well? You think removing her from Gilroyd House could remove her from my heart?"

There were tears sparkling in Doctor Powell's eyes, but that could not stop him, not now the dam had been broken. All the pain and struggle that had been building up from the moment Adam found Dottie on those cobbles, cold and hurt and alone, came rushing out.

"Don't you dare even think about taking her from me," Adam said, fingers tight around his brandy glass. "When she's well and wants to leave—well, that will be different. She can go where she chooses, and I won't stop her. But until she can choose, until she is well, Dorothy Yates will stay here. Where I can . . . can love her. Even from a distance. Even without her knowing it."

Dampness. There was something damp on his cheeks.

Adam lifted a hand and angrily brushed away the tears that had somehow fallen.

And he was not alone. A single tear fell down Doctor Powell's cheek.

Chetnole cleared his throat. "You truly love her, then."

It was not a question, and so did not perhaps need a response, but Adam nodded. "More . . . more than anything."

"You said not two months ago that you never wanted to marry again," his friend pointed out.

"I never wanted to marry again until I met her," Adam snapped. *Oh, wasn't it obvious?*

Silence fell between them. The study was filled only with the noise of the fire, crackling in the grate.

It was over. Adam could still hardly believe it had come to an end this way, but it had. Everything he and Dottie had shared—it was gone. And there was no way he could get it back. No lotion, potion, remedy, or medicine could give Dottie the recollection of who he was.

He was nothing to her, just as she was everything to him. But he could not force this. He would not put her in the position of feeling guilt for her lack of recognition.

No, Dottie Yates was free to go whenever she wished. And when she did, she would take his heart with her.

"What are you going to do?" Chetnole asked quietly.

Irritation flared in Adam's chest. *Had he not made himself perfectly clear?* "As I said, I—"

"I know what you said," his friend interrupted gently. "That was about her. What about you? While Miss Yates continues to recover, what will you do?"

The question was so surprising, Adam's eyes widened. What would he do? He began to wonder, the seed of an idea beginning to sprout. "I . . . I don't know. Spend time with Dottie. If she'll let me."

There was an all too knowing look in both of their faces, and Doctor Powell confirmed his suspicions when she said, "Gilroyd, if you think you can once again—"

"Well, why not?" Adam said, the idea taking root now as a small flicker of hope sparked in his chest. "Somehow, and I am still not sure how, we fell in love once. Who is to say that we cannot do it again?"

CHAPTER EIGHTEEN

17 December 1811

The First Noel the Angel did say
Was to certain poor shepherds in fields as they lay,
In fields where they lay keeping their sheep,
On a cold winter's night that was so deep . . .

Dottie closed her eyes as she listened to the Christmas carol being sung somewhere out in the streets of London. It was pleasant to remember there was a whole world out there. A world that, one day, she may rejoin.

For now, she had managed to make it downstairs to the morning room, and that was being considered by Doctor Powell as a great victory.

"It's only coming downstairs," Dottie had pointed out an hour ago, when Doctor Powell had actually applauded when she had reached the room in the house which received the most wintery light.

"It's wonderful, tangible progress," Doctor Powell had said smartly, as she had tucked the blanket around Dottie's legs as she sat in the large armchair. "And after last week's dizzy spell, something worth celebrating."

Dottie smiled wistfully as she watched carriages go by

through the large windows of the morning room. Perhaps the doctor was right.

It had, after all, been most disorienting when she'd tried last week to get up from bed and walk around. Lying in bed all day for weeks on end had become tiresome, and Dottie had been determined to get up.

Her body, on the other hand, had not seemed to agree.

After the third fall, Doctor Powell had given the instruction that she was not to be permitted to go downstairs yet. Not until she'd practiced.

Practiced! It had made Dottie's blood boil that she had to be treated like such a child. But she had acquiesced and submitted to the ridiculous charade of standing up and sitting, standing up and sitting, over and over again in the safety of the bedchamber where she had been living for over a month.

Dottie had not ever admitted to Doctor Powell that it had helped, but she had seen in the triumphant gleam in the woman's eyes that she knew precisely what Dottie had been thinking, even if she did not say it.

And today was the second day in a row Dottie had managed to get up, walk on her own two feet across the bedchamber, along the landing, down the steps, and into the morning room.

Her legs had felt like jelly by the time she half sat, half fell into the armchair, but still. Progress.

"Now, you sit here," said Doctor Powell sternly, waving a finger under Dottie's nose. "I want you to just relax for—"

"You're not going to leave me here alone?" Dottie had said, heart sinking.

Company. That was what she missed. Hours alone in that bedchamber had driven her to distraction. No number of books could compensate for truly excellent conversation.

"I have offered Doctor Walsingham my help in visiting the poor today, and Moses is accompanying me," Doctor Powell said briskly. "He makes a poor assistant, but don't tell him I said that."

"Why?" Dottie said with a grin. "Because he already knows?"

If there were any silver linings to all this, and after a few weeks she had been forced to look for them, it was that she had grown to know both the Chetnoles well and greatly liked them.

It was difficult not to like such a caring, intelligent woman as Doctor Powell—or, as she supposed she could call her, the Duchess of Chetnole. And the duke was charm himself, utterly besotted with his wife, and more than happy to obey almost any order given by her. The pair of them were delightful.

Though it did make Dottie feel . . . odd sometimes. As though she had been about to say something, but just as the words left her mind and made it to her tongue, they melted, like a sugar sweet.

Most strange.

"Moses is fully aware he makes an excellent basket carrier, and not much else, when it comes to the world of medicine," Doctor Powell said with a grin. "Remind me to tell you about the time when I had to stitch up a patient and I asked for candles, and he brought them to me unlit with no matches."

Dottie snorted. "That sounds about right."

"Until this afternoon, then," said Doctor Powell, giving the blanket on Dottie's knees another hearty tuck, as though that would protect her from all the world's ills. "I've left your bell here in case you need anything. I am sure Mrs. Sharp will be happy to help."

The instant she heard the news that Dottie was awake, she'd ordered the Brighton coachman to bring her to London. She'd been a whirlwind of help since she'd arrived.

But the silver bell had been one of the Duke of Gilroyd's ideas. He was a quiet man, not shy exactly, but reticent. Dottie had never met a man who hung back in quite the same way.

His idea, however, had been a good one. Dottie knew she could not be waited on hand and foot—there were still the Glasshand Gang leaders to catch and the traitor to root out. The silver bell therefore was a way for her to attract the attention of Mrs. Sharp or a passing maid, without getting in the way.

Dottie shifted uncomfortably in the tight embrace of the blanket as Doctor Powell quietly closed the door behind her.

In the way. It was impossible not to feel in the way when you were staying in a man's house for an undetermined amount of time.

And by the light of that same star
Three Wise men came from country far;
To seek for a King was their intent,
And to follow the star wherever it went . . .

Dottie sighed. It was all very well for the Duke of Gilroyd to say she was welcome to stay in his house for as long as was necessary, but it did rather make one feel uncomfortable. She hardly knew the man, after all. And then to have a first meeting when you were ill in bed and he was suggesting you had once been . . . well . . .

"I don't remember anything. Not our meeting in London, not going to Brighton together, not—"

"Not falling in love?"

It was very irregular. And her letter, perhaps, could have made things worse.

Guilt pressed on her, but Dottie pushed it aside as best she could. Well, she had acted in good faith, hadn't she? She'd been certain in that moment that the Duke of Gilroyd absolutely had to be the traitor, so she'd written to Mr. Snee.

As she ought, Dottie told herself. *What if he had been the traitor and she hadn't done anything because she'd felt indebted to him? That was no way to serve one's country!*

As it was, Mr. Snee had come to visit her and laughed just a little at her suggestion that the Duke of Gilroyd could be anything but the height of honor.

"Disappointed as I am to see that you cannot recall anything of your mission with Gilroyd," Mr. Snee had said with a smile, "I can assure you the Duke of Gilroyd is most definitely not a traitor."

Dottie had not asked if Mr. Snee had told the Duke of Gilroyd of her suspicions. It would be mortifying in the extreme! She had decided it was better not to know.

He certainly had not acted as though he knew. No, the Duke of Gilroyd had been nothing but kindness itself. No request was too difficult, no measure of hospitality too much. No doctor-required food was too complex, no medicine too expensive.

Some feeling curled around her heart, but before Dottie could decipher it, the sensation was gone.

Strange.

The Christmas carol wafting through the window ended, and Dottie smiled ruefully. It was almost Christmas. Perhaps she could have a mince pie or some sort of cake. Yes, that would be marvelous. Even if she had to sit here alone without Doctor Powell's company.

Dottie's hand reached over to the console table beside her, and the tinkling of the silver bell rang out.

The door behind her opened.

"Cake," Dottie said firmly. "I need it. Lots of it."

She had expected Mrs. Sharp's laugh to follow. The woman had been eager to see to Dottie's comfort, though she occasionally said things that did not made any sense to Dottie. But then, apparently, they had become close while she and the Duke of Gilroyd had worked together in Brighton. It was strange to think a person could know you while you had little knowledge of them.

But it was not the housekeeper's light tones that rang out into the morning room.

"Cake. I see," it said, low and clearly amused. "Well, I suppose we shall have to see what we can do."

Dottie whirled around in the armchair as quickly as she was able, craning to see who had spoken—though why, she did not know. There was only one person whose voice was like that.

Adam Seymour, the Duke of Gilroyd, stepped over to the bellpull by the fireplace, tugged it, then moved to stand before her.

Dottie's cheeks darkened. *She had certainly not intended to speak to the master of the house like that!* "I-I . . . I did not mean to—"

"Ah, Mrs. Sharp," the Duke of Gilroyd said smoothly as the door once again opened behind Dottie. "Cake, please."

"Cake?" came the puzzled reply.

Dottie could not help but smile as she watched the Duke of Gilroyd nod seriously.

"Yes, all of it. Every bit of cake you have in the house, in here, please. With two plates. And two forks."

"Right. Cake, indeed," came Mrs. Sharp's vague response.

The door shut, and the Duke of Gilroyd's gaze moved from the unseen housekeeper to her.

Dottie's cheeks burned. There was something incredibly . . . incredibly *something*, about the way the Duke of Gilroyd looked at her. An intensity she could not put into words. A familiarity that never stepped beyond the bounds of decorum, but certainly gave the impression that it could.

That was the trouble with losing one's memory, she supposed. She would always be at a slight disadvantage around those with whom she had spent time in those missing weeks. And yet, for all that he was a tall man, and evidently proud, and most certainly a duke, Dottie had been surprised to find she was quite relaxed in his company.

She knew dukes. Knew several of them. Many of them had become, if not friends, then at least people she knew she could rely on in a fix—not that she had ever permitted herself to get in one. Dottie prided herself on that.

But the Duke of Gilroyd was different. There was no sense that she had to put on airs around him. No feeling that she was inferior just because she had no title. Dottie could not have described it, even if she'd had someone to confide in.

Sometimes, the way Doctor Powell looked at her . . .

Well. As though there was something Dottie did not know.

"May I sit?"

Dottie blinked. The Duke of Gilroyd was asking her if he

could sit. In his own house!

"Why do you ask?" she said as brightly as she could. "This is your morning room."

"It's yours, whenever you are in it," came the quiet reply as the Duke of Gilroyd sat in a comfortable looking chair across from her. "I would not wish to intrude."

Dottie swallowed.

And yet he did intrude, didn't he?

Not that the Duke of Gilroyd knew that, of course. Dottie had been careful never to let anything slip and had been most guarded in the way she spoke to him. He knew her far better than she knew him, she could see that. Sense it, in the way he looked at her.

But that did not excuse the most erotic dreams she had been having about him.

Dottie wet her lips as she recalled what she had shared with the dream version of the gentleman sitting before her only last night. Why, the man had come up behind her and kissed her, just below the ear. He had told her that she needed to ask for it, that he would only give her what she wanted.

"Please, Adam."

"Please what?"

"P-Please rip off my buttons."

Dottie shivered. And he had. Her mind had supplied her with such sensations, such heady giddiness—

When she had awoken, it had been all she could do to put the dream from her mind and remind herself that the real Duke of Gilroyd would surely have been mortified to learn she had been dreaming of him in that manner!

It was therefore quite bizarre to find herself calmly sitting opposite him mere hours later.

"Miss Yates," the Duke of Gilroyd said quietly. "I—"

"This is all the cake I could find, Y'Grace, but I can send out for more or bake some this afternoon, if nothing suits," panted Mrs. Sharp as she burst into the morning room. "Come on, then!"

Dottie stared. The last few words had not been spoken to herself or to the duke—they were instead for the trail of footmen following in the housekeeper's wake.

"Excellent," said the Duke of Gilroyd smartly, as a maid stepped forward and pulled several small tables together so that the plethora of cake could be placed between them.

And plethora was the right word. Dottie had never seen so much cake together in one place. Pound cake, sponge cake, rout cake, drop cake . . .

"But will it be enough?" Mrs. Sharp said, biting her lip. "Y'Grace? Miss Yates?"

Dottie stared. "You think I can possibly get through all this?"

Relief swept across the housekeeper's face. "Ah, good. I was worried that it might not be sufficient—you must get your health back, Miss Yates!"

"I'm not sure Doctor Powell thinks that can be achieved through the power of cake," Dottie pointed out.

There was something akin to teasing on the Duke of Gilroyd's face. "If you wish, we can take it away—"

"You can take this cake out of my cold, dead hands," Dottie said with a laugh. "Thank you, Mrs. Sharp."

She had intended the words to make them smile. It certainly amused a few of the footmen, and Mrs. Sharp beamed as she left. But out of the corner of her eye, Dottie saw a shadow move across the Duke of Gilroyd's face. A shadow of real pain. Of agony, of twisting hurt that had struck him so swiftly, he had been unable to hide the effects.

And then it was gone.

The door snapped shut behind her, and the Duke of Gilroyd was holding out a plate. "Help yourself, Miss Yates."

"You have the pound cake," Dottie said, pushing the plate toward him. "It is your favorite."

The words had slipped out before she could interrogate them—but she did not need to. The duke was going to do that for her, it appeared.

"How the devil do you know that?" he breathed.

Dottie swallowed. She did not know. It was not a conscious fact she could have pulled from her mind, and yet there it was. She just . . . knew. "I . . . I'm not sure."

He examined her closely for a moment, and her breath hitched in her throat, until—

"Well, thank you," said the duke quietly. "I will have some."

And so here they sat. Dottie had expected it to be awkward, sitting in silence and eating cake with a duke who knew her in a way she just did not understand. Yet there was a warmth to him, even in the silence. Dottie could not describe it. It was like sitting with someone she had known all her life, somehow. Someone who knew her and liked what he knew.

It was most disorientating.

Thankfully, the pound cake was sufficient a distraction. All they had to do was exchange a few pleasantries, and—

"Lady Romeril sends her regards," said the Duke of Gilroyd quietly. "She hoped it would not be too long before you would be dancing at one of her balls again."

Lady Romeril? Dottie had heard of the doyenne of the *ton*, of course, who hadn't? Had she truly danced at one of Lady Romeril's balls?

"I think there are quite a few things about our time together in Brighton you will have to tell me about," Dottie said awkwardly, helping herself to another slice of cake.

Well, if not now, when?

"I suppose so," said the Duke of Gilroyd pensively. "You will have to think about whether you want to hear about the mission, all the details I can give you, or whether you want to know . . . know all of it. Everything."

Dottie met his dark, serious gaze. "Everything?"

What else could there be to know? The mission had been everything—the very reason they had gone to Brighton. Dottie could recall how carefully she had planned it: spotting the messages in the obituaries, noticing the clues, putting them all together. She was certain—had been certain that the answers were in Brighton. Mr. Snee had been certain, too.

Was it possible there were answers in Brighton, not only to finding the traitor behind these secrets spilling out, but also to who she was? Who she had become in the company of the Duke of Gilroyd?

He was smiling hesitantly. "It is up to you, of course. I would not wish to . . . I mean, it is your choice."

And the room seemed to darken and fade, and it was as though Dottie was pulled back in a rush by a hook in her stomach. Images, words, sounds, they all flashed past her as though she were traveling in time. And of course she wasn't, but her mind was reeling and memories, memories which had been gone and yet were slipping into place, were filling her mind.

Memories of Adam.

Adam, glaring, telling her he didn't want a partner.

Adam, glowering as she made a point that was both insightful and clever.

Adam, staring as she stepped down a staircase she did not recognize in a gown she'd never seen before.

Adam, close to her, holding her in his arms—were they dancing? Why else would she be this close to him?

And words she could not remember speaking or hearing were echoing in her mind, and Dottie grabbed at them eagerly, hungry for any pieces of memories that had been withheld.

"Do you have any idea how distracting it is to have a grumpy duke—"

"I am not grumpy!"

"You absolutely are, you know you are. And yet I still . . . I still care about you, Adam."

Dottie blinked.

The room rushed back around her. She was in the morning room, sitting opposite the Duke of Gilroyd, and the memories were fading as swiftly as they had come.

Desperate, Dottie tried to cling onto them. She had to remember, she could not forget again that she loved him, that Adam loved her, that they were everything to each other.

She blinked again, and the memories faded like a sunset. A tinge of their color remained in her mind, like an echo of a bell. But the substance of them, the detail, it was all lost.

"Dottie?" Adam breathed.

He had placed his plate and fork down on the table and had reached out to her.

Dottie looked down. He was holding her hand.

It felt right. His fingers slotted into place around hers as though . . . as though they had been made for one another. As though they had done this before.

Dottie swallowed. She could not recall . . . not precisely. She had remembered something, something important. Something to do with Adam.

Adam?

Her eyes met his, and something warm sparked in her heart.

"Adam," Dottie whispered, half nervous, half certain.

Tears sparkled in the corners of his eyes. "Dottie."

"I-I don't remember exactly . . . something just happened, I think I remembered . . . but then it slipped away . . ." *How could she explain the confusing sense of comfort and confusion? Would he understand, be patient, as she tried to remember precisely what had happened between them?*

Adam's voice broke, but only slightly, as he squeezed her hand. "I thought I'd lost you."

"I'm still here," said Dottie quietly, hardly knowing why she was comforting this man, but certain deep in her soul that she wanted to. "It's all in here, somewhere. I just haven't found it yet. But I will."

Adam closed his eyes, just for a moment. Two tears fell, but there was joy in his gaze as he looked at her once more. "I know. I know you will."

CHAPTER NINETEEN

4 January 1812

"AND YOU'RE NOT too cold?"

"Adam, I—"

"Or too hot? I can dampen down the fire a little, if you are overly—"

"Adam, you don't have to—"

"If you're hungry, I can—"

"Just sit down!"

Adam grinned as the fiery Dottie emerged once again in the seemingly calm face of the woman opposite him.

What a change just a few weeks could make.

For a start, Dottie's hair was growing back. Doctor Powell had been right. A few more weeks, and you would barely be able to tell there had ever been a cut on her head at all. The scab had gone, leaving behind it a shining scar that he could only just see if the light was right. Soon the curls would be long enough to hide it. No one would ever know, unless Dottie chose to tell them.

But that wasn't the only change.

Dottie gave him a knowing look. "You're evaluating me again."

Adam threw up his hands in surrender. "I can't help it."

"Try."

"I don't particularly wish to," he admitted, watching as Dottie carefully walked up and down the library, as per Doctor Powell's orders.

It had been a compromise. Dottie had wished to take her daily exercise—at least thirty minutes on her feet, walking—outside. Adam had vetoed it.

"You don't actually get a vote," Doctor Powell had reminded him only yesterday.

"Oh yes I do," Adam had said darkly.

He'd caught Dottie's eye at that moment, and wished he hadn't said it aloud. It was a tad presumptuous, after all. Dottie was only still getting the last few bits of her memories back.

She could now recall almost all their preparations before they had left for Brighton, and most of the journey there. Her introduction to Mrs. Sharp and the other servants had come back completely, much to the housekeeper's delight, and Dottie had recounted, almost perfectly, some of the earliest invitations they had accepted as "the Duke and Duchess of Gilroyd." She'd even remembered just how irritated he'd got with the Earl of Chester, worse luck.

Lady Romeril's ball was taking longer to resurface. It appeared, at least from what Doctor Powell said, that the closer the memories were to the attack, the harder it was going to be for Dottie to recall them.

Adam had swallowed hard at that. Dottie still had not recalled anything of the eight and forty hours before the attack. Lady Romeril's ball, their conversation afterward, their admission of affection, their lovemaking . . .

Even the green silk dress he had treated her to.

None of that had returned.

Which, Adam thought darkly as he watched Dottie turn at the end of the room and make her way back past the bookcases, *was perhaps not the worst thing in the world.*

A warmth was growing between them with every passing

day. Partly because Dottie was remembering more of the friendship, or at the very least, basic respect that they had built together in Brighton, and partly because of the respect and rapport they were building now.

But if she was to recall what they had shared that night, on that rug before the fire in his Brighton drawing room . . .

The last thing he wanted was for Dottie to feel beholden to him.

And besides, whispered a dark part of him. *What if she no longer felt that way?*

"I hope you're impressed."

Adam smiled, his thoughts interrupted by Dottie's wryness. "Very impressed."

"Because it's not everyone who can walk for thirty minutes together, up and down, up and down in a library," Dottie said tartly, throwing him a deeply irritated look.

His smile broadened. "I said before, and I'll say again. When I'm confident you are stronger on your feet, then we can go outside."

"I'm not going to fall—"

"You fell yesterday," Adam pointed out. "And it's icy out there. The last thing I would want is for you to fall and get hurt again."

His stomach lurched.

The investigation into who precisely had attacked Dottie Yates just outside his Brighton stables was still ongoing, but he was no fool. Unless they found the traitor in their midst, were able to track down the Glasshand Gang leaders themselves, they would never know. It would have been a lackey, someone who was given the order.

Though his heart demanded vengeance, his mind knew better. He had to focus on Dottie. Make sure that she was safe, healing.

Even if that healing meant that, eventually, she would leave him.

Adam breathed in slowly, trying to force down the panic that rose whenever he thought about Dottie leaving. She was free to do so, of course. He would never try to hold onto her if she truly wished to go.

Although sometimes, every now and again, Adam was almost certain he saw a hint of desire, of affection in Dottie's eyes. The way she looked at him. When they were dining together or laughing together. When they were discussing the traitor, who on earth it could be . . .

But he could be deluding himself, couldn't he? There was no reason to think Dottie could fall in love with him, even if she had done something so wonderful in Brighton.

"And yet I still . . . I still care about you, Adam."

Adam cursed his own caution. Why had he been so reticent, back in Brighton, to speak of the feelings he had known but been afraid to name? Why had he missed out on what could have been his only chance to tell her—

"You're thinking of something important, aren't you?"

Adam started. So lost had he been in his thoughts, he'd forgotten where he was.

Dottie was grinning as she passed him, walking with firmer steps than she had just a few days ago. "Aren't you?"

Well, it wasn't as though he could bring himself to lie to her. "Yes."

"About the traitor?"

Adam shrugged. "In a way, yes."

It was a roundabout way, but it was still true. Whoever had hurt Dottie had done so knowingly—and whoever had ordered it must have known she was on the right track. Whatever epiphany she'd had, that morning after they had made love, must have been correct.

It didn't make sense, otherwise.

"I keep thinking about it, too," Dottie mused, reaching one end of the room and turning back on herself. "I wish I had seen more of that Glasshand Gang leader that I glimpsed. If I had only seen a little more of him . . ."

Adam leaned forward in his chair. He couldn't help it. There was so much locked inside Dottie's mind that he could not see, and there were times when it frightened him. If Dottie ever remembered what they had shared together, they would need to have a difficult and perhaps emotional conversation about what happened next.

But there was more in there. The answer to who had been betraying them, time and time again, was also in her mind. And that meant—

"It must be someone we know," Dottie said slowly.

Adam groaned as he leaned back in the armchair. "We've been over this a dozen times!"

"Well, I would like to go over it again," she said firmly, turning on her heel as she reached the large bay window. "We know he is close to the center of things. How else would he have known—"

"We don't actually know that he's a he," said Adam ruefully. "There was a time when I thought you, perhaps . . ."

His voice trailed off. Perhaps it wasn't the most politic thing to say. It was rather offensive, after all, to accuse someone of being a traitor when they most certainly weren't one. He wouldn't like—

"How interesting," said Dottie, a mischievous grin on her face. "At one point, I thought it could be you."

Adam's chest puffed out at the affront. "Me? I have done nothing but give service to my—"

"Yes, yes, very impressive," said Dottie dismissively, waving a hand in that way only Dottie could. "But that's the trouble, isn't it? Everyone we know who has been involved in this one way or the other—even Dulverton who, bless him, simply doesn't have the brains to serve in the same way you do—" Adam ignored the slight on Dulverton, choosing instead to enjoy the warmth in his chest caused by Dottie's implied compliment "—even Dulverton would not be so foolish as to let anything slip."

Adam shook his head. "It must be someone we already trust."

"But there are so many of us," Dottie said darkly. "Penshaw,

Sedley, Wincham—and we must look beyond even those I have worked with! There must be others, I suppose. Others that Mr. Snee has worked with who I don't know."

Shrugging, Adam nodded. "I suppose so."

Dottie sighed as she paced past him. "It's like looking for a needle in a haystack."

"Like looking for a needle in a field full of haystacks," Adam added helpfully.

"And we don't even know if we're in the right field," Dottie said with a laugh, turning on her heel again. "Oh, hell, Adam! What are we supposed to do about it?"

Trying to focus on the conversation at hand, and not at how pleased he was that Dottie had slipped so easily back into using his first name, Adam shrugged again. "I am not sure."

It did his heart good, however, to see her move about so freely, to see her mind move so swiftly. Doctor Powell had been very careful in her estimations, and she had been right to do so, though her prognosis had been rather full of doom and gloom.

But this Dottie? This woman, sparking ideas, waving her hands about as she talked as she always did? This was the woman he had thought lost forever. This was the woman he loved.

Even if she was not quite ready to hear it yet.

"—just a figure, really, though I could see he was a gentleman," Dottie was saying. "I wish I had seen more of him. Perhaps then I could have . . . could have . . . have . . ."

Adam looked up swiftly. His gaze had drifted to his hands, but the change in her voice was enough to grab his attention immediately.

Dottie was no longer walking. She had paused mid-step, her left foot ahead of her right. Her eyes were unfocused, her mouth open, and her hands were spread out either side of her, mid-flourish.

"Dottie?"

She did not answer. She did not move.

Adam rose hastily. Doctor Powell had warned him, privately,

that there may be setbacks. *Was she about to fall?*

"Dottie, are you quite all right?"

He was standing right before her now, clutching her hands in his, heart pounding. Adam didn't know what he would do if Dottie lost some of the memories she had only recently regained. What should he do—ring the bell? Call for Doctor Powell?

"Dottie?" Adam breathed.

And then she came back to him. Her eyes sharpened, focusing on him, and Adam's breathing calmed, his lungs loosening.

She was fine. She was—

"Mr. Snee," Dottie breathed.

Well, she had obviously exerted herself. Adam would have to carry her upstairs, not that having Dottie in his arms was much of a hardship, and send for Doctor Powell. Together they could—

"Snee, Adam. *Snee*," Dottie repeated, tightening her grip on his hands. "It was Mr. Snee I saw that day. Snee is a Glasshand Gang leader. He's . . . he's the traitor."

For a moment, Adam just stood there, unable to take in what she was saying.

Snee? Old Snee? Bumbling, well-meaning, sharp as knives Snee? The man was an enigma of course, none of the dukes knew much about him, save that he was a magistrate. He was bumbling with Penshaw because that's what Penshaw expected, and sharp with him because Adam would only tolerate a smart man.

So he was a chameleon. That did not make him a traitor!

"Dottie," Adam said quietly, as kindly as he could. "I think it's time you had a little rest. You must be exhausted—"

"Botheration, man, listen to me!" Dottie said firmly. "I am not out of my wits, nor overly tired by a little wandering around a library. It's Snee!"

"Snee is the one who brought us all together—he gives us missions from the Crown," Adam said quietly. *Oh, bless her.* "He isn't—"

"He is the one I saw, Adam, I would swear to it," Dottie said, her voice strong and steady. "That pipe! That dragon pipe, I knew

I'd seen it somewhere. That flash of light—he was smoking that pipe of his! Besides, who else has more information about us all? Who else could ensure some missions succeed and some fail?"

Adam blinked.

No, it couldn't be. The thought that the very man who had brought him into service to the Crown was the same one sabotaging them, sacrificing truth for a little coin . . .

No. It would reshape the world Adam knew so well. *Break it.*

"Who sent us to Brighton?" Dottie said quietly.

Adam swallowed. "Well . . . well, Snee did. But that was because—"

"Because we were getting too close," she said, her words almost tripping over themselves, she was speaking so hastily. "And of course the last thing I was going to do was question Mr. Snee! The very idea! But he wanted us out of London, Adam, don't you see? And he must have warned the Glasshand Gang—of course he did, he's probably in league with them just as he is with the French—and that's why we couldn't see anyone in Brighton!"

His mind was whirling as new approaches to the same old information made Adam's head hurt. "We . . . we didn't see anyone in Brighton—"

"And none of our informants had seen anyone from the Glasshand Gang either," Dottie said, speaking over him. "Of course they hadn't! Because Snee had told them we'd be coming!"

It was a terrible thought. *Mr. Snee, the magistrate?* Someone right in the center of the judicial power in London? *Dear God, the man had actually met with Prinny!*

"And I saw him."

Adam's gaze sharpened and he looked closely into Dottie's eyes. "You are sure?"

"Positive. I saw that dragon pipe. I just didn't realize it."

"Because you have not been sure before," he said quietly, hating that he had to point this out. "You know what some will say—that it was the knock on your head confusing you."

Dottie wrenched her hands from his. "If you don't believe

me, just say—"

"I do—Dottie, I do believe you!" Adam said hastily, grabbing her shoulders before she could move away. "It's not something I like, but it . . . damn and blast it, it makes sense."

The moment Chetnole had found out about the traitor, he'd come back to England—but he hadn't gone to London. It had always confused Adam, that bit. He'd put it down to the fact that the poor man had been injured and robbed, but perhaps it was more than that. Perhaps he'd known going straight to London wasn't the best idea, if . . . if Snee was the traitor.

"Chetnole went to you," Dottie said quietly. "About the traitor. And you—"

"I went to Snee, of course." Adam's heart was sinking. "Straight to the man who had already betrayed us. Oh, Dottie, you're wonderful!"

She was. Despite everything that she had suffered, everything she had endured, she had been the one to work it out. She was the one who had seen him and remembered him.

And it all made sense.

"We need to tell them," Adam said quietly. "All of them."

There was a sparking light in Dottie's eyes. "So that we can go and accost—"

"Arrest is probably a better word," he amended.

There was such fire in this woman's bones! Oh, he could not hope to be as sharp as Dottie Yates, but he would have to hope he had more of a chance to know her. But first, they had to sort out Snee.

"We'll write to them," he said slowly. "All of them. I'm almost certain Wincham and Sedley are still in London—the two of them can go."

"You really think the four of us can subdue him?" Dottie said, doubt in her voice. "He's a clever man, Adam. If he's avoided notice for this long—"

"Sedley and Wincham will be more than enough to take Snee into custody," said Adam firmly.

Dottie frowned. "What, and we aren't going?"

Adam shook his head slowly.

No. No, if recent experience was going to teach him anything, it was that he simply could not continue on from this moment without saying something.

Though he had told himself he would not. That Dottie had to come to that memory on her own. That it would be unfair of him to tell her, outright, that he was in love with her and that she had given herself freely to him.

"Want me? Well for goodness sake, Adam. If you want me now, why not have me?"

But Adam could no longer in any conscience have these feelings without revealing them to her. It was not fair to her. And perhaps she would leave Gilroyd House, but he would have to take that chance. Because Dottie Yates needed to know he loved her.

"We're not?" Dottie was frowning. "Adam, that man is perhaps the most important person in the whole of London at this moment!"

"I have someone far more important here," said Adam slowly, his heart thundering.

Was this the right time? Could she see in his eyes just how desperately in love with her he was? Would he regret this in just a few minutes?

Dottie met his gaze and her cheeks pinked. "You . . . you do?"

His ribcage could barely contain his thundering heart, and Adam hardly knew how he managed to nod, but he did. "You."

For perhaps a few seconds, Dottie did nothing but stare in clear astonishment. Her lips parted, her eyes widened, and Adam thought he actually heard the hitch in her breath.

And then she was kissing him. Dottie had stepped into his arms and kissed him hard on the mouth, and the world finally made sense again. They had started out in friction and distrust, had seemed to end in glory, then shattered in heartbreak and pain, but this made all things right.

Adam pulled her to him, holding tightly onto her waist as though she could be taken from him at any moment. She tasted sweet, and her skin burned against him as she clung to him, and Adam could have wept with the pleasure of knowing that just for this moment, she was his.

When Dottie broke the kiss, she beamed and stayed in his arms. "I think we should make love."

Adam almost dropped her. "I beg your pardon—"

"You heard me," Dottie said, eyes glittering. "I can't believe it's taken me this long to say it."

Now it was his breath catching in his throat. *It wasn't possible—she hadn't—*"You . . . you remembered?"

"Two days ago," Dottie said promptly, laughing as Adam's eyes widened. "I thought, how long will it take Adam to crack before kissing me, as he so clearly wants to?"

"You minx!"

"Probably," said Dottie, lifting her lips to be kissed again.

Adam was hardly going to deny her. A tingling ache was building in his manhood which had already stood to attention. *How could he say no?*

But before that—

"You are going to marry me, aren't you?" Adam said, breaking the kiss just long enough to start trailing kisses down Dottie's neck.

She shivered as her hands moved swiftly to his buttons, wrenching them undone. A shudder worked its way through Adam as he recalled the last time buttons had flown off between them. *Oh, if they were about to experience something like that . . .*

"Of course I'm going to marry you," Dottie breathed, such longing in her voice that Adam had to work hard not to just drop her onto the floor and ravish her immediately. "I thought you'd never ask."

Adam groaned with restrained desire. "I was so worried—I thought you'd never remember—"

"So did I," Dottie admitted, pushing his waistcoat to the floor.

How had she managed to get his jacket off without him noticing? "But you were patient, Adam. I know you would have waited."

His heart contracted painfully as her gown slowly fell to the floor. "I thought we'd never get here."

"Oh, I knew we would," Dottie said happily. "In the end."

EPILOGUE

24 March 1812

"I F YOU DON'T calm down, I will have you shot," said Dottie sternly.

The Duke of Wincham grinned. "Won't be the first time."

"I mean it! When I asked you to give me away—"

"Ahead of every other duke who had served the Crown, I might add," said Wincham, his grin broadening. "I made sure to tell Penshaw. I hear he's devastated."

Dottie rolled her eyes. "You are impossible!"

It was precisely why she had chosen him. There were a great many dukes she had interacted with in the past, though some of them did not even know she had been a part of their stories. Caelfall had been remarkably astonished, apparently, to hear that his old college hadn't been champing at the bit to welcome him back, that it had been her intervention that made it possible.

But when it came to choosing one of them to walk her down the aisle, Wincham had been the obvious choice. He'd been the rudest to her when he'd first got back to England without his leg, and therefore the most contrite when he'd written to tell her he was getting married.

Besides, he loved the idea of being chosen. It wouldn't have mattered, really, to the others.

"How can I be calm? It's your wedding day!" Wincham said as the carriage trundled along the London streets. "My Hattie says I've been quite the irritant the last few days."

Dottie rolled her eyes. "I can't imagine why."

Still, she could not deny there was a certain excitement in her own heart. After so long, after having the stuffing knocked out of her and losing all sense of who Adam was—after he so patiently cared for her, waiting for her to feel comfortable in his presence before he did so much as hold her hand . . .

It was all coming to an end today. Or at least, perhaps it was more accurate to say, they were coming to a new beginning.

"There it is!"

"Yes, there it is," said Dottie with a smile as the carriage pulled up outside the church. "Did Hattie ever tell you that you're like a puppy?"

"Only the once," shot back the Duke of Wincham. "She's right, of course. I was nothing when she found me, and now . . . I wouldn't even know who I am without her."

Dottie's stomach tightened. Truer words had never been spoken—but now she came to think about it, Wincham was not alone in her acquaintance to have experienced such a thing.

The double doors of the church porch were thrown open, and she heard the heavy sound of hundreds of people rising to their feet. *This was it.* As organ music floated through the air, Wincham offered her his arm and leaned heavily on his cane.

"Ready?"

Dottie nodded. "Born ready."

There were numerous familiar faces in the wedding congregation. She had been most surprised that so many of her old acquaintances and new friends were willing to come to see her wed—but then, most of them did owe her a favor.

There were the Duke and Duchess of Penshaw and their twins, gurgling away. Beside them, the Duke and Duchess of Dulverton. Henry looked particularly exhausted, though Minny looked radiant, her newborn asleep in her arms while little Henry tugged at his father's cravat.

The pew ahead of them held old Caelfall, his stick resting between himself and his wife who was, as far as Dottie could make out, was scribbling something in a notebook. *Another notebook aficionado.* She would have to speak to her at the reception and inquire as to where she purchased her paper.

Alongside Caelfall were the Duke and Duchess of Sedley. Dottie smiled warmly at them, and was rewarded with a little wave from Sedley, and a sob into a lace handkerchief from the duchess. Her sister, Beth, was beside her, and her husband Martock beside her. Dottie did her best not to scowl at the irritating man. He had proven to be quite difficult to manage, though Beth had let slip that there would soon be a reason to keep the man at home.

Wincham's wife, Hattie, was seated in the next pew. Her eyes were shining with tears, though Dottie was certain the tears were for the man escorting her down the aisle, rather than herself.

The next pew held one of Society's beauties, Miss Joanna Bettencourt as was—now the Lady Hebblethwaite. Her husband and father were seated either side of her. Dottie shook her head. Some fathers could not change.

She had not expected the Duke of Chantmarle. He had been assigned to a most interesting case in Dublin and had not been predicted to complete it until the height of summer. Evidently he had been successful. Perhaps his wife, beaming beside him, had something to do with that. She was swollen with child, near her confinement time, if Dottie was any judge.

Next to them in the pew were the Duke and Duchess of Thornfalcone. Dottie had barely had time to speak with poor Daniel after the loss of his brother, but he appeared content with his beautiful new bride beside him. It was difficult to believe it had been less than a year since their own wedding.

The Duke of Ashcott and his wife could not be sitting more closely to each other if they tried. Dottie had heard they were truly sickening to be with at the moment, though it did not look as though that was going to change soon, if the slightly swollen stomach of the Duchess of Ashcott was any indication.

And there was Chetnole, the duke who had brought the news of the traitor back to England, though by a remarkable detour. The result of that detour was sitting beside him. Lady Genevieve Cotton-Powell, as was, was making a remarkable duchess. Dottie made a mental note to speak to her later about the doctoring she was doing in Chetnole Wayleigh. It all sounded most fascinating.

And there was Lady Romeril, and the Earl of Chester, and Viscount Braedon, and the Earl of Armstrong. The Duke of Axwick glowered alone, and the Marnions, and the Howarths—

And there. There he was.

Dottie's heart skipped a beat. The whole pack of them were dear to her, in one way or another, but if not a single person other than the vicar and Adam Seymour, Duke of Gilroyd, had come, she would have been content.

"You've taken forever," he muttered as Wincham handed her over to her future husband.

"I was just enjoying my freedom," Dottie teased under her breath, to the chagrin of the vicar, who immediately spoke over her.

"Dearly beloved, we are gathered here today . . ."

Dottie had promised herself she would recall every single moment of their wedding, and in a way, she did. She could recall the vows, spoken calmly and with pride. She remembered the way Adam slipped the gold band onto her finger, and how she felt such a happiness it could not be contained. She remembered the soaring hymns, the way everyone had beamed as they processed back down the aisle, and the joy of the brisk sunshine, and the flower petals cascading over her.

But the part she remembered the most, the part seared into her heart, was when Adam pulled her into his arms outside the church as their guests started to make their way to Gilroyd House for the wedding reception.

"You're mine now."

Dottie kissed him. "I've been yours for quite a while."

There were only two topics of conversation at their wedding reception. Well, three, if you counted everyone's astonishment at the transformation of the place.

"Cobwebs gone, windows replaced, flowers in every room—it's a vision, Your Grace," said the Duchess of Martock warmly.

But the main things everyone wanted to discuss could be divided equally amongst the guests, and the first was babies.

"Oh, isn't she just adorable!" cooed the Duke of Thornfalcone, holding the Dulverton baby. "And she has your eyes, Minny!"

"Thank goodness, poor little Henry has already got to suffer mine," said the Duke of Dulverton proudly.

Dottie smiled as she walked past the gaggle of guests talking about the boredom of confinement and when to expect first words and how precisely to name a child when every single family member has an opinion.

In the next room was the second main topic of conversation.

"—such a wonderful wedding—and I knew of course that the whole thing was a trick!" boomed Lady Romeril. "Oh no, these Gilroyds couldn't pull the wool over my eyes!"

Everyone seemed to claim that opinion, Dottie thought, and they were all fibbing. Or at least, she was almost sure they were. Lady Romeril most definitely had not known. There had apparently been great consternation in Society, particularly in Brighton, when it was revealed that the Duke and Duchess of Gilroyd they had all met had not, actually, been married. Not yet. Hopefully, the furor would die down now and Society would come to forgive them for their little spot of mischief.

It was in the library that she found another topic of conversation. One rather less cheerful.

"—can't believe we didn't see it," Chantmarle was saying with a heavy sigh as Dottie slipped, unnoticed, into the room. "I trusted him!"

"We all did," said Penshaw, shrugging. "Perhaps I more than anyone. I put my very life in danger!"

"I think we can quibble about that," Sedley interjected. "It was my father who died at the hands of the Glasshand Gang, my damned brother who joined them!"

"The point is, Snee has been caught, tried, and will swiftly be learning just what it means to serve one's country," said Adam with a laugh in the center of the room. "Hanging's too good for him, if you ask me, but he has friends in high places so will be spared the gallows. A penal colony will do very well for a man who had us all serving our country—and his interests."

Dottie beamed.

Yes, Mr. Snee had been caught. After spending years at the very center of the Glasshand Gang and in the midst of those who wished to protect the country they loved, the blackguard had been caught.

It could not remove the pain of the treachery they had all endured, but it was enough, perhaps, that the culprit had been detained, tried, and found guilty.

"Come now, this is hardly the topic for a wedding!" Wincham said, slapping Adam on the back. "Besides, I think now that I've given Yates away, that makes me your father-in-law!"

Dottie stifled a giggle as she watched Adam make a face and the rest of the gentlemen laugh and clap him on the back.

"Lord save you!" said Ashcott with a dry laugh. "I wouldn't want this rake—"

"Who's calling who a rake?" Wincham said hotly, never able to see the joke in an insult. "I'll have you know—"

"Ahem," Dottie said, clearing her throat delicately.

Every eye turned to her.

"Oh blast, she's got another mission for us," one of them said, and they all laughed.

Dottie joined with them. "I do indeed, gentlemen, if you are bold enough to accept it. There is dancing required in the ballroom."

There were some laughs, some groans, and Wincham shook his head. "Try as you might—"

"I know your wife has taught you how to dance with a cane," Dottie said severely. "Now out, all of you. Except you."

None of the gentlemen seemed particularly surprised at who she'd picked out to stay.

As the door closed on the last of them, Adam shook his head with a wry smile. "I don't think I'll ever grow truly accustomed to having you order everyone about."

"I don't see why not," Dottie said lightly, stepping toward him and kissing him quickly on the mouth. "I like giving orders."

"You like having them obeyed," he pointed out, pulling her into his arms and sighing happily. "What's even stranger is that I like obeying you."

"Good," she said, happiness soaring into her chest. *Had anyone ever been this happy?*

But Adam's smile faded. "You are absolutely sure you are up to it?"

She did not have to ask what he meant. The topic had been spoken about constantly the last few weeks, attempting to approach it from every angle. Dottie was determined to have considered all the variables before making a decision. After all, it was a huge step to take. For both of them.

She took a deep breath. "I think this is the right decision."

"I know you can do it, that's not what I am concerned about," Adam said seriously, gazing deeply into her eyes. "I just . . . it will take a toll on you."

"I know," Dottie said quietly. "But I can think of no better thing to do with my life than to take over what Mr. Snee started—but without the taint of treachery."

It had been Prinny's idea, apparently, which had been rather a shock to the system. Dottie had not even known Prinny knew about Mr. Snee and all the dukes who had formed his network. Let alone her.

Still, he had, and he wanted it to continue. With someone at its head, Prinny had said in the note sent to Adam just weeks ago. Someone who could be trusted. Someone beyond reproach, beyond suspicion. Someone who knew how to work with people, how to run a mission. How to spot the signs of interest and how to write a snappy report.

There had only been one suggestion on everyone's lips, apparently.

"I just hope . . ." Dottie swallowed. It had to be said, even if it was painful. "I just hope you will not worry too much. After . . . after Louisa, and then my fall—"

"Your attack, more like," Adam said darkly, but there was softness in his expression. "She would have approved of you, you know. Louisa. I think you would have liked her."

A lurch in her stomach, one Dottie could not ignore. "I hope so."

"And now you're at the top of the tree! I rather like the idea of being given orders by you, I must say," Adam said, a teasing air creeping over his face. "Though don't tell the others I said that."

Dottie laughed, joy curling around her heart. "And I rather like the idea of you as the parent who stays home and takes care of the children."

She had spoken lightly, but her heart hammered now she spoke the words. It had been on her mind all day—seeing all the other duchesses with growing stomachs and growing families. Had anyone guessed? Did anyone except Madame Jacques, the modiste, know how delicately those tucks had been taken out?

Adam evidently had not understood her. "I think we've got plenty of time to worry about that!"

His laughter faded slowly as he took in her expression.

"We . . . we have time to worry about that, don't we, Dottie?"

Dottie allowed herself a small smile. "Oh, yes."

She permitted him a moment of relief.

"About five months."

Adam stiffened, his arms rigid around her as his eyes sought hers. "You—you're not—"

"I am," said Dottie ruefully. "I may still not remember the moment of conception, but—"

"You can't be," Adam breathed, his face a picture of shock.

She nodded. She'd intended to tell him before, of course, but what with setting up the network for the Crown, rooting out the final few traitors, planning a wedding . . .

Well. There never seemed time.

"But—but that's wonderful news! Oh, Dottie, a baby!"

And Adam was crushing her, his embrace so tight she had to wriggle out. "Careful!"

"Oh, right," he said hastily, glancing at her stomach as though it was now the eighth wonder of the world. "And you still don't recall the first time we . . ."

Dottie shook her head. It was frustrating in the extreme, but there it was. "You said it was pretty spectacular. I am sorry to have lost the recollection."

She should have known in that moment. There was such a look of wicked mischief in Adam's eyes, she should have known precisely what he was going to do.

Stepping from her, Adam swiftly reached the door to the library—and locked it. Then he turned around, leaned against the door, and fixed her with a wicked look.

"Well, there's no time like the present," he said softly.

Dottie's jaw fell open—even as warmth rushed between her legs. "Adam Seymour—at our own wedding reception?"

"All good dukes come to an end," he said quietly as he stepped toward her, every footstep increasing Dottie's heartrate. "And you have ended me, Dottie Yates. You've made me your own. Now it's time to make you my own."

"And changing my name wasn't enough?" she breathed, reaching for him and reveling in the warmth of his chest, the strength in his arms that wrapped around her. "Marrying you, carrying your child?"

"There's always more," Adam said roughly, kissing her neck.

"More love. More passion. More pleasure."

Dottie shivered, eyelashes fluttering as his hands pulled her hips toward his own. "I rather like the sound of that. Beginnings not endings."

"Oh, don't you worry. You'll also be finishing very, very soon . . ."

About Emily E K Murdoch

If you love falling in love, then you've come to the right place.

I am a historian and writer and have a varied career to date: from examining medieval manuscripts to designing museum exhibitions, to working as a researcher for the BBC to working for the National Trust.

My books range from England 1050 to Texas 1848, and I can't wait for you to fall in love with my heroes and heroines!

Follow me on twitter and instagram @emilyekmurdoch, find me on facebook at facebook.com/theemilyekmurdoch, and read my blog at www.emilyekmurdoch.com.

www.ingramcontent.com/pod-product-compliance
Lightning Source LLC
Chambersburg PA
CBHW060443310726

48977CB00001B/303